What Were You Thinking, You Thinking, Paige Taylor?

A BELLES OF ST. CLAIR NOVEL

D1713693

What Were You Thinking, Paige Taylor?

A BELLES OF ST. CLAIR NOVEL

AMANDA ASHBY

Entangled Publishing, LLC
2614 South Timberline Road
Suite 105, PMB 159
Fort Collins, CO 80525
rights@entangledpublishing.com

August is an imprint of Entangled Publishing, LLC.

Edited by Candace Havens
Cover design by Elizabeth Turner Stokes
Cover photography from iStock and Shutterstock

Manufactured in the United States of America

First Edition November 2018

To Sally and Karen, who have both been there right from the beginning. This book is for you.

Chapter One

"It's never too late to say no to the things that don't serve you. Apart from chocolate. Chocolate serves us all." **Just Say No**

Paige Taylor had a theory. If you were going to start your life over, you should do it in style. Which was why she'd planned to arrive in St. Clair wearing her favorite jeans and a pair of cute brown boots, to show that while she was New York born and bred, she was ready to fit in. Her eyebrows would be perfect, birds would be singing, and this lovely new chapter of her life would welcome her with open arms.

Nowhere was there any mention of her wearing a skintight outfit and the towering heels she'd bought in one of those 90 percent off sales that made a woman temporarily lose all reason.

She blamed the packers. The moving men, not the football team. At least she thought they were a team.

They'd taken her carefully prepared "I'm driving almost three thousand miles across the country to start my own business" wardrobe and left her with the "I once lived in New York and will never *ever* wear these clothes again" collection earmarked for the thrift shop.

Still, right now her outfit was the least of her problems.

"Please, just give me a little bit of signal. Just one more bar," she coaxed, and waved her phone in the air.

The gas station she'd pulled into was closed, and there was no sign of a payphone. *Do they even exist anymore?* She could just wait until she reached her new home. But it had already taken her bank manager three days to return her call regarding the line of credit she'd requested to help pay for her new life.

She balanced herself on the bonnet of her old Toyota, and the signal increased by a fraction. An improvement. Now she just needed to get somewhere higher to return the call.

There were no steps or benches she could climb on, and the only other vehicle in the place was a black pickup truck. It wasn't quite Mount Everest, but it might do. She peered around. There was no sign of the owner. She hurried over, praying her East Coast bank manager hadn't decided to go home early.

The uncomfortable shoes rubbed against her heels as she reached the truck. The back was almost as high as her chest, with only a trailer hitch to help her up.

See, if she *had* been wearing her jeans and boots, climbing would've been easy. *Okay, easy-ish.* Definitely better than the tubular black skirt she'd bought at Patrick's request last year.

No. Rule number one of her new life—no thinking about her ex-fiancé. She pushed him from her mind and awkwardly clambered up in a penguin-like fashion. She was rewarded by three flickering bars of signal. Gold dust.

Thank you, thank you, thank you.

She hit the number with her finger, the ragged, chipped

manicure a victim of her cross-country trip.

"First Square Bank, this is—" her bank manager answered before the call once again dropped.

Noooo.

She held the phone even farther up in the air, but the no-signal bars just flickered back at her. All red and taunting. She reluctantly lowered herself into a sitting position at the edge of the truck and discovered her next problem. Getting back down. No way she could jump in the shoes. She flexed her ankle to try and ease them off. It didn't work. Of course not, because it was becoming more obvious by the moment that Satan himself had designed the damn things.

She leaned forward to tug the first one off. Almost there. Just one more—

"Problem?" a voice said just as her foot finally released the shoe and sent it flying over to the owner of the voice. He easily caught the purple suede monstrosity before it could hit him in the head. A flash of impatience threaded across his mouth.

He was in his late thirties with dark hair, starting to pepper, and silvery gray eyes. His face was tanned, and beneath the plaid work shirt and plain jeans, his body was firm and strong, like it had been carved from the Oregon hills that flanked the deserted gas station. Oh, and there was no wedding ring.

Wait. That was old Paige talking. New Paige wasn't interested in men of any description, single or not.

He coughed, and the frown deepened.

It didn't take a rocket scientist to guess he was the owner of the truck.

"Hi." She plastered on a bright smile, while at the same time hoping he wasn't a crazy person. He didn't look crazy. A bit pissed, maybe. Then again, she was sitting in the back of his truck. He had every right to be mad. "You're probably wondering what I'm doing. You see, I was in the middle of an important phone call when it dropped out."

The gray eyes darkened, as if to suggest her excuse wouldn't stand up in a court of law. She gulped.

I should probably stop talking now.

"We're in a gully. There's never much signal," he finally answered. "You should hit some in five miles."

"Good to know." She licked her lips and decided to risk lowering herself to the ground while still wearing one shoe. She wriggled her bottom forward and tucked her phone into the front of her skirt before gripping the deck of the truck with both hands. The pitted steel was cool against her palms as she eased her way down, while wishing she hadn't skipped so many yoga classes.

The only thing that would've made it worse was if he'd offered to help. He didn't, and while she was grateful, trying to finish the task while her core muscles were screaming wasn't fun.

Sweat beaded the top of her lip, and her arms shook as her heeled foot hit the ground, closely followed by her other leg, which was a good three inches lower. She steadied herself by pretending her bare foot was also in a shoe, all under the guy's disarming gaze.

If undignified dismounts were an Olympic category, I'd be a gold medal winner.

"I should get going." She plastered on another smile.

"You might need this." He held up the shoe. His hands were tanned and the nails neatly clipped, and they seemed to mock the frivolous stiletto, making it look out of place and useless.

Definitely not how Day One was meant to go.

"Thanks." She reluctantly slipped it back onto her foot. At least the world was no longer lopsided. "And sorry about standing on your truck."

"Forget it." He shrugged, as if already deleting the encounter from his mind. She swallowed and walked back to her own car, heat rising in her cheeks, as the black truck pulled out of the gas station and headed in the direction she'd just come from.

At least I won't ever see him again.

She slid into the driver's seat and thrust her keys into the ignition, humiliation humming in her veins. For goodness' sake, she was a thirty-six-year-old woman, and most of the time a perfectly sensible person.

Yet here she was making a fool of herself in front of the most beautiful man she'd seen in a good long while.

Correction.

Humiliating herself while wearing a bad outfit was a good a thing. *Great* even. Because, as her favorite author, Dr. Penny Groves, was fond of saying, *"If you want to change your story, then stop auditioning the same cast members."*

And Gas Station Guy was definitely a cast member she'd auditioned before. She had no proof he was a two-timing cheater who was sleeping with other women the *entire* time they were engaged. But those kind of knee-knocking good looks never seemed to go to the nice guys who liked hand-holding and long walks on the beach.

Not that it mattered.

She turned to the passenger seat. It was covered with the evidence of her cross-country trip. Multiple packets of M&M's, sunscreen, empty water bottles, the cute vision board she'd made to inspire her on the trip, along with her well-thumbed copy of *Just Say No—A Journey from Servitude to Freedom*, by Dr. Penny Groves.

The book responsible for her new philosophy on life.

Put quite simply, whenever she wanted to say yes, she'd just say no instead.

No to her landlord who kept putting up the rent without

fixing the heating. No to her ex-boss who sat in her corner office while Paige tried to get publicity for a tween YouTube star whose latest book was about posing with a blow-up unicorn in front of public monuments (she didn't get it either). And definitely, *definitely* no to men.

From now on she was a *no* machine.

The old Paige was gone. Dead. Buried under a mountain of yeses.

She kicked her shoes off, pumped the gas, and pulled out. As promised the reception improved farther down the road, but her call went straight to voicemail. She left her bank manager a long message, hoping it didn't sound too much like she was begging.

The last miles flew past in a blur of colors, until she reached a winding road with tall thin poplars flanking either side, allowing dappled sunlight to filter onto the road, while the smudgy blue sky was host to fat, lazy clouds. The road widened, and she caught her breath as her new hometown swung into view.

St. Clair, Oregon. Population two thousand and twenty.

Make that two thousand and twenty-one.

The town was as picturesque in real life as it had been on the internet, with colorful wooden houses dotting the landscape like a child's painting. To the left was a small inlet with a couple of boats bobbing merrily against the tide and a few rustic boatsheds, haphazardly perched in the water on long wooden stumps.

The heavy fall colors that had marked her cross-country trip were still evident, but the oranges and browns were tangled up with late-blooming summer flowers. She slowed down as a tractor pulled out in front of her, not minding it was only driving five miles an hour as it allowed her to drink in the glory of the place. But it wasn't until it abruptly turned up a driveway that she found herself in front of three old

Victorian houses.

They were squished side by side, as if trying to stay warm. It was the one at the end she was interested in. A bookstore called *Fireside Books*.

The bookstore she now officially owned. And, despite having stopped far too many times to deal with her sister-in-law's increasingly snarky phone calls, she'd managed to arrive a day earlier than planned.

She climbed out of the car.

The air was salt laden with a hint of late jasmine from the vine lazily creeping up the framework around the front window. The building was pale peppermint, slightly faded but still endearing, and the sign swung in the faint breeze. It was so dang cute she was surprised gingerbread men with candy canes weren't plastered to the walls.

The other two businesses were equally adorable.

One was a coffee shop, painted blue with a bold modern sign, while the florist store in the middle was a soft yellow. The large window was filled with fall flowers, and an old bicycle was propped against the outside porch, also crammed with a riot of blooms.

It was something out of a dream.

A dream I'm now part of!

Her old life might've sucked, but her new one was going to be amazing.

Her heels sunk down into the soft grass that flanked the pathway leading up to the old wooden door with frosted glass. She fumbled for the front door key. Diana, the previous owner, had FedExed them once the sale had been completed.

A CLOSED sign was hanging there, and under the doormat were several notes, but before she could scoop them up she caught sight of the brass doorknocker.

It was in the shape of a fox's head, with wide eyes and a long nose, while one paw was held up in a welcoming gesture.

Call her crazy, but the way the brass twinkled in the sunshine, it was almost a smile. Like it was saying:

"Welcome, Paige. Say goodbye to the past. From now on it's going to be book-scented happiness, as you engage in long and amazing conversations about literature, while sipping coffee (or wine. Because this is your imagination and I'm not here to judge.) It's everything you want, Paige. And nothing will ever go wrong—"

"It's her. It must be her," a voice cut through the welcoming address in her mind. She swiveled as two women spilled out of the yellow florist shop next door.

One was tall and lean with a pixie cut and a resting bitch face that made Paige want to stay on her good side. She was wearing faded jeans and a plaid shirt. The second was petite with auburn curls and dreamy blue eyes. She was dressed in a navy polka dot dress, and in her hand was an armful of flowers, white, purple, and pink all blended together, wrapped in an old dressmaking pattern and tied with string.

"Yeah, I think the key in her hand gives it away," the tall girl drawled as they walked across the lawn, their sandals making a padding noise against the grass. Up close the hard jaw softened, and the girl gave her a reluctant smile. "Hey, I'm Sam."

"And I'm Laney." The petite girl thrust the flowers in Paige's direction and gave her a smile. "We're the Belles."

"The Belles?" Paige blinked as she took the flowers. "Is that like a girl band or something?"

Laney laughed. "I forgot you're not from here. These buildings were once owned by three sisters and were nicknamed the Belles of St. Clair. I'm surprised Diana didn't tell you when you bought the place."

"I'm not." Sam snorted as she scooped up the notes peeking out from under the doormat, while Laney made a growling noise. "What? I'm just saying Diana wasn't known for her conversation skills."

Paige had to agree, and after her original call with the owner, she'd quickly discovered Diana was a straight-to-business type of woman, and the rest of their correspondence had been via their solicitors. Still, the price had been right, and the deal fast, which was all Paige had cared about.

"She wasn't so bad," Laney protested, though it lacked conviction. "I know you're going to love it. We've been hoping you'd be nice, and I can already see you are."

"You can?" Paige said in surprise, recalling the inappropriate outfit. "I promise I don't normally wear this kind of thing. Well, I did in my old life, but now I'm here—"

"Now you're here you can wear whatever you want," Laney said in a firm voice. "Besides, I like what you're wearing. It shows you have spunk."

"Trust me, spunk's the last thing I want right now," Paige confessed as she adjusted the band of her skirt and wished she'd said no to the breakfast taco. "There was a mix-up with the moving boxes, which means I've traveled across America looking like an extra from *Dynasty*. All power suits and earrings the size of satellite dishes."

Some of the reserve fell from Sam's face, and she grinned. "I'm guessing you're from New York."

Paige nodded. The intoxicating aroma from the flowers in her arm flooded her senses, easing the tension in her shoulders that had built up from thinking about her old life (which, for the record, was only six hundred times a day). Laney was obviously a floral ninja. She took in another deep breath.

"Did you have a bookshop there?" Sam asked.

"Not exactly. I am...I mean I *was* a book publicist, but I've always loved reading, and when I saw this place it just seemed perfect."

Not to mention three thousand miles away from all my

problems.

"And it will be," Laney agreed in a cheerful voice, making Paige wonder if she was perpetually happy.

"I hope so." She fiddled with the key in her hand. "Do you want to come inside? I'm dying to look around."

Laney's smile dropped a quarter inch as she tucked her arm into Paige's. "You know, while that does sound fun, I have a better idea! Why not come over to my place and have a welcome glass of wine?"

"It's eleven in the morning." Paige blinked. "Aren't you still open for business?"

"Er, yes, but how often do we get a new neighbor?" Sam appeared on Paige's other arm "We can fill you in on life in St. Clair."

"Yes. There's so much to tell you," Laney echoed.

Paige pushed her lips together. She might not have owned a bookstore before, or lived in a small town—but thanks to dating Patrick for the last six years, she had a PhD in shifty behavior.

"What's going on? Is there a reason you don't want me to go inside?"

"What? No. That's crazy talk." Laney shook her head, but Sam sighed and let go of Paige's arm.

"We might as well just tell her. She's going to find out eventually."

"Find out what?" Her grip tightened on the flowers as her mind filtered through all of the things that could've possibly happened. It wasn't hard. Her friends in New York had been listing them with great frequency ever since she'd announced her plans. "Please don't tell me that Diana didn't own the place and I've been duped. Or she's taken all the stock and only left fishing books? Or—"

"I swear it's not so bad," Laney said before wrinkling her nose. "Hey, are you sure you don't want that wine?"

"One hundred percent," Paige said in a grim voice.

"Okay, here's the deal. Two nights ago, there was a storm and we both heard a crashing noise. Long story short, one of the back windows was broken. We boarded it up before there was too much damage, and Len reckons it won't cost much to replace it…" Sam trailed off.

"Unfortunately—" Laney rushed in before Paige could comment or ask who Len was. "That's when we discovered the other stuff."

Other stuff?

The breakfast taco churned in her stomach as repair bills flashed through her mind.

Buying the bookstore had taken all of her life savings, and a hefty mortgage from the bank. Which meant she'd hardly left anything to fall back on, hence her request for the line of credit.

She shut her eyes, searching for a backup plan. None came to mind. She couldn't ask her family for money. Her relationship with her mom had always been strained, ditto with her pompous brother.

There was the small inheritance she'd received after her estranged father died last year, but she couldn't bring herself to touch it. After all, he'd made it perfectly clear she wasn't part of his new family. Spending his money seemed like she was forgiving him for years of pain and rejection.

"Like what?" She swallowed her panic. Dr. Penny Groves always said to breathe through it. Breathing, hyperventilating. They were the same thing, right?

"The place needs a bit of maintenance."

"This is the quiet time of year." Laney paused and twisted her mouth. "And…well—"

"Diana didn't exactly get on with the local community, which affected her cash flow." Sam reluctantly held up the notes that'd been tucked under the doormat. There were five of them—all complaints from local residents about the bad service.

"I'm guessing by the look on your face, her accounts didn't reflect this."

Paige scrunched up the notes and shook her head. Though to be fair, she'd been so smitten (fine, desperate) she hadn't paid close attention to the bottom line.

"As far as we can tell, she let things slide in order to make ends meet. That or the local contractors wouldn't do business with her."

"What kind of maintenance?" Her stomach dropped.

I wonder what the going rate for a kidney is?

"Nothing major. It's more a shopping list of small things. Not to mention the mess," Laney added in a slightly less sunny voice, before sighing. "We wanted to call, but no one had your number, and Diana hasn't been answering her phone. We were going to finish tidying today, but you got here early."

"It seemed like a good idea at the time." She gulped before frowning at the keys in her hand. "Wait, how did you get in?"

"Yeah, we were hoping you might not notice that part." Sam flushed. "My fourteen-year-old nephew has an interesting skill set, and I'm not sure he's quite decided if he's playing on team good or team evil. He picked your lock."

"Though I swear it was only because we asked him to," Laney added. "Do you still want to see inside?"

No. Yes. Maybe.

But there was only one answer. She'd left her old life behind, so abandoning her new one on the first day wasn't really an option.

"Let's do it." Paige swallowed hard and thrust the key into the lock. The air was damp and heavy as she stepped across the threshold and scanned the room.

Stripped pine shelves were crammed with books, while

long wooden tables ran down the middle, piled high with a colorful collection of coffee table books, stationery, and notepads.

Along the back wall a large board had been nailed from the outside to cover the smashed window. Someone—she was guessing Laney—had cleared away the glass, though it couldn't hide the broken plaster around the window frame. While on the sidewall was a magnificent fireplace that had no doubt given the store its name.

That was the good news.

The bad news was most of the floor area was covered by cartons of books, plastic bags overflowing with paper, and *was that a half-eaten sandwich*? Her eyes drifted to the counter, stacked high with old newspapers and magazines. The walls had once been painted pink, but it had been done a long time ago, and chipped paint marked nearly every surface, while a highway of spiderwebs claimed the ceiling.

She picked her way over to the light switch and flicked it on, hoping it would be less gloomy. Nothing happened, and one look at the overhanging pendant light confirmed there was no bulb.

"If it's any consolation, it was a lot worse yesterday," Laney said as the whole floor rumbled, like a jet plane about to land. A loud screech followed, sending Paige's heart into overdrive.

"What was that?" she croaked, wondering where her nice new relaxing life was.

"The radiator." Sam pointed to the ancient roadmap of metal tubes attached to the far wall. "Its bark's worse than its bite. And it won't stop you from running the business. Last year I had a bucket in the middle of my dining room for a week."

"I had no power for five days during my busiest period," Laney chimed in. "It comes with the territory of owning a historic building and being a Belle."

Paige sucked in her breath and tried to stay calm.

The mess could be cleaned up. The radiator and broken window fixed, and yes, it was a slight problem Diana seemed to have burned her bridges in the small town, but Paige was sure once they got to know her, things would be fine.

She could do this.

More importantly, she *had* to do this.

"I'm an unstoppable force who says no to fear," she reminded herself in a soft voice.

"Wait! Did you just quote Dr. Penny Groves?" Laney demanded.

Paige blinked. "You've heard of her?"

"Heard of her? Are you kidding me?" Sam rolled back her sleeve to display a small tattoo of the book title scrolling up her arm. "She completely changed my life."

"And mine," Laney added before wrinkling her nose. "Though I wasn't brave enough to get a tattoo. But we both love *Just Say No*. I can't believe you do, too."

"It's actually what helped me decide to buy this place," Paige admitted as the mess and repairs faded away. Despite the book being a *New York Times* bestseller, none of her friends had shown the least interest in reading it. Probably worried it might cause them to end up in a tiny coastal town, too.

"And it's what going to help you start your new life," Laney said in a firm voice.

"You're right." She gave Laney and Sam a small smile. "Thanks for trying to spare me the shock."

"Rule number one of living here. People help people," Sam said with surprising candor considering how scary she'd looked just twenty minutes earlier.

"I know what it's like. I moved to this town ten years ago and immediately panicked about whether I was doing the right thing," Laney added.

"And were you?"

"Absolutely," Laney said before her bright smile faded. "Well, there were tough times, but I survived, and you will, too. Now we'll leave you to settle in, but just shout if you need anything, and if you're not too tired swing by at five o'clock for a glass of wine."

"I'll see how it goes," she said.

Once her new neighbors had left, she put her purse down on the counter and searched for cleaning supplies. After all, she'd spent most of her life trying to please other people and clean up their messes.

At least this time it was entirely for her.

Me first, from now on. With that in mind, she got to work.

Chapter Two

"On those days when you can't find your ass from your elbow, remember that clarity is just a no away." **Just Say No**

Luke Carmichael rubbed his jaw.

Thanks to an overzealous party down at the beach, then a frantic call about a missing cat, there hadn't been a lot of sleep last night. Not to mention the three stiches when the oversize tom had taken exception to being carried down the old fig tree behind the school. Still, at least there'd been a happy reunion. As for the no sleep part? That's what coffee was invented for.

He'd started the community patrol a couple of years ago when the small seaside town had been hit with a string of arson attempts during the tourist season. Nothing had burned down since, and the good folk of St. Clair had once again been able to sleep easy in their beds.

"Let me guess." Patsy sashayed over and held up her coffeepot, as her sharp eyes took in his bandaged hand. "Cat duty?"

He nodded. "He didn't like being woken mid-nap. Even when he was up a tree."

"Can't say I blame him." Patsy poured a cup of her famous coffee, the bitter aroma filling the air. "Want your usual breakfast?"

His stomach rumbled, but he shook his head. "I'm due on site in half an hour." He ran his uninjured hand through his hair. Yet another resident had fallen victim to the Airbnb craze. This time it was an expensive cottage conversion, with three bathrooms.

He could've told them accommodating more tourists in the small town wasn't going to fix all their problems, but he had mouths to feed—okay, one mouth to feed. And so, he'd kept his opinion to himself and got on with it.

Besides, the job would soon be finished.

"I heard Olive's on the mend. That's good, right?" Patsy said.

At the mention of his grandmother, he smiled.

To the outside world the Carmichaels looked like a tight bunch, despite the fact his mom had walked out when he was ten, and his dad had died a year later. Technical reason was pneumonia, but they all knew it was a broken heart. Yet, Olive had woven together a new life for him, Jacob, and Trina, making them think she was indestructible.

The flu, which had really slowed her down, had given them all a scare.

"Yeah, yesterday she was testing vodka punch recipes for her eightieth birthday, not to mention conning me into installing a hot tub. Should I be worried?" He slugged back the rest of his coffee as his lethargy faded. He fumbled for some notes to pay.

"Not if you know what's good for you." Patsy shook her head to wave away the money. "She wouldn't thank you for it."

"Ain't that the truth."

Patsy gave him a nod, then lifted up a curious eyebrow. "Have you met her yet?"

His jaw flickered.

Ever since Diana had announced she'd sold the bookstore to someone from New York, the town had been speculating about the new owner, but Luke hadn't given it much thought. It'd just be another city fool with more money than sense.

Stood to reason. Who bought a business this time of year?

Except now he knew. Paige Taylor. The woman who'd been randomly standing on his truck, wearing a pair of purple heels that showed off her endless legs while trying to make a phone call. Glossy blonde curls had tumbled down her shoulders, and the faint scent of vanilla had surrounded her. Not exactly what he'd expected to find after coming back from helping Old Joe put up an extra wall in the gas station workshop yesterday.

He'd assumed she was passing through. *Hoped* she'd been passing through, since the curve of her chest and dark navy eyes had done sinful things to his body. He needed a relationship like he needed a stiletto-shaped hole in the head.

But it had only taken one trip to the post office—where gossip spread like butter—to discover she was the new owner of Fireside Books.

Still, it wasn't like it would be a problem. He'd been so busy that the reading pile by his bed had hardly been dented. By the time he needed to buy more, she'd be long gone, following in Diana's footsteps. And until then, avoiding her shouldn't be too hard.

"Just in passing." He studied his hands.

"Really?" She quirked an eyebrow, but before she could comment, one of her servers called her over.

He stood up, leaving the money on the table despite her

protests. She might want to support the community patrol, but she had bills to pay just like everyone else.

"You coming to the town meeting?"

"Wouldn't miss it for the world." Her eyes gleamed, though it was hard to tell if she was concerned about the future of the small-knit community, or just liked seeing the new mayor get hot under the collar every time she ogled him.

Not sure I want to know the answer to that one.

She took her magical coffee back to the counter, and Luke walked outside.

The diner was covered in flat slate tiles with an asymmetrical roof, once designed to lure the interstate traffic, but these days it was mainly patronized by locals. He shrugged off his jacket and climbed into his truck.

Yesterday's rain had passed, and the promise of sun hung in the air as he drove to his latest job. A long, sweeping driveway led up to the main house, while the cottage was off to the left.

Several vehicles were parked up, and the blaring radio and cacophony of voices let him know his crew was already hard at work. He'd never planned to be a boss, all he'd wanted was to work for himself, but after he'd taken on a large contracting job a few years ago, he'd quickly realized the only way he could ensure his crew could afford to live in St. Clair was to keep the work coming in.

Sometimes it was an uphill battle, but one he was determined to win. With a sigh, he climbed out of his truck and put on his hard hat.

• • •

"What's that noise? I thought you bought a bookstore, not a construction company," Zoe complained from down the end of the phone, as the hell spawn radiator shrieked in greeting, the sound bouncing off the walls and rattling Paige's jaw.

They'd met on a book tour for a celebrity chef ten years ago. Paige was a junior publicist and Zoe the stylist, before she'd set up her online home wares store, which had taken her from being just another struggling city girl to a bona fide businesswoman.

"Nothing. Just a few teething problems," she lied and counted to five in her head until the noise let out a final shudder before stopping. Her new friends had given her the names of contractors, but she hadn't wanted to admit how tight her budget was. Not helped by the phone call she'd had with her bank manager.

Turned out she wasn't the only one saying no to things.

There was no line of credit.

Besides, why pay someone when the answer was lurking on YouTube? Not that she'd quite found the right tutorial to stop radiators from screaming like a pissed off demon, but she would. It was only a matter of time.

Then she'd figure out how to replace the broken window.

"Doesn't sound like nothing. What's going on?" Zoe demanded, in a voice Paige knew well. An exercise machine whirled in the background, and a twinge of nostalgia hit as she pictured Zoe at the gym, swiping her Tinder app, while closing deals and raising her cardio. That had once been Paige's life, too.

Minus Tinder, and plus a cheating fiancé.

"Okay. The place wasn't quite what I expected." She adjusted her Bluetooth headset and wiped the dust away from her eyes. Still, if the dust was in her eye, it was one less piece on the shelves, right?

"How bad?"

"Think of the worst hoarding show you've ever seen on television. Then double it. Please don't say you told me so."

"I won't. But, honey—" Zoe paused as if weighing up her

words. That was bad. Her friend was normally known for her blunt talking. Which could only mean one thing. *She thinks I've messed up.* "No one would judge if you wanted to come home."

No one but me.

Besides, what was there to go back to?

Saying no to her old life hadn't just been a figure of speech. She'd quit her job, given up her apartment, and even canceled her library card.

If she went back, she'd be worse off than when she'd left.

"It's fine. Everything's fine."

"You said that about wearing clogs when they blipped back into fashion. And we both know how that turned out."

"They were great shoes," Paige protested. "I know I'm doing the right thing."

Which was almost true.

The last three days had been a blur of cleaning, a backyard filled with trash bags, and opening up the doors to her new business. Not that she'd had many customers.

Well, no paying customers. There'd been numerous curious locals who wandered in and out without giving her a smile. The handful of tourists who'd come in earlier had been more promising. But they'd only wanted the latest Dan Brown book, which despite showing up on the inventory, Paige couldn't find anywhere. She was quickly discovering Diana preferred to shelve books by color and size rather than content.

On the plus side, the rest of her belongings had arrived, which meant she could retire the power suits, and was now wearing her favorite jeans and boots, along with a soft white blouse with embroidery around the neckline.

"Look, you know I love you like the sister I never had."

"You have three sisters," Paige reminded her in a dry voice.

"And you're trying to change this subject, but you can't. I'm worried. Running away from your problems doesn't work."

"I'm not running away. I'm starting over. There's a difference."

"I beg to differ. Most people would just slash a couple of their ex's suits and spend quality time with Ben, Jerry, and a bottle of gin. But you decided to blow all your money on a place you've never even seen, three thousand miles from your nearest and dearest."

"Don't make it sound so extreme," she protested.

"Sorry. You're right. It's completely normal. Besides, if you don't come home, Patrick will think he's won."

"He has won." She stood up, her knees aching from the exertion.

Habit forced her to look at her naked finger.

She'd had her suspicions he'd been cheating almost from the start, and while he'd always sworn it wasn't true, she'd reluctantly concluded it wasn't because he was a great liar, but more because she was desperate to have her own family. To give meaning to her life, which only seemed to revolve around her soul-destroying job, her reserved mom, and her crappy apartment.

It explained why she'd managed to ignore the perfume on his suits, the impossibly hard password on his cell phone, and the numerous late nights he worked at his photography business. Unfortunately, she hadn't been able to ignore it when she caught him and his assistant Poppy, hard at it against her own pantry door.

Worst thing was he wasn't even sorry.

He consoled her by saying it was probably for the best. *The best for whom?* Paige had wanted to scream at him. To tell him what she really thought. But even then, the people pleaser in her hadn't managed it. She'd just let him pack up his belongings and walk out of her life, without her saying a word.

That was when she'd dragged out her copy of *Just Say No*, drunk a bottle of wine, and done what any sane, newly single woman in her mid-thirties would do. She looked for a new life on the internet, and two weeks later found herself in possession of a bookstore.

A bookstore with no customers and a broken radiator.

"Patrick's scum whatever way you slice it, but that doesn't mean you can't live in the same town together. New York's a big place. And I swear I'm not pressuring you, I'm just worried you're throwing your life away. Why not just stay down there for a few weeks, sow your wild lady oats, and then come back home?"

She shut her eyes. It was useless to argue with Zoe, who thought all problems could be fixed with a large drink and rearranging the decorative pillows on her minimalist couch. Or to explain that even if there was a chance to sow her *wild lady oats*, she'd be saying no to it. Just like she'd be saying no to everything that didn't involve setting up her new business.

Me first, from now on.

The radiator once again screeched to life, and the entire floor rumbled.

"Paige," Zoe groaned as the door chime played, and the old wooden floorboards creaked with footsteps. A potential customer!

"Gotta go, but I promise I'll call you."

"No, you won't," Zoe prophesized. "You'll read another chapter of that damn book and decide you need to say no to all of your old friends."

"Don't be silly. There's no such chapter." Paige crossed her fingers since the book had suggested she get rid of all the people who held her back. Thankfully Zoe didn't fall into that category. Her friend was just a bit worried about her.

"Love you, bye."

Paige put her phone down as a woman in a ginormous hat made a tutting noise and looked around.

"So, you're the new Diana?"

"My name's Paige. Nice to meet you," she said with her brightest smile. It was wasted on the woman, who ran a finger along the counter, though her gaze suggested Paige was the one being inspected. "Is there anything I can help you with?"

"I highly doubt it. If I want a book, I'll order it from the internet." The woman continued to peer around, sharp blue eyes taking in all of the spiderwebs Paige hadn't quite got to yet, not to mention the broken window.

At least the radiator was quiet.

"Well, have a great day." She amped up the smile and pretended to busy herself with the old-fashioned cash register, which contained all the money from her wallet. On top of it was a note reminding her to go to the bank later and get change.

So far it hadn't been a problem.

The woman didn't reply. She just gave a final sniff and walked out of the shop, leaving only her disapproval behind. Paige let out a pained sigh and reminded herself Rome wasn't built in a day. Or even in three.

"Don't worry about her. That's Mrs. Devon, and everyone knows she's grumpy." The disembodied voice of a young girl broke the silence.

The hairs on the back of Paige's neck shot up as she scanned the store.

It was empty.

"Who said that?" she asked, trying to shake away her panic. She glanced around for a weapon but only found the missing Dan Brown. She picked it up, her palm moist.

Please don't let it be haunted.

It would explain why Diana had been in such a hurry to

sell. Why there were no customers. Why the radiator sounded like it was eating the souls of the dead. Problem was, she wasn't sure if there would be a YouTube tutorial on how to clear a ghost. Not to mention—

"Me." A head appeared from under the wooden display table at the front of the store. It belonged to a girl. She was about thirteen or fourteen, with sun-kissed caramel-colored hair tied back in a messy ponytail and a pale yellow T-shirt. Her green eyes were fringed with dark lashes, and there was a smattering of freckles across her nose and cheeks, while her awkward limbs suggested she wasn't done growing.

More importantly, she was 100 percent corporeal. Crisis averted. There was no ghost.

"How long have you been under the table?" Paige loosened her grasp on the Dan Brown as sanity trickled back into her mind.

"I came in with the German tourists about an hour ago. I'm Kira." The girl held out her hand, and Paige found herself shaking it. "I was going to say hi, but then Cal walked past the window, and obviously I had to hide. Luckily Diana hadn't found my book, and since I'd left Suzette and Aaron in the middle of a djinn attack, I wanted to make sure they were okay."

"I see." Paige nodded, no closer to understanding what was really going on.

"I thought you would," Kira agreed as she pulled out a bag of gummy bears and offered them up. "By the way, I like your top. I wanted one like that, but my dad vetoed it. He gets one veto a year."

"Only one?" Paige said as she waved away the candy, while trying to decide if it was a good thing or bad thing that she shared the same fashion sense as a teen.

"It use to be three, but I negotiated a better deal."

"Nice work," Paige said, appreciating a good hustle when

she heard one. Then she frowned. "So, Kira, two questions. Who's Cal, and what's a djinn attack?"

The girl dimpled. "Cal's my OTL. That's One True Love if you don't speak internet. He's been staying with his aunt above the cafe."

"Ah!" Cal of the lock-picking notoriety. She'd met him in passing while getting a coffee, though his hoodie had been pulled low, and with his monotone replies, it had been hard to form an opinion.

"When he first moved in there I was stoked," Kira confided. "I mean my OTL *and* my happy place all in the same block. But then I started to worry he might think I was stalking him. Especially since he doesn't know I exist."

"It can be a fine line," Paige was forced to admit. "Though I'm sure he knows who you are."

Kira shook her ponytail and let out a mournful sigh. "Nope. He only knows the girls with hips and boobs. Like Tess Jenkins."

"I bet Tess Jenkins isn't half as interesting as you are. Though I'm still not clear where the djinn attack fits in?"

Kira scampered back under the table and reappeared with a hardback. "It's book three in the *Desert Witches of Numara* series. Would you believe Diana refused to sell it to me because she didn't think it was appropriate reading material for someone my age, and my dad wouldn't buy it online because he has a thing about supporting local businesses. Which is fine for him because *he* doesn't care what happens to Suzette and Aaron."

"There's no accounting for taste." Paige couldn't help but smile as she recognized a kindred spirit. Well, she'd never hidden beneath a bookstore table to read a banned book, but she'd spent most of her high school years tucked under the bleachers, in her own little world.

"Right!" Kira gave a vigorous nod that sent her ponytail

flying. "Oh, and get a load of this, when I told him Trent Burton, *my all-time favorite actor*, is going to play Aaron in the movie, he just stared and said, 'Who's Trent Burton?'" Her lips puckered before she hit Paige with a level stare. "Please tell me that you know who I'm talking about."

"Cute with an English accent and to-die-for eyes. I hear he's just broken up with Tara McGuiness. If Cal's playing hard to get, this might be your chance."

"You *do* know." Kira clapped her hands. "I love him so much. And not only is he born in March like me, but we both love the color yellow. Isn't that great?"

"Great," Paige agreed, stupidly pleased her time spent trailing around after the tween blogger had an unsuspected silver lining.

She jumped as the door chime went and a man in a fishing jacket stalked in.

"I won't be a moment." She excused herself and wove past the newly stacked shelves toward him. "Can I help you?"

"Diana promised she'd order in book two of *Game of Thrones*. I mean what's the point of having book one and three, but not book two?" the man challenged, as if daring her to contradict him.

"I couldn't agree more." She murmured an apology and walked over to the ancient laptop she'd inherited with the store. She'd done a couple of tutorials on the software last night and tapped in the title. There was one in stock, but like she'd learned with the Dan Brown book, it could be anywhere.

"Let's check if it's on the fantasy shelf." She tried to project confidence.

"I can see from here it's not," he said, his tone matching his frosty expression.

"Perhaps it's in general fiction?" She was clutching at straws.

"Actually." Kira walked to a half-sized bookshelf filled with Agatha Christie mysteries and wriggled it away from the wall to inexplicably reveal a stack of books. "She kept all the customer holds in here."

Of course she did, because it made no logical sense.

She took the book and handed it over to the customer.

It was hard to tell if he was happy or disappointed, but after examining the cover he pulled out his wallet and passed over some notes.

Her first sale.

Yes, it was only ten bucks, but metaphorically speaking it was very significant.

"My change?" The man coughed.

Oh, right. She knew that.

She counted it out before discovering she didn't have any bags. Then again, no bags were better for the environment. She handed him the book along with the change.

"There you go, sir. And have a great day."

"Humph." He was still grumbling as he left the store.

"Don't mind him," Kira advised. "That's Mr. Tanner. You should see what he's like at the library. He's always complaining the newspapers are too crumpled."

"In that case, I'll pronounce this a success. All thanks to you. Any other secret hiding places I should know about?"

"She kept the romance books in the big safe in the office, and all the celebrity biographies in a box down in the basement. And don't even try looking for vegetarian cookbooks. She wouldn't stock them."

Explains why customers aren't banging down the door.

"I'd better make sure I order some. Hopefully by the time they arrive I'll have everything shelved properly."

"You know, if you wanted, you could give me a job here." A thoughtful expression gleamed in Kira's eyes.

"Oh—" Paige opened her mouth. Her budget was already

tight; paying a schoolgirl hadn't been on the list. Even a precocious one like Kira, who seemed to have a decoder key to Diana's unique cataloging system.

"You don't have to pay me in money. You could pay me in books," Kira said as she looked longingly at the Young Adult section, despite the fact it was mainly filled with road maps. "If I was working here, I'd have a legitimate reason to see Cal every day."

"What about your parents? I'm not sure they'd like it."

"It's only me and my dad, and he'll be pleased at my initiative. He's always telling me how important it is to contribute to the community. And if I help you with the books, then the people who come in here will be able to find what they want. That's contributing, right?"

"I'm still not sure." Paige faltered as a pair of wide green eyes stared at her.

"Please, please, please." Kira clasped her hands together. She was probably lonely if it was just her and the father—who sounded a bit dull. Paige could relate. Her dad had walked out when she was six, and her mom had become distant, as if it was Paige's fault he'd gone.

Perhaps it was?

After all, his new wife had never warmed to Paige, only to her older brother, James. Because of it, Paige had spent a good deal of her time alone. Her resolve faltered as Dr. Penny Groves flashed into her mind, randomly wearing a kaftan and holding a cocktail in one hand.

Paige, honey, don't forget no man-slash-woman is an island. It's okay to ask for help.

I do ask for help, she mentally replied.

You mean like fixing the radiator and the window by yourself? Sam and Laney tried to give you the number for a contractor, but you turned them down.

Okay, that's true. In my defense, I'm broke. Plus, I did let them give me wine. That's got to count for something, right?

Do you really want me to answer? The imaginary author gave her a challenging stare. *What's the worst thing that can happen?*

I'll turn into my mother. Or my ex-boss, she promptly replied.

Dr. Penny Groves took a sip of her drink, as if to punctuate the point.

Paige took in a deep breath and turned back to Kira.

"Okay, but only if your dad says yes," she clarified, which sent Kira racing around the store like a soccer player who'd just scored the winning goal.

It probably wasn't worth mentioning her decision was based on an imaginary conversation with a best-selling author. Not to mention that Dr. Penny Groves was notoriously private. She never did book signings or publicity, so the chances of her having a one-on-one conversation with Paige were low to not-going-to-happen.

"He will." Kira continued to grin as her phone beeped. She pulled it out of the strawberry-shaped purse hanging over her shoulder and studied the screen. "We can ask him right now. He's here. Come and meet him."

"Sure. I guess." After all, it wasn't like there were any customers to serve.

Pale September sunlight danced around the climbing roses while bees lazily darted in and out of the flowers as she walked down the three steps, just as a vaguely familiar black truck pulled up.

She frowned. *Why* was it familiar?

Then she let out a soft moan as a dark-haired man climbed out.

Gas Station Guy.

She tried to force her gaze down to her boots, but it didn't last long. Her eyes zeroed in on him.

The dark shadows had gone from under his eyes, and the plain gray T-shirt did nothing to hide his rippled torso and arms, but there was still a rumpled look to him. Like he was too busy to do more than just run a hand through his hair before putting on whatever random piece of clothing he could find. *It suited him.*

Her heart pounded.

This could be a problem.

A definite problem.

"Dad, this is Paige. Paige, this is Dad. I mean Luke," Kira giggled before continuing on like a freight train. "And guess what? She said I could work at the bookstore. Isn't that great?"

The way his mouth tightened suggested otherwise.

"I said it was only okay if your dad agreed," she clarified, trying and failing not to be offended at the dark look he was sending her way. And his name was Luke. It was a nice name. Strong, simple, masculine.

And totally on my "no" list.

"You've offered her a job?" His voice was lower than she remembered, and a whole lot hotter. Damn.

"Not exactly, it's just—"

"Diana left the place in a big mess." Kira was now standing on one leg, executing a ballet move, her gangly arms swinging outward for balance. "And on account of all the table hiding, I know where everything is! It's perfect. Besides, you're the one who told me to get a paper route."

Luke's jaw clenched, and she found herself trapped in his gaze.

Her stomach tightened, and heat pooled lower down.

This was all Zoe's fault for mentioning wild lady oats.

And Dr. Penny Groves's fault for mentally telling me to give Kira a job.

Okay, and my fault for finding him attractive.

Even his withering gaze didn't seem to cool her down. Which was yet more proof she couldn't trust her instincts. She shut her eyes and assessed the problem. It could still be fixed if Luke just said no.

Perhaps I should lend him the book?

"Fine," he eventually muttered, obviously no match for his exuberant daughter.

See, this was the problem with men. They could never be trusted to do what you wanted them to do.

Well, she'd just have to make sure she avoided him from now on. Which, considering the pained expression in his heavenly—er, sardonic—eyes, shouldn't be hard. With that in mind, she plastered on a smile and waited until they drove away before heading back into the store.

Her phone beeped, and her brother's name flashed up on the screen. She failed to say no to Kira, but she was definitely saying no to him. She hit delete before she could change her mind. It was quickly followed by yet another text message from her old boss.

What's Darren Lester's favorite color?

Her fingers hovered over the keys. It was orange, and he was obsessed with it to the point of refusing to do any book signings unless he had an orange coffee cup and pen. *And it's all written down in the thirty-page dossier I left behind.* It was time she started "owning" her nos.

She sucked in some air and deleted it as Laney waved from next door, holding up a bottle of wine.

Paige gratefully nodded her head and flipped the CLOSED sign over. Perhaps wine would help her ignore the fact that right now her new life was just as complicated as her old one.

Chapter Three

"Don't underestimate the power of no. It will stop you from buying that one-size-too-small dress on sale, from eating the extra piece of pie, and telling your piece of crap ex it's not okay to leave his stuff at your place anymore." **Just Say No**

"Hi there." Paige smiled as an old man with snow-white hair shuffled toward her, dust mites dancing in his wake. He was dressed in neatly pressed red overalls and had a long grizzly beard, the same color as his hair. Santa Claus in a hardware store. It was promising.

"You're the new Diana, eh?" He came to a halt and studied her. "I'm Floyd. Not much of a reader. Last book I picked up was about some poor kids locked in an attic. Enough to put a person off donuts for life."

She tried to ignore the irony that apart from Kira, Floyd was the first person who'd actually talked about a book with her. Even if it was forty years old. She held out her hand.

"I'm Paige, and I'm not much of a hardware expert."

"Seems we'll get on just fine." Floyd gave her a toothy

grin and took her hand. His skin was papery against hers. "How can I help?"

She smiled and consulted her list. "I'm looking for an adjustable wrench, a soldering torch, and a shutoff valve. Oh, and some gloves."

"Sounds like you need a new toilet valve." He leaned against the counter, studying her face. "If you want my advice, save yourself the bother and call Charlie Higgins. He'll do the job for you."

"That's okay," she said in a casual voice, as if replacing toilet valves was second nature to her. Who knew? Maybe after she was finished, they would be. More to the point, she'd already spoken to Charlie, and according to him the job would cost one thousand dollars. One thousand dollars she didn't have. "I can manage."

He took off his glasses and rubbed his eyes, as if trying hide his skeptical stare. Then he shrugged. "The wrench and valve are in aisle three." He pointed to the far side of the store with an arthritic finger. "And I keep the torches out back. Any kind in particular?"

The cheap kind.

"Er, whatever you recommend," she said as he shuffled away at a glacial pace. She turned to inspect the store before realizing that unlike Fireside Books, Floyd's hardware was busy with people. A young couple were looking at paint colors as an elderly woman in a red apron hovered nearby. *Mrs. Floyd?*

A middle-aged man was examining the wheels of a trolley, while several other people drifted past, arms full of items.

She plastered on a smile and found the aisle Floyd had pointed to.

There were shelves of strangely shaped brass fittings. None of them looked like the valve she'd seen in the YouTube clip. No doubt Charlie Higgins would know what they were. Still, she was a strong, modern woman who had driven across the country on her own. She could figure it out. She picked up the two most likely candidates as a familiar voice drifted over from another aisle.

"Jacob, relax. I'm just picking up a few things from Floyd's. I'll be there in half an hour."

She stiffened. Luke Carmichael.

Before she could question it, Paige dropped down to the ground and pressed herself against the shelf. It had been five days since she'd met the man, and despite the fact he'd been into the store twice to collect Kira, she'd successfully avoided him by using much the same tactics.

Straight out of a middle schooler's playbook.

"Luke," another voice suddenly said. Female. Possibly elderly. Not that it mattered. Obviously. "Would you be a doll and show me where you got that fire bucket from. I've been in this darn store for fifteen minutes looking for one."

"Probably because this is the last of them," Luke said.

"Isn't that typical of Floyd. Trust him not to restock just as the weather's about to turn. Now I'll need to drive all the way to Portland," the woman grumbled.

"Don't be silly. Take this one. I'll grab one when they're back in stock," Luke said. The other woman tried to protest, but he dismissed her. "It's fine, Brenda. Give my love to Tony and I'll see you both at the town meeting."

The woman murmured something that might've been about turnips. Or turtles. Then she headed to the counter, and Paige risked peering through the shelving. Brenda was indeed in her sixties.

Not that I care.

She waited until Luke had made his own way to the counter before standing up. Then let out a soft groan as he suddenly turned back around, as if he'd forgotten something.

Crap.

His eyes flickered in surprise. "I didn't realize you were here."

That would be because she'd been hiding.

I wish I was still *hiding.*

Because no good could come from talking to a good-looking man who was nice to little old women in need of a fire bucket.

"I just had to get a few things." She idly waved her hands in the air before deciding that was stupid, especially when she was still holding the two potential shutoff valves. She thrust her arms back down by her side.

"I see," he said, his eyes focusing in on the brass contraptions. "You need a hand with something?"

Only with my life.

"No. I've got everything under control," she assured him, then let out a sigh as he shrugged and returned to the aisle where he'd been. This time she stayed right where she was until he'd taken his items up to the counter and finally headed out the door. At least she'd said no. That was something, right?

• • •

"Remind me why we're doing this?" Luke's brother, Jacob, demanded as they finished chopping up the heavy branch that had fallen down by the church on First Street. "Because I believe your invitation was for beer and pretzels."

"I never promised pretzels," Luke countered and took a step back to inspect their handiwork. Last week's storm hadn't just taken out half the windows in town and numerous trees. It had also taken down Daryl, the local tree surgeon, leaving him with a broken ankle and a bad temper.

Problem was more than thirty properties needed trees

removed, and if they all used the alternative—a brashly marketed national chain called Deadwood Timber, based forty miles away—Daryl wouldn't have a business to come back to.

And St. Clair would lose yet another long-time local to the turning tide.

As head of the Rejuvenation Committee, it was his job to stop that happening.

It was fall, but the weather was muggy. He wiped his forehead, thick with sweat and sawdust, while the alpine scent of the cut wood hung in the air like a blanket.

"Yeah, and you never promised hard labor either." Jacob dragged off his T-shirt, exposing his tanned flesh. It was a well-practiced move, and Luke raised an eyebrow. His brother was a man whore. An out-and-out exhibitionist who worked on the premise you never knew who'd be walking by at any given moment.

The fact he'd slept with every eligible (and a few non-eligible) woman in the town meant the peacocking was wasted.

"It's good for your soul." Luke gathered up the chain saw while his brother busied himself loading the logs into the trailer. They could use them for the town bonfire the following month.

"Said no one ever," Jacob retorted as he flexed an arm and winked at Mrs. Raine, who was out walking her poodle. She also happened to be ninety-three years old. "Sex is good for the soul. Isn't that right, Mrs. R?"

"At my age, waking up is good for the soul," the old woman corrected.

"Worth a shot." He flashed a smile and turned back to Luke, who'd finished putting the tools away. "And while we're on the subject of sex, I think I speak for the whole town when I say you need to get laid."

"And I speak for the whole town when I say you should worry less about my business and more about your own." Luke didn't bother to point out that discussing his sex life in front of a church—*the* church—he'd been married in wasn't ideal.

Then again, there was no good place to have this conversation.

Not that it ever stopped his brother or sister from trying. In fact, recently it had become their specialty subject.

How to get Luke laid according to Jacob and Trina Carmichael.

His siblings had way too much time on their hands.

Plus, he had enough on his plate. Between his contracting business, restoring the old marina, and bringing a heartbeat back to the town, not to mention his grandmother's party, there was no time for anything else.

"That's where you're wrong." Jacob offered up a serene smile, reminding Luke just how futile it was to argue with his brother. The guy had a back like a duck. "Too much work and not enough play makes Luke a total—"

"Pain in the ass?" he finished off.

"I was going to say butt, but ass will do." His brother effortlessly lifted the second chainsaw and carried it to the truck. "And all this abstinence is bad for your health. There must be someone you're interested in."

"Nope." He snapped his eyes shut to dislodge the image of Paige in her faded jeans and soft white blouse that was almost see-through in certain lights. She was cute. More than cute.

All the more reason to stay away.

Especially since his bookworm daughter had managed to get a job there.

Something she hadn't stopped talking about since. Which was all part of the problem. Paige would get sick of St. Clair, just like Diana had. Then she'd leave, and Kira would be hurt.

He'd seen it happen too many times.

City folk who bowled into town, hoping the charm and rustic quaintness of the sea change would fix whatever was wrong with them. Using his town for therapy, rather than seeing it for what it really was.

Another dying dot on the map, trying to stay afloat.

Not to mention it interfered with his plan to avoid her until she left town. She was a temptation he couldn't afford.

Besides, it wasn't like he *never* had sex. He was just careful to make sure it was casual and didn't encroach on his life in any way. More to the point, his daughter's life.

"Hey, here's Melanie. She'd be perfect for you. She's cute. Kind. Funny—"

"And *she* can hear you. Jacob Carmichael, you have a voice like a foghorn," Melanie Banks announced as she joined the brothers. She was a couple of years younger than Luke with straight dark hair, a wide mouth, and large doe eyes. At one time she'd flirted with the idea of moving to Los Angeles, but then her mom had become sick, and she'd stayed back to care for her. And while she appeared happy enough, every now and then a veil of bitterness shimmered around her, as if reminding her of another life she could've had.

"And you, Melanie, have the face of an angel," Jacob countered in a flirty voice, which earned him a frosty look. "Which is why I thought you and Luke would be perfect together. Why haven't you ever dated before?"

"Hmmmm. Let's see. It probably has something to do with the fact I was Joanne's best friend. As in Luke's wife?" Melanie arched an eyebrow, and this time Jacob did have the good grace to wince.

"Ex-wife," Luke corrected in a controlled voice, while making a mental note to never go out in public with his brother again. He turned to her. "How are you, Mel?"

"Fine." She nodded before seeming to lose an internal battle. She sighed. "Okay, not fine. Have you met her yet?"

"Met who?" Jacob looked up at the mention of a female pronoun and promptly flexed his pecs in preparation.

"The new owner of Fireside Books."

"No, is she cute?" Jacob said before catching Melanie's furled up mouth. "Er, I'm guessing that's not the right question to ask."

Normally Luke enjoyed watching his cocky brother squirm, but right now he was tired, hungry, and still had wages to do.

He threw Jacob a metaphorical lifeline.

"Mel wanted to buy the store."

"I made a fair offer, and I'm fourth gen St. Clair born and bred. But Diana didn't care, she just took the money and ran."

"She always was a weird one. I'm sure the new owner's much nicer."

"As usual, you're missing the point." Melanie folded her arms and gave Jacob a withering glare. "Oh, and listen to this, I was talking to Len before. He turned up to fix a broken window only to have this Paige Taylor tell him she could do it herself."

"Let me guess." Jacob rolled his eyes. "Somewhere in the St. Clair Rejuvenation Committee Handbook is a subsection on supporting local businesses, making fixing your own window punishable by whipping."

"It makes economic sense. A rising tide lifts all boats. And put your shirt back on. We've all seen your abs, Jacob. It's getting old," Melanie retorted before her cell phone beeped. She sighed and turned to Luke. "I gotta go make sure mom's taken her tablets, but tell Olive I'm pleased she's on the mend. Are you going to Carol and Nina's engagement party?"

"I'm not sure I can make it." He shrugged.

Disappointment flashed across her mouth, but an instant later it was gone. "I'll see you if I see you then," she said. She paused to give Jacob a dark glare before walking away, her shoulders stiff and tense.

"Jeez, what's her problem?" Jacob bristled once they were alone. "And I take it back. Don't hook up with her."

"I hadn't intended to."

"Good. So, tell me more about the new owner. Have you met her? Is she cute?" his brother demanded, like a missile-seeking puppy, the sting from Melanie's verbal burn obviously fading.

Hell, yes.

"I didn't notice." He shrugged as they both climbed into the truck. "And let me save you the time. No, I'm not going to sleep with her. Or anyone else."

"Ever?" Jacob demanded.

"At least until Kira's older. And speaking of which, she'll be on her way home from Girl Scouts, which means it's my famous mac and cheese night. Want in? I might even throw one of those beers your way, if you play your cards right."

Despite being the biggest matrimonial flight risk this side of Seattle, Jacob took his uncle duties very seriously, surprising just about everyone with how much he doted on his niece. Everyone but Luke, who had no trouble believing anyone could fall under his daughter's charm. She was literally the greatest kid in the world and was the reason he worked so hard to rebuild the small coastal community to what it had once been. He wanted her to experience just how much St. Clair had to offer. And to prove to his ex-wife that while the town wasn't big enough for her, it was plenty great for their daughter.

• • •

"And this is one of our breakout stars for the season." The sales rep waved a kiss-and-tell autobiography in front of her, forcing Paige to look up from the list she'd been working on. *How to get more sales.* Though actually she'd be better off changing it to *How to get any sales.*

"I'm not sure it's right for my customers," she lied, wishing the guy would go away. He'd been sitting in her back office for half an hour showing her book after book she couldn't afford.

"Yes, but that's where you're wrong. These'll walk out of here like hotcakes."

Hotcakes? Hmmm. That was an idea. Perhaps she should just turn the place into a hotcake store? Then she frowned as she realized it would clash with Sam's business. Plus, her baking wasn't much better than her ability to get sales reps to finish their pitch.

It had been two weeks since she'd opened her doors, and she'd sold ten bookmarks, a dozen paperbacks, and the fox doorknocker to a smitten tourist who offered her a hundred bucks. Somewhere in there was a life lesson, but she wasn't sure she wanted to know what it was.

Finally, the rep packed up his boxes, leaving her with a catalogue and the promise to call in next time he was in the area.

Once he was gone, she wandered into the store.

The polished floorboards gleamed, the shelves were dusted, and the gorgeous fall flowers Laney had created were on the counter. On the display table were piles of books enticingly displayed on the cute old wooden boxes Kira had found in the basement the previous day.

All that was missing were the bags of gold she assumed would follow.

The old cuckoo clock sprang into life, ringing out five times to remind her it was closing time. *Another day, another seven dollars and thirty-two cents.*

She locked the door and turned the sign over before heading to the stairs behind her office, which led up to her apartment.

Cardboard packing boxes sat around her small collection of furniture. Most of which had come from Zoe's store.

It was all ash blond wood, with a nod to Scandinavian simplicity, bought for her New York apartment. Unfortunately, while it fitted her old life perfectly, it was out of place against the patterned carpet and the yellow walls a previous owner had painted.

She was sure she'd figure out a way to make it look better, but now was not that moment. She studied the contents of the fridge. A healthy salad she'd made up yesterday to go with her equally healthy quinoa and salmon. There was also a jar of olives, a bottle of green juice, and a pot of soup.

Oh, and a slice of cherry almond pie Sam had dropped off yesterday.

Her new neighbor wasn't just a great barista, but one hell of a baker, as Paige's waistline was discovering.

Her stomach seemed to nod in approval at the pie, but she ignored it. Her metabolism wasn't what it once was. And she was a grown woman. She couldn't eat pie for dinner.

Soup it was.

She poured it into a saucepan and set the temperature on low before going in search of her vitamin tablet she took every night. She found them underneath a stack of book catalogues and shook one out before wandering to the front window of the apartment.

It overlooked the horseshoe bay the small community was built around. Wooden remains of an old jetty jutted out of the slate gray water like toothpicks, and several swimmers were penguined-up in rubbery black wetsuits, braving the cooling waters to freestyle their way out to a floating platform. The Belles had told her they were octogenarians who'd started the tradition a few years ago to raise money for charity, but had kept it up for health reasons.

Personally, Paige didn't get the appeal of swimming in freezing cold water. Then again, she wasn't eighty.

No, I just feel like it sometimes.

She took her vitamin and was about to go back to the kitchen when the theme music from *Jaws* rang out.

Her shoulders tensed.

James.

She'd spent the last two weeks ignoring an increasing number of calls from both her brother *and* her ex-boss, but James's last message implied if she didn't answer, he'd fly from Boston to see her. Not because he cared, but because he hated to be ignored.

"Hey, how's it going?" she said by way of greeting.

"How's it going?" His voice was sharp. "Well, let's see. I've had to stop Audrey from buying a leather sofa, five pairs of boots, and a worm farm. How do you think it's going?"

She resisted the urge to remind him it was his idea for their mom to move from New York to Boston. Or that he'd spent the past year insisting she was imagining their mom's increasingly erratic behavior. Or that since their mom treated James like a demigod, perhaps it was time for him to actually earn the title.

Her brother settled the decision by carrying on in a pompous voice. "I need you to talk to her. Poor Fi's exhausted."

"Me?" Paige stared at the peeling paint on the wall and picked up one of the decorative pillows to see if it would look better on the other chair. "Since when has she ever listened to me?"

"You practically lived next door to her for the last sixteen years. You're a lot closer to her than I am."

"A forty-minute trip by train is *hardly* next door," she

retorted. And as for being close? That was laughable.

Not that Paige hadn't tried over the years.

But after her dad left, her mom (who'd insisted on being called Audrey because *mom* made her feel old) had thrown herself into her nursing career and built a wall of ice between herself and the world, waiting for him to return. He never had, but his absence had filled the room even more fully than his presence ever did.

That was until last year. It had been Paige's job to deliver the news he'd died. She'd braced herself with a large whiskey and had an even larger one for her mother. But, instead of tears, she'd burst into hysterical laughter.

Two weeks later Audrey had booked a singles' cruise to go around Florida.

Paige tried to remind her she hadn't dated in almost forty years, and once you got on the cruise, you were stuck. But nothing had changed her mind. That had just been the start of the year of acting strangely.

The only un-strange thing she'd done was sell the two up, two down in New Jersey, and declare she was moving to Boston to be closer to James and the grandchildren.

It wasn't a surprise. Her mom had spent a lifetime telling her just how amazing James was with his very own law firm and his equally successful (bitchy) wife Fiona. Not to mention the two postcard-perfect children called, wait for it—James and Fiona. It made sense she wanted to be near the child she actually liked.

The silver lining was it had made Paige's own decision to leave New York easier.

Something her brother seemed to have forgotten.

"Look. She's probably still adjusting to life in Boston. Moving can be hard." She glanced around the messy apartment. "Just give her time."

"It's all very well for you to say, with only yourself to

worry about," he retorted. "Which is why Fi and I think the best solution is for you to move to Boston."

Her jaw went slack. Though she wasn't sure why she was surprised at her brother's narcissism. Their father had been exactly the same. Anything outside of their own wants and needs didn't register.

"I've just bought a business on the Oregon coast." She forced her voice to stay calm.

"Please, you only did that on a whim because of Patrick. Everyone knows retail's dying."

"That's not true," Paige said, crossing her fingers and trying not to remember James was summa cum laude at Harvard.

"Really," her brother retorted, his voice so cutting she was certain he could see down the phone directly into her profit and loss spreadsheet. "Tell me, how are you managing to buck the trend of a nation in a tiny, backwater town with almost no business experience under your belt?"

I really walked into that one.

She pressed her lips together and didn't answer.

Zoe wanted her to move back to New York, James wanted her in Boston, and the good folk of St. Clair didn't seem to care where she went, as long as she did.

Her stomach tightened as a familiar panic caught in her throat. She swallowed it down.

"Look." James's voice was softer, as if sensing victory was near. "There's no shame in making a mistake. The trick is to stop before it gets worse. Besides, you love Boston. And if you come back here, the whole family will be together. Just like old times."

"What old times are you remembering?" She frowned.

Beeeeeeeeeeeeeeep.

"What the hell's that?" he muttered as a waft of hazy black smoke billowed out of the kitchen.

Crap. It was the soup.

"Nothing," she said as the fire alarm beeped again. "And to me moving anywhere back east, the answer's no. Give my love to Audrey, Fiona, and the kids. I'll talk to you later."

"Paige, don't hang up. I want you to think about what I—" he started to say, but she ended the call and raced into the kitchen. She pulled the saucepan off the stovetop and threw open a window. Then used a tea towel to fan away the arid stench. The alarm stopped beeping, and she let out a long sigh as she went to the fridge. This time she didn't even try and talk herself out of the cherry almond pie.

It had been that kind of day.

Chapter Four

"The best things in life begin with N. Netflix, Nachos, and No." **Just Say No**

"Dad, come in. I want to show you what I made," Kira said, her heavy school bag weighing down one of her shoulders. He'd parked his truck outside the bookstore just like he'd done for the past week. His daughter had already dragged him into the store twice, but thankfully there'd been no sign of Paige. He didn't want to push his luck.

"Sorry, not tonight. We're due at Olive's in five minutes," Luke said, not bothering to add that his grandmother wouldn't have minded if they were a little late. The point was—

Wait. Don't answer that.

A flash of disappointment crossed her face as she climbed into the front seat of the truck. "Lucky I took photos of it," she said, fastening her seatbelt.

"Great. You can show me at Olive's." He flicked the engine on. "How was school?"

"The same." She gave the standard teenage response,

and he resisted the urge to smile. Up until middle school she'd come home everyday full of conversation, all sparkling eyes and pink cheeks. Olive promised him it would pass, and considering his own monotone answers at the same age, he believed her. Then she brightened. "It's Paige. Hang on a minute."

So much for a quick getaway. He cut the engine and schooled his features as the new bookstore owner walked toward them, clutching something in her hand.

"Hey," Paige said in a breathy voice as Kira wound down her window. "I'm glad I caught you."

"We're in a hurry," Luke said, and then regretted it as red splotches rose onto her cheeks. "Sorry. Long day."

"It's fine." She shrugged, as if battling to control the rising color on her face. She turned to Kira and held out a slim schoolbook. "Thought you might need this before your math class tomorrow."

"I could live without it," Kira deadpanned before grinning. "But Mr. Holmes might not be happy."

"Hell have no fury like a math teacher scorned," Paige quipped, which sent Kira into a peal of laughter. She then gave Luke an apologetic grimace. "I'd better not keep you both."

"Thanks for returning the book," he said, his voice sounding gruffer than he'd intended. She didn't answer. Just stepped back from the truck and gave Kira a small wave before walking back to the store.

"You forgot your homework?" He raised an eyebrow since his daughter was normally meticulous with her schoolwork. Even the subjects she didn't like.

"It must've fallen out when I was packing my new books," Kira admitted. "You'll never guess how many Paige gave me."

"Two?" he said in a cautious voice. Despite the original deal to pay Kira in books, his daughter had already come home with her first week's pay packet.

"Ten." She unzipped her school bag, and it became apparent why it had been so heavy. A stack of books spilled out, and Kira lovingly patted them. "Isn't that amazing? I'm going to write reviews on them, which Paige will put in her newsletter."

"That's great," he made himself answer in a light voice, which didn't seem to fool her.

"You don't like her?" Kira said, though he couldn't decide if it was a statement or a question. His fingers tightened around the steering wheel. Truth was it was impossible to dislike someone who made his kid so happy. Who took the time to talk to her. Not to mention give her a job. *And yet no matter how nice she is, she's still going to leave, and my kid will get hurt.*

It was a conundrum he hadn't quite figured out.

"What makes you say that?" he said.

"I don't know." Kira shrugged as she continued to pat the pile of books in her lap. "But you should. She's really nice. Plus, can you believe she ships Amira and Renarto?"

"Really?" Luke said. He'd just about figured out what "shipping" was, but had no idea what book Amira and Renarto were from. "That's great."

"Great." Kira made a clicking noise. "It's more than great. They're not even in the same series, which makes it hardcore. She's so cool."

"Almost as cool as you," Luke said, swallowing down his unease. It earned him a groan and a smile all the same time. It was enough for him, and he returned his daughter's grin. Besides, it didn't matter if he did or didn't like St. Clair's newest resident. All that mattered was his daughter's happiness.

• • •

Paige stepped back to inspect her handiwork. She'd set up a display of cookbooks along with some brightly colored pots and pans she'd bought several years ago on a whim and never used since. In the middle was a plate of Sam's killer salted caramel cookies on an ornate cake stand with a glass lid over them. A little bribery never hurt anyone.

The door chime rang, and an elderly man slowly pushed open the door. It was raining outside, and a gust of wind almost sent him flying into the store. He was dressed in a navy jacket and had an old-fashioned deerstalker hat on his head that glistened with raindrops.

His face was a weathered road map of lines, but his eyes were lively as he peered around. "Bookstore, eh? I remember a time when this place sold bicycles."

"That would explain all the oil cans in the basement." She smiled. "Can I help you look for anything?"

"No, no." He waved a hand and nodded toward the window. "I just got a text from Myra, she's half an hour late and didn't want me to wait in the rain. The woman fusses like a hen."

"Is Myra your wife?" She blinked.

"Lord, no. My Elizabeth died three years ago, bless her. Myra drives the bingo bus, and this is my stop. Though we're always late thanks to Alan Rankin. In the seventy years I've known him, he's never been on time. They say age makes you wiser, but in Alan's case it just makes him forget where he put his teeth."

"Probably best not to leave home without them." She only just repressed a laugh as she held out her hand. "I'm Paige."

"Geoffrey Jones, but everyone calls me Smith, because I make horseshoes. Well, I did," he said and held up his hand. It was shaking. "Damn medication. These days I can barely hold a pen."

"Nice to meet you, Smith. And you're welcome to wait for Myra. Come and sit down."

She nodded to the reading nook she'd set up over by the fireplace.

There was a wooden table with four mismatched chairs around it and a pile of random coffee table books all stacked up, while in the other corner were a couple of wingback reading chairs, one dusty pink and the other a plush dark green velvet, both with long-armed lamps bowing over them.

Smith frowned. "I don't want to take up any of your space. Wouldn't want to scare off your customers."

Something was scaring them off, but it wasn't the sweet old man in front of her.

"Nonsense."

She led him over and let him get settled just as the door chimed again. It was another elderly man. Unlike Smith, he didn't have a hat on, and his bald head and thick walrus moustache were slicked with rain. He caught sight of Smith and ambled over.

"That Alan and his teeth. I swear one of these days I'll glue them in," the man said before looking over to her. "And you must be the new owner. Nice to meet you. I'm Marlon."

"Paige," she said as Marlon eased himself down into one of the wooden chairs.

"The other one looks comfortable, but you'd need a forklift to get me back up," he explained. "You're a book person, eh? What do you think of the latest Reacher?"

"I've heard it's very good," she said, not quite wanting to admit she read more romance than thrillers. "I take it you're a fan?"

"Keeps me out of mischief." He winked before plucking out a large handkerchief and wiping his wet scalp.

"Really? Who was it that spiked the punch at the last town dance, then?" Smith quirked an eyebrow, and Marlon looked like a kid caught raiding the cookie jar.

"In my defense I wanted to get Myra to go on a date with me. I swear she's been playing hard to get for the last twenty years."

"Perhaps if you wooed her with candy and flowers instead of limericks and brandy you might get somewhere," Smith retorted.

"Hey, there's nothing wrong with limericks," Marlon protested before clearing his throat. "There once was a girl from St. Clair, who always got things caught in her hair—"

"I'm not sure Paige's virgin ears are ready for what's going to come next." Smith held up his hand, and Marlon looked contrite.

She grinned as the cuckoo clock chimed. It was eleven o'clock. She normally stopped for a coffee. The two old men were bickering between themselves about whether "fanny" rhymed with "any" while she busied herself brewing a fresh pot.

They'd moved onto a lively discussion of last week's bingo, and since no more customers had walked into the store, she poured two extra cups.

"Well, aren't you a doll." Marlon grinned and glanced over to the display table. "Do I spy Samantha Harris's cookies? That girl has the touch. She's the only one in this town who comes close to Patsy."

"Now Marlon, don't you go mooching."

"Who says I'm mooching? This is a medical emergency." Marlon pulled out a plastic pillbox and rattled it like a maraca before shaking a couple of lethally sized capsules into his hand. "That new doctor insisted I take 'em with food. I'm just following the rules."

"Please, you make up the rules as you go along. Paige, sweetheart, just ignore him."

Again, she smothered a smile as she carried the cake

stand filled with cookies over to the two men. They might not be buying anything, but at least they were keeping her amused.

Half an hour and four cookies later, Smith and Marlon both eased themselves up to their feet, leaving a trail of crumbs behind them as they tottered to the door, where a bright orange minivan was waiting for them.

Behind the wheel was a tiny woman with long black hair. It was obviously Myra, and Paige giggled. Marlon's crush was probably about half his age. No wonder his limericks hadn't been working.

Myra gave Paige a friendly wave and then hurried the two men into the van before roaring off, no doubt to make up time after the missing teeth saga.

She drifted inside and tackled the debris left behind by her elderly visitors, when a young woman came in, a golden-haired toddler in her arms. Paige perked up. She'd just received a new shipment of picture books that she was itching to talk about.

"Hi." She beamed, but the woman just shook her head.

"No time for talking. Which way to the restroom?"

"I don't have a public—" she started to say before noticing the green tinge to the toddler's face. "Er, through the office and to the right."

Somewhere in her mind Dr. Penny Groves was laughing at her, but Paige hummed to block the noise as she returned to her tidying. She stacked the mugs onto a tray and wiped the wooden table. There were more crumbs on the seat of the chair, along with a small folded note where Marlon had been sitting. She carefully opened it.

Roses are red,
Violets are blue.
Cookies are good,

And so are you.
(p.s. though next time I prefer ones with cherries)

She smiled and tucked the note into her pocket. Okay, she wasn't quite making millions yet, but she'd just received her first limerick. That had to mean something, right?

• • •

"Son, you look like hell. Let me guess, another night of community patrol?"

"Volunteers are thin on the ground for Tuesday. No one wants to miss two-for-one tacos. Not to mention the margaritas," Luke said as he walked into Do or Dye hair salon on Elm Street.

"They're good margaritas. You should take a night off and try them."

"Then who'd drive home Lucy Granger and Neil Oslow?" Luke replied, which was exactly what he'd done when he'd found the two elderly residents toddling along the esplanade singing show tunes.

This earned a throaty laugh.

At sixty-two, with sharp dark eyes and a handlebar moustache, Victor Hathaway was the unlikely owner. An ex-biker with a sleeve of tattoos and a colorful history, he'd moved into the small town twenty years ago, and far from causing trouble like people predicted, he'd taken over the salon from Luke's aunt and had been primping and preening the folk of St. Clair ever since. Five years ago, he'd also bought an old bar five miles up the road, but it was strictly for cowboys and bikers, and seemed to circulate in a different orbit to the rest of the town.

"I take it you're here about the cottage conversion."

"You guessed right." Luke held up his clipboard.

"Okay, let's just finish up here." Victor whirled his

scissors around his finger like a gunslinger and motioned Jessica Harris over to the dryers. Once he'd set her up, with the timer going, he headed to the front of the store, where he picked up the coffeepot. "Want one?

"Sure." He took the coffee, and they both walked out to the bench seat that ran the length of the storefront. "What's on the agenda for today?"

"Plumbing's going in next week, which means you need to sort out your fittings, and we need to lock in Jason for the tiles. Please tell me you've made your final decisions."

The guilty look on Victor's face didn't fill him with confidence. "I swear I'll get it done this week. Things have been crazy here."

"I know, but if you want this conversion finished before winter, we need to make the decisions now." He took a slug of coffee, then wished he hadn't. It was bad. Like burned mud bad. He suspected it was because Victor's receptionist and right hand had recently moved over to Europe to join her fiancé. "Still haven't found a replacement for Sandy?"

Victor shook his head and poured his own drink into the nearby potted plant. "You try convincing anyone to drive to St. Clair when they can earn twice the money in Portland. Maybe when this conversion is finished I can shut down the salon and just operate the Airbnb and the bar."

Luke winced, trying to imagine what the town would be like without a hairdresser in it. Bowl cuts flashed into his mind. "I'm sure you'll find someone. I'll leave these here for you."

Victor took the catalogues. "Thanks. And I meant what I said. You need to relax. In fact, it's probably time you got—"

"If you say laid, then I swear to god I'll bury fish bones in the cottage that you'll never find," Luke warned. Victor let out a bark of laughter and held up his hands.

"Okay, well at least get a massage. Or a scented candle."

"Right," Luke said, trying to reconcile Victor's tattooed arms with the advice in question. "I'll see what I can do."

Ding.

"No rest for the wicked." Victor winked and eased himself up at the sound of the dryer timer going off. "I'll decide on the fittings tonight."

"Thanks." He made a mental note to follow up again tomorrow. Then he consulted his list.

First port of call was the hardware store to order wood for the decking around his grandmother's hot tub, then he'd swing by Patsy's for lunch. He nodded to several people as he turned left on Ryan Street. The shops he'd known all his life were decorated for fall. Large pumpkins of all colors and sizes were stacked on upturned boxes, while cornhusks trailed around doorframes like spiked feather boas.

None of it quite matched the bright blue sky, but the wind, as if feeling the need to cooperate, lazily drifted in small eddies, half-heartedly picking up crisp orange and brown leaves as it went. Still, the nights were definitely getting cooler, and by winter the skies would lose their brightness.

And what the hell was she doing?

He stared at the sight in front of him.

An old wooden ladder was pushed against the side of Fireside Books, and at the top of it was Paige Taylor, precariously leaning forward, trying to reach the guttering that had blown loose. A couple of male tourists were admiring the curve of her body as she stretched out her hand, but neither of them appeared interested in stopping her.

He blinked, not sure whether to be amused at the spectacle or worried she was going to kill herself. *Or admire her determination.*

It was obvious she had zero experience with either ladders or guttering. He was surprised she wasn't wearing the same inappropriate shoes that'd almost hit him when they first met. The ladder swayed in the wind, and Luke swore as he shouldered past the tourists.

He steadied the ladder as best he could, while trying not to look directly up. He failed and was rewarded with an even better view of her long legs, covered in tight jeans that left little to the imagination. Or at least to *his* imagination. He tightened his grip and focused on the broken gutter hanging out at a drunken angle.

She wasn't aware of him as she continued to lean forward, chanting to herself, "*I say no to fear. I'm an unstoppable force. An unstoppable force who absolutely isn't scared of heights. I say no to being scared of heights.*"

"How about you say no to heights from down here?" He tried to use the same coaxing voice he'd once used on Kira to convince her to eat carrots. Mainly because if she *was* scared of heights, the last thing he wanted to do was startle her.

It didn't work, and the whole ladder wobbled as she awkwardly looked down. Her eyes narrowed in dislike at the sight of him, and he sucked in his breath.

Yeah, I probably deserve that.

All the same, while he might not like her, and she most *definitely* didn't like him, he didn't have any desire for her to get hurt.

"I'm fine, thank you."

"You don't look fine," he replied. If any of his crew tried something so spectacularly stupid, he would've bawled them out on the spot. Instead, he had to content himself with keeping the wooden frame steady.

"You'd think that." She shrugged before letting out a sigh. Her teeth were white against her full lips, and something in him stirred. "Please go away. I have everything under control."

Which was probably the same answer Mrs. Gilbert's tree-loving cat, Trevor, would've given him, if in fact the cat could talk. Unfortunately, it didn't make it true.

He suspected it was the same with Paige.

"I'm not disagreeing, it's just I can't see where your crane wrench is, and since that's what you need to fix the guttering, I was going to offer you mine."

"I really hope that's not a euphemism," she retorted, but the bluster had gone from her voice, and her knuckles whitened around the wooden uprights. Uncertainty flared in her blue eyes. "D-do I really need a wrench?"

"To go dancing, no. To fix a gutter, yes," he agreed in a soothing voice, while trying to ignore the way her hip was pressing into the wooden frame. Just pretend she's a cat stuck up a tree. Or the time Trina needed to be rescued from the high diving board at the local pool. Or any of the other community mishaps he came across while doing his patrol.

"Okay." She shakily lowered one leg to the next rung. He let out the breath he didn't know he was holding as her second foot followed. Her face was now the color of marzipan, while her neck and shoulders were stiff.

"You're doing great," he coaxed as she slowly made progress. Seven rungs to go. Six. Five. "Just take your time."

She didn't bother to reply. With a shuddering breath she bent her knee, and her right foot found the rung below. "Unstoppable force," she mumbled as she eased her way down.

"Nice, well done," he said. "You're almost—"

He was cut off as the wood groaned and creaked. Probably from the shock of being used after such a long time. Paige, who'd just been in the process of stepping down, stiffened, and her foot missed the rung.

Instinct kicked in, and he wrapped his hands around her legs, her body slithering down into his arms.

Mistake.

Big freaking mistake.

A hundred volts of electricity raced through him as her soft body pressed against his chest. A tangle of coppery golden hair brushed his skin, and the faint scent of flowers caught in his nose. A distant voice in his head thundered to let go, but he continued to hold her tight, knowing the shock would fade faster that way.

"It's okay," he murmured as the shaking subsided and she took a wobbly step away from him.

One of the buttons on her soft gray blouse had come undone, displaying just a hint of a white lacy bra. Something slammed against his chest at the swell of her breast.

Should I tell her about the button? Yeah, I should tell her.

He didn't tell her.

Color returned to her face, and she shook her arms, as if trying to get rid of excess energy. Luke longed to do the same, but he didn't want to show he'd been affected. Think of tax bills. Think of standing on a nail. *Think of the promise I made the day Joanne walked out on us.*

Always put my daughter first.

His pulse abruptly curveballed back to standard operating procedure.

"You okay?" His voice came out harsher than intended.

"I'm fine. Sorry for the mid-ladder freak out." She clamped down on her lower lip.

"It happens to the best of us," he replied as the background noise filtered into his head. A small crowd had gathered on the other side of the street. He scowled. "Let's get you inside."

She nodded and walked to the front door. He followed her, stopping only to flip the CLOSED sign over and lock the door while she sank down onto a dusky pink reading chair that had been set up in a little nook. It was new, along with the embroidered decorative pillows and the framed book quotes hanging on the walls.

She stared at her hands, as if unsure what to do with them.

"Can I get you a cup of tea?"

"No tea." Her long blonde hair had escaped from behind her ears and was hanging down around her face. "Sorry for being a bother."

"What made you think it was a good idea to go up there?" He glanced at the second chair, but it was too close. Too intimate. He leaned against the counter, arms folded.

"It looked easy in the YouTube tutorial." She sighed before wrinkling her nose. "There was no mention of a special wrench."

"Yeah, I might have made that up," he admitted.

Her blue eyes darkened as her mouth upturned into one of outrage. "Is this some alpha male thing where you think only men can fix buildings?"

He shook his head. "I just wanted to get you down from that old ladder. It could have collapsed at any second."

"Is it really that old?" Her anger faded.

"Yes. Where the hell did you even find it?"

"In the shed at the back of the yard. I figured Diana left it there."

"I'd say the dinosaurs left it there," he retorted and was surprised when she let out a soft laugh. Gorgeous and had a sense of humor? He needed to get out of there. Fast. "I'll give you Dan's number for the guttering. He's a good guy. He won't rip you off."

"Please, it's fine," she said as she stood up from the chair and moved farther away from him. "I just got a bit freaked. I'll watch a few more tutorials before I try again."

His head jerked up.

"You'll try again?" He raked his hand through his hair, and she swiftly glanced away. His brother did the same thing when he flirted with someone else's girlfriend.

But what did Paige have to hide?

And why would anyone scared of heights, with a ladder

older than carbon dating, try again?

He glanced around the store. On the surface, it was looking better than when under Diana's management. But he'd done enough work on Sam's building last year to know how much maintenance the Belles needed, and since Diana had never spent a dime on the place, he bet Paige had a shopping list of—

Floyd's hardware. She'd been in there holding valves.

There was only one reason someone with no experience bought valves or tried to fix their own gutters.

"You're broke, aren't you?" It wasn't even a question, more of a statement. He kicked himself for not figuring it out sooner. After all, half the town was suffering from the same problem.

"What? No. I mean, I just bought a bookstore. How can I be broke?" she said before sighing. "Okay, look, I'm not broke. I…have access to backup funds if I need it. Though, it's a last resort. I wasn't expecting there to be as much maintenance. Or for business to be slow. It's almost been three weeks. I hoped…" She trailed off with a shrug.

Which was why she didn't belong in St. Clair. Like most coastal towns, it earned its money from the tourists. The off-season was tough. Especially without the support of the locals. And if she hadn't prepared then she'd be gone even sooner than he'd predicted. Something else hit him.

"Why did you give Kira a job, then?"

"You mean I had a choice?" She raised an eyebrow. It was disarming, and despite himself he let out a rueful chuckle.

"I admit my kid can be quite convincing. Especially when it comes to books."

This time it was Paige who smiled. "She's been amazing. But I do owe *you* an apology. I never should've offered her a job without asking first. She was just so excited, and I've got to admit she's completely incredible. See that display—"

he followed her gaze over to a stack of orange books built to create a pumpkin. "—it was all her idea. I wish I'd half as much initiative when I was her age."

A stab of pride went through him, and his animosity faded.

It was hard to be distant with someone who could see how great his daughter was.

It was also hard to ignore the fact Kira had hustled Paige into giving her a job.

And impossible not to admire her grit.

"Makes two of us. Look, about that gutter, let me fix it tomorrow. With a ladder built this century."

She stiffened, and the small truce that had been building up evaporated. "I couldn't let you do that for free."

The irony wasn't lost on him. He'd accused her of treating his town as therapy, without regard for the people who lived there. Yet now she wasn't accepting a handout, he was pissed.

Not pissed, he corrected. *Just a concerned citizen.*

It made sense not to let a greenhorn from the city climb up a rickety old ladder.

He would've done the same for anyone. *Yeah, keep telling yourself that.*

He slammed down the voice and folded his arms. "I'm the head of the St. Clair Rejuvenation Committee, and part of the deal is we help maintain historic buildings."

She opened her mouth as if she wanted to protest before a wave of color hit her cheeks. "Okay, well, thank you," she said as she dusted imaginary fluff from the pale gray shirt, before discovering the top button had popped open. She quickly did it up along with the next two. Luke didn't need to be a psychologist to figure out the conversation was over.

Which was good. Obviously. And with a shrug he walked to the door and let himself out. He had no idea what had just happened, but he was pretty sure it could only lead to trouble.

Chapter Five

"There's a whole world waiting to be explored, and the key to entering this new kingdom is one little word." **Just Say No**

"Can I help you?" Paige said for the third time, but the woman at the counter didn't answer. She was probably in her mid-forties with streaky blonde hair and bright cheeks. She was also completely obsessed with something outside the window.

Okay, fine. It wasn't something, it was someone.

And if you dare look, I'll make you drink beansprout smoothies for a week.

The threat didn't work.

She swiveled her head to the front porch of her bookstore. Luke was talking on his phone and walking back and forth, looking far too gorgeous for a man dressed simply in a plaid shirt and denims.

And I told him I was broke.

So much for her plan to be a strong, independent businesswoman.

She'd let him know she was financially strapped and couldn't climb a ladder to save her life. Humiliation tickled her skin. Not to mention the whole button incident.

Okay, incident wasn't the right word, since it wasn't like he'd noticed it was undone. But she had, and had fantasized undoing the next one, and the next, until the whole blouse was gone. And—

"Oh my goodness." The woman dragged her gaze away and offered up a rueful smile. "I can't believe I've just been ogling Luke. If anyone tells Nina, she'll leave me at the altar."

"Your secret's safe with me." Paige tried to act like she hadn't been ogling, either. She didn't have a marriage to worry about, but she did have her own ironclad promise to say no to men (which, for the record, appeared to be made out of putty rather than iron at this particular moment in time).

Not that it really mattered.

Luke had made it painfully obvious that she was an outsider who didn't have the survival skills to make it in the picturesque town. Even more humbling, he was repairing her guttering because he was sorry for her.

"Phew!" The woman grinned. "And I'm Carol. Laney's doing the flowers for the engagement party and wedding. She said I'd like you. I can see she was right."

"Thanks. I'm guessing you already know my name's Paige."

Carol nodded. "Word spreads fast. Now, I was wondering if you could help me. Diana had the most glorious set of Jane Austens, but refused to sell them to me, because—" Her voice faltered. "Well, that's neither here nor there. But if you still have them, they'd be such a perfect gift for my fiancée…"

"I sure do." Paige swallowed back the dark thoughts on Diana as Carol followed her to the far end of the store. The books were stunningly gorgeous, the covers a rainbow of colors ranging from pastel pink to a lush shade of purple. *As if Jane Austen wasn't dreamy enough.* "And I can't think of a better present you could give your fiancée. I was tempted to keep them, but I'm pleased I didn't."

"They're as glorious as I remembered." Carol's face was a vision as she carefully inspected the exquisite books. "I'll take them."

"That's wonderful."

Her sales had been steadily increasing. Not in a way to make her accountant happy, but enough to take the tension out of her shoulders. Unfortunately, most of the sales had come from the trickle of tourists visiting the town on the off-season. Selling something that cost more than a couple of dollars to a local was a definite win.

She walked to the counter just as Kira raced up from the basement.

There was a smudge on her face, and her hair was dragged back into a ponytail, while under her arm was a gigantic piece of cardboard, bigger than the girl herself.

"Paige, you'll never guess what I've found. I mean it's totally unbelievable. Oh, hey, Carol," she said.

"Hi, sweetie." Carol picked up the carefully wrapped books and waved goodbye. "I'll leave you both in peace. But Nina and I would love for you to come to our engagement party on Friday. Everyone will be there."

"Oh." She'd quickly fallen into the routine of having a coffee, a cup of tea, or something of the grape variety with the two Belles, but she hadn't ventured into the town to socialize. "Sure. I'd love it."

"Great. I'll see you then. Bye, Kira."

But Kira was too busy dragging the cardboard into the middle of the store.

She carefully leaned it against a shelf and then stood back, her face a picture of ecstasy. It was a cutout of a teenage boy wearing desert brown trousers and a robe that showed a hint of youthful chest, while dark smudges of black ran under each of his eyes.

"It's Trent Burton," she yelped, obviously not satisfied at how quickly Paige's brain was working. "My favorite actor."

"Of course." Paige tried to regain ground. "And he's going to play Aaron in the upcoming *Desert Witches of Numara* movie. Hence the costume."

"Exactly." Kira lovingly wiped the dust off the cardboard figure. Once she was happy with her handiwork, she looked up, eyes wide. "Can you believe this was sitting in a big pile of trash down in the basement?"

"Sacrilege."

"Totally! So, where should we put it?"

Paige gulped. Would it make her a bad person to not want a cardboard cutout of a teenage heartthrob anywhere in her store? Kira had a protective arm around the figure, as if unsure of Paige's response.

"Well—" she said cautiously. "Instead of keeping him here, you could always take him home."

Kira's mouth dropped to a perfect *O* shape as a strangled gasp emerged. Then she threw herself at Paige, enveloping her in a hug. Something primal caught in her throat as Kira's arms stayed tight.

She'd never wanted kids.

Not after her own lonely childhood. Patrick hadn't been interested, either, and since she'd spent the better part of her early thirties dating him, it hadn't even been a conversation.

She sucked in her breath as the door swung open and a guy about her age wandered in. He was tall with sandy blond hair, a body to die for, and strangely familiar eyes. She frowned, trying to place him. It had happened a lot lately. Seeing someone she thought she knew, only to remember she was in St. Clair and not New York.

"Hey, kiddo, I can see you're hard at work," the guy said,

and while Paige didn't know him, Kira obviously did because she untangled herself and went charging over.

"Jacob. You're *never* going to believe what's just happened. I mean it's like the wildest *most* crazy dream ever."

"You sure?" A playful smile danced across his mouth. "Because I've had a few wild and crazy dreams. There was this one time—"

"No," Kira cut him off without ceremony, obviously well used to his teasing. "Not your dreams, *my* dreams. Look. It's a cutout of Trent Burton. Isn't it amazing? And even better, I'm allowed to keep it. Oh, by the way, this is Paige."

"Anyone who gives my niece cardboard cutouts of Trent Burton is obviously my kind of person. I'm Jacob, Luke's brother." He joined her by the counter while Kira put her arm around the cutout and took a selfie, before heading outside to no doubt show her father.

That explained why he was familiar.

He was bigger than Luke, with broad shoulders, an easy smile, and eyes that twinkled on command.

"I didn't know Luke had a brother."

"It happens a lot." He flashed a dimple. "He tries to keep me under lock and key. On account of my incredible good looks."

"And modest personality?" Paige added, but it was hard not to smile. Jacob was as sunny as Luke was grumpy, and she'd forgotten how enjoyable it was to flirt. Especially when that person didn't turn her stomach into a shredded mess of emotions.

"Modesty's overrated." He fiddled with a basket of bookmarks on the counter, restless energy spilling out of him, surrounding him like a cloak. "How're you finding life in St. Clair? Because if it's a bit slow for you, I could always—"

"Would you give it a rest." Luke appeared in the doorway, his arms folded tightly across his chest.

"What's your problem? I actually came over here to help. Olive told me where you were." Jacob's voice was innocent enough, but the smile tugging at his mouth suggested there was more to the conversation.

"Too late. I'm all done, and Kira's already in the car. I have a bad feeling she's put a seat belt on the newest addition to the family." This was directed at her.

"Road safety's important," Paige said, not sure why there was such a tight expression around his mouth. "I hope you don't mind I gave it to her. Diana earmarked it as trash."

Jacob seemed to study Luke's face before grinning. "Well, you know what they say. One man's trash is another man's treasure. Isn't that right, brother."

"You talk too much," Luke muttered before marching back to the door and disappearing, all before Paige could even thank him.

"Don't take it personally," Jacob said with a parting smile before following his brother out of the store, leaving Paige to go and serve a group of Australians who were browsing the art books. At least they weren't looking at her like she'd just been scraped off the bottom of someone's shoe.

• • •

Luke pushed back the safety glasses and stowed his miter saw in his truck before carrying the lengths of wood to the front of the historic building. He'd finished fixing the guttering yesterday afternoon—while Jacob had lounged around flirting with Paige. But while he'd been working, he'd discovered several of the exterior boards were riddled with dry rot.

None of which was his problem.

Why didn't I just tell her what I'd found and give her a quote?

No comment.

It wasn't like it was such a big deal. He really was in charge of the St. Clair Rejuvenation Committee, which meant historic buildings fell under his jurisdiction. Plus, he had plenty left over from when he'd worked on Sam's building last year. And so what if he'd left Victor's cottage an hour early to get this done? Like he said, no big deal.

He clipped his tool belt around his waist and climbed the ladder, figuring the sooner he got started, the sooner the job would be done and he and Kira—who was working inside—could head home.

Afternoon sun filtered down on his back, and it didn't take long to cut out the rotten boards and replace them. The familiar aroma of sawdust and the trickle of sweat on his forehead calmed him down.

He was just tidying up as Paige joined him on the small lawn in front of the historic building. He tried not to look at her.

Problem was while he could ignore the physical attraction—well, to a degree—it was getting harder to ignore her kindness.

Not just with his own kid, but with Carol, who'd walked out of the store yesterday hugging the books like a trophy. He focused on packing away his drill.

"Hope they're okay. I'll swing by in the next couple of days and paint them."

"You really don't have to." Her eyes clouded with indecision. "I know you're busy."

"And I know what you're like on ladders," he countered, trying not to read too much into his offer. *I'm just being neighborly. Yeah, right.* "Seriously, it's fine."

She chewed on her lip, still worried. "Are you sure I can't pay you?"

"I'm sure." He finished gathering up his tools and walked

to his truck. "And since it's almost closing time, I'd better take Kira off your hands."

"Sure." She beckoned him to follow her back into the store. "Smith and Marlon have been helping her sort books into colors for a reading rainbow display to celebrate Carol and Nina's engagement."

"Wait. You've got Smith and Marlon in there?" He rubbed his chin, searching for an explanation for why two of St. Clair's most mischievous residents were in the bookstore helping make rainbows. None sprung to mind.

"Myra picks them up out front for Bingo, and they've started dropping in while they wait." She seemed to sense his confusion.

"Really? And did they bother to mention there's no Bingo this afternoon?"

"I've discovered." A rueful smile tugged at her mouth, and she let out a laugh. It was low and melodic. And the fact she could laugh at herself was damn sexy.

Hell.

"Played you, did they?" He tried to hide his reaction by keeping his voice cool.

"Like a fiddle," she agreed in an affectionate voice. "But that's okay. They're like the greatest double comedy act the world's never known."

"Say that after you've seen them with a couple of drinks under their belt," he said. Her navy eyes flooded with amusement.

"Let me guess. There's limericks?" There was that laugh again, and despite himself, his good intentions faded.

"Among other things. I'd tell you, but I wouldn't want to shock you," he said before sucking in a breath.

Am I flirting with her?

Danger bells rattled in his head.

"I'm not sure I want to know," she confessed.

"Dad!" Kira called from the table in the window where she'd stacked up a pile of red books on top of a long red cloth (which looked suspiciously like one of his hand towels). At her feet was a pile of orange books, and over in the reading nook Smith and Marlon were carefully selecting green books from the nearby shelves.

He blinked.

This was taking surrealism to a whole new level.

"Ah, Luke. Just the man. Come and see what Paige found for me." Smith pushed back a strand of snowy white hair and picked up a large book in his frail hands. His wrists shook under the weight, and Luke plucked it from him. "Isn't it marvelous? It's the history of horseshoeing in Oregon. And I'm in it!"

"You think folks would have something better to write about," Marlon chimed up, but there was pride in his voice as they both watched Luke expectantly. He turned to Paige and raised a confused eyebrow.

"Page thirty-two," she murmured, her arm brushing his as she joined him. Sizzle hot-wired its way down his spine, and it took all his willpower not to react. "I had no idea he'd be in it when I dug it off the shelves to show him."

He flipped open the book to a grainy photograph of Smith. He was probably about twenty when it had been taken and was standing next to a dappled gray, a hot poker in his hand.

"Pretty good, eh?" Smith chuckled.

"There was an old horse from the sea." Marlon's wrinkled face broke into a grin. "Who didn't know where he should p—"

"Marlon Evans, I hope you're not about to say what I think you're about to say." Myra appeared in the doorway, her ebony hair twirled around her head in two neat braids. "And what are you two even doing here? Don't you have a community art class this afternoon?"

"Pah. They're making us do string paintings. We're not first graders. Plus Paige has better cookies," Marlon explained with a wink, as he slowly got to his feet. "But I suppose while you're here, you could always drive us both home."

Myra let out a long-suffering sigh. "Fine, but it's only because I'm between pickups, and because I'm sure Paige has plenty of other things to do."

"They're really no bother," Paige said as Myra hustled the pair of them outside, letting them stop just long enough to say goodbye to Kira before they left in a wave of grumbles and laughter.

"I think you've got a fan club," he said, once they'd gone. Paige shook her head as she wiped down the table where they'd been sitting. Her nails were painted a pale blue with tiny silver stars on them. It was unexpected.

Just like her.

Hell.

He stalked over to where Kira was still piling up the colored books. "Come on, kiddo. I just remembered we're meant to be somewhere else."

"Where?" his daughter demanded.

Very good question.

"Just somewhere," he quickly answered as he gave Paige a brief nod and moved to the door. From now on he'd just have to avoid the store. It was safer that way.

• • •

Paige woke with a start. She'd been having a dream. A really great dream involving a gorgeous but grumpy contractor, and a bookstore owner who looked remarkably like herself. Not that she'd changed her mind about men, but this was a dream, and therefore she had a free pass.

She closed her eyes again, trying to recapture the fine tendrils of sleep, hoping they'd carry her back. Instead, the music to *Jaws* rang out. She fumbled for her phone, not quite ready to open her eyes.

"James?" she croaked, not even attempting to sound awake, considering it was only—*seven thirty on Thursday morning*? "What's going on?"

"I'm hoping you can tell me. Have you seen Audrey?"

"What do you mean?" Paige wriggled into a sitting position, and the last hazy shard of her dream faded away. "Why would I have seen her? She lives in Boston. With you."

Her brother was silent.

"James." Paige stood and wrapped herself up in an old dressing gown before rubbing the sleep from her eyes. "Please tell me you haven't misplaced our mother."

"Hardly. She's a grown woman. She can come and go as she pleases."

"Well, it sounds like she's been doing more going. When was the last time you saw her?"

"Yesterday. Fiona and I took the kids to New York to see a Beethoven concert, and we returned late last night. But it wasn't until this morning we realized she wasn't here."

Panic spread in her belly. She wasn't close to her mother. Not by a long shot. But that didn't mean she didn't care. Not to mention how erratic her mom had been lately.

"Have you tried calling her? Calling her friends?" she said, which earned her a scathing reply.

"As astonishing as it is, I did actually think of that first."

"Hey, don't get mad at me, I'm not the one who misplaced her," she said. "Okay, well try Aunt Ginger. They've become close lately."

"Actually, that's a good idea. I'd forgotten about Ginger," James admitted, but before she could answer, a crunch of tires echoed through the quiet morning air.

An uncomfortable sensation churned in her stomach as she walked to her bedroom window. She peered out.

No. No. No.

Yes.

It was her mother. And judging by the number of suitcases the poor driver was unloading, she wasn't planning on a short trip.

"Paige?" His voice broke through the ringing sensation in her ears. "What's going on?"

She swallowed and reluctantly walked downstairs to the front door. "You can call the search party off. I've found her."

• • •

People always said she took after her mother, but she'd never been able to see it. Audrey's hair was strawberry blonde, though these days it was thanks to her hairdresser rather than nature. Her face was longer than Paige's, and her mouth was pinched from years of telling patients to take their pills.

Oh, and they didn't have much in common.

Especially when it came to eating the breakfast muffin Sam had rushed over. And while the muffin had saved Paige the embarrassment of having nothing in her fridge, it was now turning into a never-ending torture weapon as she watched her mother eat.

Each bite was meticulous. A tiny speared section, delicately lifted up to her mouth, chewing it at least seven hundred million times before repeating the process all over again.

At this rate she'd be finished by Easter.

Her patience faded. "Are you going to tell me what this is all about?"

Her mother's mouth twisted into a disappointed sigh, as if trying to figure out how she'd managed to raise a daughter so lacking in etiquette. Then she carefully put down her cutlery and dabbed her lips with the napkin Paige had managed to find from the un-emptied boxes.

"I thought that was obvious. I'm here for a visit."

"When most people visit, they actually call first. James has been frantic," she said, not quite sure that her brother's cool voice had reached those heights, but considering how unperturbed her mother was, she couldn't help but needle her.

And, if her mother *had* called first, Paige would've had enough time to consult *Just Say No* and formulate all the reasons why it wasn't a good time to have visitors. But it was a bit difficult when the person just turned up on the doorstep.

I bet even Dr. Penny Groves wouldn't have been able to say no.

"Nonsense. James is fine. Besides, I've always wanted to visit this part of the country. It will be a nice way to relax. Now, if you don't mind I'd like to get unpacked." Her mother stood up, her gaze flicking over the numerous cartons still dotted around the room. She got to her feet. In order for Audrey to unpack, Paige would first have to drag out all the things she'd been dumping into the spare room. It was going to be a long day.

Chapter Six

*"In this life there are only three things you need to remember.
You catch more flies with honey than vinegar. Red wine's
a bitch to get out of fabric. And saying no will always be
harder than saying yes."* **Just Say No**

"And then he had the nerve to tell me it was my fault. I mean,
seriously?" A tall blonde woman took another bite from one
of Sam's hazelnut choc-chip cookies and sat upright in the
pink chair of the reading nook.

"That's terrible," Paige agreed.

"I know, right. Let me tell you, it's the last time I'll get
one done while I'm on vacation." The woman shrugged off
her black leather jacket and lifted up her shirt to reveal a
large tattoo of a rose with some Japanese symbols running
down her rib cage. "How was I meant to know it said 'bite my
big juicy peach'?"

"I've got no idea." She shook her head, not sure how else
to answer.

Should I try and sell her a Japanese dictionary?

The woman dropped her shirt and flexed her arm, which was covered with a gun-wielding skeleton, complete with blazing red eyes.

Okay, scrap that idea.

An elderly couple looking at gardening books glanced over, and the woman made a clucking noise before dragging her husband out of the store. They were quickly followed by another woman who'd been studying the back of a Nora Roberts.

Talk about killing two birds with one evil-eyed tattoo.

"Well, I won't be tricked again. My next one's going to be of a gargoyle fighting a dragon, and there won't be any words at all."

"That's definitely one way around the problem," Paige said, but the woman frowned as if expecting a more substantial answer. She licked her lips and glanced over to the chalkboard she'd hung up on the wall. She'd randomly picked one of her favorite *Just Say No* quotes to put up for inspiration. "But you know...*the people who care about us will always see our inner beauty.*"

Silence engulfed them.

A prickle of discomfit lodged in her throat as the woman flexed her arms, inflating the skeleton. Then she let out a throaty laugh. It ricocheted like a machine gun, but apparently it was genuine because when she finished, she stood up from the chair and grinned, revealing several gold-capped teeth.

"You're all right. Let me know if you ever want to get one. My regular guy's in Portland. He'll look after you. Plus, he's a good speller."

"Oh. Um, t-thank you." She swallowed.

"Hey, us ladies gotta stick together." The woman fist-bumped her, dragged her leather jacket back on, and sauntered out of the store without another word.

She began to clear up the remains of the cookie that she'd

planned to have for lunch when the doorbell jingled and Myra the bus driver walked in.

"Hey, I was just driving by and saw Nancy Trevor walking out. Just wanted to make sure you were okay."

"W-what do you mean?"

"Nancy's nice enough on a good day, but she hangs with a bad crowd, and…well, like I said. Just wanted to check you're okay." Myra's eyes scanned her, as if searching for broken bones or blood. Paige gulped.

"I'm fine. She just chatted and showed me her tattoo." *And scared off two potential customers.* "But thanks for checking."

"Sure." Myra shrugged as her phone beeped. "I have to collect everyone from the library. But you might want to be careful. Nancy's a loose cannon, and I know you're trying to be helpful, but it's okay to not feed everyone who comes in."

She's right, you know. Dr. Penny Groves appeared behind the counter, leaning forward, her chin cupped in her hands. *I thought we'd talked about people-pleasing?*

Paige waited until Myra left the store before frowning. *I'm not people-pleasing. This is customer relations. There's a difference. A big difference.*

Um, no there's not, sweetie.

The door jangled, and the bestselling author disappeared as a delivery guy with a straggly red beard walked in with a large box.

"You Audrey Taylor?"

"I'm her daughter," she said.

"That'll do." The guy gave her a form to sign, then put the box on the counter and left. She studied the box and frowned. It was from a company called Live Your Dreams Home Shopping. It didn't fill Paige with confidence that her mom was planning on leaving in a hurry.

Audrey had been strangely vague about the length of her

visit, since she'd turned up yesterday morning. More so after James had called in the evening.

If her brother ever wanted to change careers, he could probably get hired as a bull in a china store.

"Is that for me?" Audrey appeared at the bottom of the stairs. Her hair and makeup were immaculate as ever, but the neat trousers and blouses she normally favored had been replaced by a brightly embroidered kaftan similar to the one Dr. Penny Groves had just been wearing.

She nodded. "It just arrived. Do you want a knife to open it?"

"No, it's okay." Audrey produced a penknife from somewhere in the voluminous dress and flicked it open, slitting the packing tape in three quick motions. Packing foam fell around the counter like gigantic snowflakes as she plunged her hands in and carefully lifted out an ornate white porcelain clock. Her mother's face broke into a smile. "Oh my! Look, it's a sixteenth century replica clock. There's one just like it in Versailles. Isn't it gorgeous?"

Paige blinked. As far as she was aware, her mother had never shown any interest in antiques of any kind. Not even replica sixteenth century clocks.

"Is everything okay?"

"Why wouldn't it be?" Her mom hugged the clock to her chest, burying it in the folds of the kaftan, a challenging light in her eyes.

Because you turned up here unannounced. You're wearing a kaftan and seem to be ordering weird things online.

If James were there, he'd push further. Demand answers, but Paige didn't feel up to it. A day of not selling anything was exhausting, and she still had to go to the engagement party that evening.

"No reason," she said.

In the background she could hear Dr. Penny Groves

make a snorting noise. She ignored it as Audrey swept back up the stairs with her new clock, the Styrofoam packing beads dancing in her wake from the static energy. Paige sighed and began to tidy up for the second time that day.

Her phone rang. It was James, but she ignored the call. In a day of yeses, at least she'd managed to say no once. It should've made her feel better, but it didn't.

• • •

"Well, that settles it. I'll have to pay a visit," Olive said as Luke walked back into the dining room.

His grandmother had been living in the same bungalow for the last sixty years, and while Luke and his siblings had long ago moved out, they still tended to gravitate there every Friday night for dinner. Tonight, it had been takeout pizza.

"Who are you visiting?" He almost tripped over the cutout figure Kira had insisted on bringing with them. Still, he supposed he shouldn't complain. After all, not only was his daughter blissfully happy, but she'd finally stopped talking about Trent Burton and had settled into her homework.

"Paige Taylor. I've just been hearing all about her."

"I see." Luke could only imagine what the pair of them had been saying. In Kira's eyes Paige had moved from cool and funny to Wonder Woman within the space of a few days. And as for Jacob, it was obvious what he thought. Then again, it was *always* obvious what his brother thought.

And me?

Yeah, let's not go there.

"I would've gone sooner, but that blasted doctor and his blasted ways," Olive continued, handing him a skein of bright purple wool. Ever since he was ten it had been his job to roll the wool into a ball, and it'd take a braver man than he to tell his grandmother the task was juvenile.

"How crazy that he wanted you to fully recover." Luke flattened out the wool and found the starting thread in a well-practiced action.

"Pah, what does he know?" Olive snorted as the slim crochet hook bobbed in and out of the wool at lightning speed, making the brightly colored afghans she sold through one of the stores in town.

"Is she defaming Dr. Robb again?" Jacob looked up from where he was lounging on the sofa. Normally Trina would've been there, too, but she and her husband were away for a week in Seattle. "Nan, one of these days he'll refuse to treat you."

"Rubbish. The man dotes on me." Olive gave him an impish grin, making her look almost childlike, with her short silver hair spiking out in all directions while her green eyes—so like his daughter's—twinkled with amusement. "And stop trying to divert the subject. I want to hear more about our newest citizen."

"Please—with your network, you probably know more than all of us," he said as the soft curve of Paige's hips slammed into his mind, while the tangy scent of her shampoo had him longing to bury his face into her hair.

Stop thinking about her.

"You'll love her, Gigi." Kira looked up from the homework table. It was the name she'd always called Olive, though no one could quite remember how it had started. "Her eyes dance when she smiles, and she doesn't mind what books people read. Even the ones you like."

"Well, that's promising. I stopped using the place after Diana refused to buy in anything that showed a bit of cleavage on the cover."

"The books you like show a lot more than cleavage. And that's just the guys," Jacob piped up, since it was a well-known fact Olive was a fan of erotic fiction. Luke preferred not to think about it too much. He busied himself rolling the wool.

"Reading expands the mind," Olive simply answered, though a smile tugged at her mouth.

"Hey, Gigi. You should get your book club to meet there." Kira abandoned her homework and bounced across the room like Tigger. "Paige changed the store around, and there's a reading corner where you could all fit."

"Ah yes. *The Fifty Shades of Grey Rinse*." Jacob sat up. "What I wouldn't give to be a fly on the wall when you all meet up."

"It'd probably make you blush," Olive teased before turning to Kira. "And that's a great idea. Poor Paige probably had no idea what she was buying into, we need to help her any way we can."

"I agree," said Jacob.

"Me, too," Kira chimed in before giving Luke the same smile she used when she wanted to stay up late on a Friday night. "You should help her, too, Dad."

"Yeah, Dad," Jacob mimicked, knowing Luke couldn't throw anything at him while his hands were tangled up with wool.

"I have been helping." Luke gave his brother a dark look and turned to Kira. "That's why I was there fixing the gutter." *And trying not to look at her.*

He shook the image from his mind.

Everything about Paige screamed city.

There was no way she'd last in St. Clair, and while he admitted she was a damn sight better than Diana, or the two owners before, it took more than just repeating a few mantras and watching YouTube tutorials to survive in a town like St. Clair. Especially when she didn't appear to have savings to get through the slow season.

"Not just repairing the building. You know what this place is like. If everyone keeps ignoring her, her business will go under," Olive said, before realizing Kira was looking at her in alarm. "Sweetheart, would you mind getting me a glass of water?"

"Sure." Kira immediately hurried out to the kitchen, oblivious to the undercurrent.

"I don't want that," Luke said defensively once his daughter was safely out of hearing. "But wouldn't it be better for her to cut her losses now?"

"Not everyone's your mom." Olive's green eyes were full of compassion for the woman her only son had married. "You're the one who wants to rejuvenate this town and improve business, so help her improve her business."

He bowed his head as memories stirred.

They'd been a happy family once. A father who smiled and took them to games. A mom who baked and insisted on walking with them to school even though they were much too old. Then, when Luke was ten, she'd met Glen Harrison. A lawyer from Texas—just in town for a week—renting out one of the manors across from the beach. He was everything that their father wasn't. That their life *wasn't*.

Worldly, rich, decadent.

And like a flash flood, the sun disappeared, and torrents of wild, untamed water had burst through the family walls, destroying everything. She told them she was leaving. To move to Texas, and she hoped they'd join her when things were settled. His father had cried, begged, pleaded. As had Luke, but nothing would change her mind.

It was the talk of the town for months after it happened, and even though she phoned and wrote, she never sent for Luke, Jacob, and Trina. Not even after their father died. Much later they found out the relationship hadn't lasted, but their mom never came back before her death fifteen years ago.

And then history repeated itself with Joanne.

The town was too small for her.

The people in it weren't enough.

I wasn't enough.

He slammed it all back down.

This wasn't about him and his lousy past. It was about Kira. She was already becoming attached to Paige, and despite what he suspected would happen, he'd do anything he could to keep his daughter happy. *Even if it was only temporary.*

"I'll think about it." He handed the finished ball of wool to Olive and stood up. The cutout was in his way again. "And you can keep your opinions to yourself," he muttered just as Kira walked back in with the water.

"Dad, you're so losing it," she informed him. And, after passing over the water, she picked up the Trent Burton cutout and carried it out of harm's way.

"She's right." Jacob threw a balled up jacket at him. "And do you want to know *why* you're losing it?"

"I really don't," Luke assured him as he caught the jacket and frowned. "What's this for?"

"Carol and Nina's engagement party," Jacob reminded him. "Tonight. At Carriage."

"I can't go." The piles of paperwork sitting at home on his desk blasted into his mind. As well as Victor's cottage, he had a couple of quotes to finish. And he was working on the plans to rebuild the old marina and restock the waters so they could sustainably fish again and bring in business that didn't rely on how cute the town looked.

"Can't or won't? Seems to me you're avoiding a certain someone."

"If you mean my brother, yeah, I am, but it's not been very successful."

"Unlike in fifth grade when you let me tag along on a fishing trip with you and your friends. You told me to wait outside the bait store, then ditched me."

"Ah, the good old days." Luke let out a wistful sigh. "Besides, I have a daughter. I can't just go out when I please."

"No, but you can go out every now and then without the world grinding to a halt." Olive, who'd been content to let them talk, looked up and nodded to Kira, who was once again taking selfies with the cutout. "My granddaughter and I would like some quality girl time. She can stay the night, and you can pick her up in the morning."

Luke opened his mouth to protest before recognizing the stubborn set of his younger brother's eyes. These days he was a lot harder to ditch. He shrugged on his coat.

"Fine, but I'm not staying late."

"Of course," Jacob said with the pious look of someone who'd gotten his own way.

· · ·

"Here we go." Sam returned with three glasses of wine and settled down at the table. The place had once been a train station, but the line had been stopped years ago, and it'd been converted into a bar and restaurant.

Paige suspected it was normally quite a big space, but it was hard to tell because there were so many people all crammed in to celebrate.

The bar was decked out in fairy lights and glorious autumn flowers billowing out of old paint buckets, while the newly engaged couple talked and laughed with their guests, their hands entwined, looking like the happiest people in the world.

It was a completely different affair from when she and Patrick had become engaged.

It had been a party at his studio with people she hardly knew. By the end of the night he'd gone out clubbing, and she'd gone home to bed.

She slammed it down. No more Patrick. He was in the past.

"I'm so happy you're here." Sam held up her glass. The mask of reserve she'd worn on the first day was gone, and Paige was already discovering what a fierce friend the café owner was to the people she liked.

"Me, too! It will give you a chance to meet everyone," Laney added. "Are you sure your mom didn't want to come?"

"She's a little tired," Paige said, crossing her fingers. The truth was Audrey was too busy taking part in an online auction to win a pair of vases to match the clock. She'd hardly even noticed when Paige had stepped out wearing a silky shirtdress with a cute cactus print. The neckline was low, but with the soft sleeves and belted waist, it was dressy without being overdone.

She wasn't sure why she'd put it on.

Liar.

"I hear you experienced the Jacob Carmichael charm offensive the other day," Sam said, saving Paige from delving too far into why she'd dressed up for the evening.

"Oh, you lucky thing." Laney let out a small sigh despite the dark look Sam was throwing her. "What? I mean, I know he's got single tattooed across his forehead, but it doesn't stop him from being cute as all heck. Have you seen the arms on him?"

"Take it from someone who's known the Carmichael boys their entire life, Jacob will break your heart in an instant and won't even know he's doing it. The guy's untamable." She looked in the direction of the bar, where Jacob was in the process of balancing a shot glass on his nose. Then she made a snorting noise and turned away.

Unlike Paige, who'd taken a quick glance before discovering Luke was standing next to him.

Do. Not. Look at him.

Follow Sam's lead and turn away.

She didn't turn away.

He'd changed from his work gear and had on a pair of black jeans and a navy sweater molded to his body. The body she'd been pressed against three days ago.

She dragged her gaze away before her friends figured out what she'd been thinking about. Correction. *Whom* she'd been thinking about.

"Er, so how long have Carol and Nina been together?" she said.

"Two years now. But they've been friends for longer. It's such a sweet story. They were walking in the park when a stray golden retriever came over to them. They searched everywhere for the owner before discovering it was an elderly woman who'd recently died. They both wanted to adopt the old boy, but in the end they decided on joint custody. The more time they spent sharing their dog duties, the more they fell for each other. And the cutest part? The dog's name is Cupid, and he's going to be bridesdog at the ceremony."

"Total case of puppy love," Sam quipped.

"Maybe it will be us next?" Laney let out a wistful sigh. Not long after they'd met, the florist had haltingly told Paige that she was a widower and that her husband had died five years ago. And while she still loved and missed him, she'd decided it was time to step back into the real world. Back into dating.

Paige only hoped her friend would find the happiness she deserved.

"Sam, there you are," a voice said from somewhere behind them, and a gorgeous brunette raced over, her long dark hair curling down her back, while her large doe eyes stood out against her Snow White complexion. As she reached the table, her entire expression shifted, and a steel wall slammed down. "Don't worry, I'll catch up with you later."

Without another word she pushed her way back through the crowd.

Paige blinked while her two friends had a silent conversation that involved a lot of eyebrow lifting and mouth twitching. Sam let out a sigh.

"I guess you're wondering what that was all about."

It wasn't hard to figure out.

"Someone else who doesn't like me being here," she said in a dry voice.

"It's not personal. Melanie wanted to buy the store and was convinced Diana would lower her price eventually. But then at the last minute—"

"A drunk New Yorker swooped in." She let out a groan. "Basically I took a business from her. No wonder she hates me."

"She doesn't hate you." Laney's sunny face darkened in alarm. "She was just a bit hurt. I swear once you get to know her, she's lovely."

Paige was pretty sure Laney thought everyone was lovely.

"Should I talk to her?" she said, before catching sight of Melanie having a whispered conversation with Luke. It made sense in a depressing way. After all, they had one thing in common. They both disliked her. "Are they dating?"

"God, no." Sam spluttered. "Luke isn't like that."

"Like what?" The words were out before she could stop herself.

"He doesn't date," Sam said.

"Ever?"

"Not in a long time," Sam corrected. "His ex, Kira's mom, was a doctor who moved here for work. It was instant love with the perfect wedding followed by the perfect baby. Then, ten years ago Joanne walked out, swearing never to come back to St. Clair. On top of the scandal, and caring for

Kira, he had to keep assuring people he was okay. He hasn't dated since. Just him and his daughter. That kid's his world."

"I had no idea." Her hand flew up to her mouth as her heart ached with sadness.

For Luke having to raise his daughter on his own. For Kira, who was growing up without a mom. Even for the unknown Joanne, who'd left behind such a beautiful family.

It explained why he didn't like outsiders.

And his fierce commitment to his daughter.

What was it like to be the center of someone's life?

She certainly hadn't been her father's world, or her mother's for that matter. As for Patrick? *Don't even go there.*

"But don't let the tough exterior fool you," Laney said. "After Simon died everyone was so sweet to me, always checking in to see how I was coping. But Luke was different. He'd just turn up and fix things. My grandmother used to reckon there were two kinds of people. Sayers and doers. Luke is a doer."

Paige rubbed her chin. The fire bucket in the hardware. Fixing her guttering. Replacing the rotten boards. Laney was right. He *was* a doer. *Even to outsiders he didn't trust.*

"His brother, on the other hand—" Sam rolled her eyes as Jacob pushed his way through the crowd and sat down at the table, his size swamping them as surely as his restless energy did.

"Sam Riley, are you using my name in vain? Because God, I hope you are."

"You wish," Sam retorted, suggesting their banter went back for years. A stab of longing jabbed her belly. "What do you want, Jacob?"

"I'm here to ask the lovely Laney to dance with me."

Laney's rosebud lips turned up in a smile, and she stammered a reply before following him to the dance floor. A moment later a tall guy with a beard claimed Sam, and Paige found herself alone.

She considered another glass of wine, but as she scanned the crowd, she wasn't sure that drunk was the way to go. Her phone beeped, and since no one was around she studied the screen. Three more messages from her ex-boss. Delete. Delete. Delete.

All around here people were talking and laughing. She clamped down on her lip, as if trying to force down the self-conscious thoughts that were battling to get out. A woman in a red dress stared at her, but when Paige smiled, she just turned away.

Okay, that happened.

"How about another wine?" Sam reappeared, her cheeks glowing.

She shook her head. "It's been a long day. I'm just going to head home."

"Let me give you a lift. Crime isn't big in St. Clair, but it's still not good to be alone."

"Don't worry, I didn't leave all my New York ways behind me. I have a whistle and mace. But thanks." She was touched at the concern. Though, considering she'd been catching the subway for twenty-odd years, she didn't think it would be a problem.

Besides, the walk might help clear her head.

"You're welcome. And try not to worry about Mel. Remember what Dr. Penny Groves says, 'If you spend all your time trying to please other people, ask yourself who's trying to please you?'"

"I will," she promised, but for once the advice didn't resonate.

She waved goodbye and then thanked the two brides for inviting her before reclaiming her jacket and stepping outside.

An orange moon hung low over the small harbor as waves ebbed and flowed, while the sky spread out in never-ending blackness, only broken by the stars. The stillness of the night enveloped her.

Across the road was angled parking, and beyond that a strip of grass and a bench seat overlooking the water. The green suede heels were pinching her toes, and she drifted over to the bench and slipped them off. She really needed to have a conversation with herself about buying inappropriate footwear.

Instead, she sighed and pressed her sore feet into the cool earth.

Every now and then a car drove past, heading along the coast road, which led to miles of Oregon beach. The sand around St. Clair was grainy and the color of burnt caramel. Sam had explained it was what kept the small town from exploding the way other beach towns had. But it hadn't stopped locals from building a strange mishmash of houses. Everything from bungalows to converted shipping containers to mansions was dotted along the road.

Yet there was something about the stillness that was creeping its way under her skin.

I really like it here.

The sound of music interrupted her thoughts as the bar door opened and shut again. Then the crunch of footsteps heading toward her. She swiveled, and instantly regretted it as Luke Carmichael came into view, walking to his truck. His face was a mask, lost in his own world, and it wasn't until he reached the curb that he looked up.

His flickering eyes clearly said, "Shit, I should've waited another five minutes before leaving."

"I...er...I didn't see you there." He was struggling to regain control of his face.

"I'm working on my powers of invisibility," she explained and then winced.

Did I really just say that?

She licked her lips. Dr. Penny Groves always recommended that when you found yourself in a bad situation, don't make it worse. She reluctantly put the uncomfortable shoes back on. "Okay, I'm going to head home now. Night."

"Wait, you're walking?"

"Well, yeah. It's only few blocks away."

"Still, it's not safe. I'll come with you."

"You really don't have to," Paige said. "I have my mace."

"Mace?" He quirked an eyebrow, letting her know what he thought about women who carried mace. It was probably up there with inappropriate ladder climbing. "I'd prefer to walk you home. Unless you'd like a lift."

She eyed the black truck, and her skin heated up. Being confined to the cab with his looming presence didn't seem like a good idea, for reasons she didn't want to discuss.

Keep your friends close and your denial closer.

"Fine." She shrugged as she began to walk, her gaze fixed straight ahead. He easily matched her step, the heat of him searing into her skin despite the space between them. She tried to break the rhythm, which caused an amused smile to cross his mouth.

"You enjoy the party?" he said.

She forgot her plan to not look at him and turned in surprise. Laney was right. He was a doer, not a sayer. Which meant if he was making small talk, it was because she made him uncomfortable.

"Sure." She shrugged and continued walking. "Carol and Nina seem lovely. I was just feeling—"

"Like an outsider?" he offered, once again matching her pace.

"Tired," she corrected, not sure whether to be touched or horrified that he'd read her. Exhaustion settled into her bones. This whole town was hard work. Everyone knew everyone. *Everyone but me.* Her shoulders sagged.

"You okay?" This time he stopped just ahead of her and turned slightly, blocking her progress. His eyes met hers.

No.

I keep stepping on people's toes just by being here.

The more I try and belong, the less it works.

She sucked in a shuddering breath, determined not to speak. But as the silence stretched around them, echoed by the stillness of his face, something inside shifted.

"It's nothing. Just a little overwhelmed. Sam and Laney told me Melanie wanted to buy the place. I didn't realize my presence here would be so controversial," she said and then flinched, remembering how they first met.

She glanced up, half expecting to meet a stony expression, but his mouth had softened, and if anything, he looked guilty.

"Would you believe me if I said it's not you?"

"What do you mean?" Her brows knitted together.

"Folks have seen more businesses come and go here than you've bought shoes." He glanced at the green suede heels. "I guess it makes us quick to judge. We shouldn't, and I'm sorry."

Oh. Out of all the things she'd expected him to say, it hadn't been that.

"How do outsiders do it? Fit in here, I mean?" she asked before kicking herself as his face darkened. *Because they don't. That's why his ex left.* Shit. "Sorry, forget I said that. Sam just told me about your wife. I didn't mean to bring it up."

Silence dwarfed the space between them, filling it with the echoes of her thoughtless words.

"I'm surprised it took you so long to find out. Gossip here moves quickly," he said. "Somehow Joanne slotted straight into everything. Working at the surgery, joining the volleyball team—and guiding them to their first win in fifteen years. Hell, she even joined a knitting circle. Everyone loved her."

This is none of my business.
This is his pain. His life.
It's not my place to ask.

"What happened?" she asked anyway, unable to stop the words from tumbling out.

The shadow of brutal memories seemed to ripple across his face.

"Honestly? I have no fucking idea. One day we were happy, and the next day, her bags were packed, and she left me with a two-page letter and a four-year-old daughter." His voice was flat and his fists clenched. He'd obviously told this story before.

Then again, she knew a thing or two about people leaving. And sometimes it was only the stories that got you through it.

She steadied her breath. There were a hundred things she wanted to say, but none of them really meant anything. None of them could fix what had been broken.

"Being left behind sucks."

"Yeah, you're right. It does suck." The lines around his mouth softened. "But thanks."

"For what?"

"I don't know." He frowned, as if trying to articulate his thoughts. "I guess for calling it like it is. It's refreshing. And…unexpected."

"Oh." Warmth skittered across her skin as the words caught in her throat. "I meant it. Sometimes there's no point trying to spin gold around things."

"Paige." His low voice sent a ripple of something illicit through her body. It was the first time he'd said her name. She had a bad, *bad* feeling she'd be replaying it over and over again in her mind. A flash of indecision raced across his face before he fixed her with a steady gaze. "Do you really want to fit into this community?"

Stars spread out across the horizon, and her skin prickled.

She loved this place, she just wasn't sure how to make it love her back.

An image of what would happen if she failed flashed across her mind. Back in New York working for another horrible boss, dating another Patrick. Or worse, in Boston with a family who saw her only for what she could do for them.

"I do." She tried not to admire the way the moonlight and shadows danced across his face. "I just don't know how. Sam has a 'Born in St. Clair' stamp on the back of her neck and can bake like an angel, while Laney's the happiest person in the world who gives flowers to everyone. Hell, I even caught her giving a bouquet to a dog the other day."

That earned her a small smile, and he took a deep breath, as if in two minds about what he was going to say.

"Let me welcome you to the community patrol team. It's a vital part of this town, and everyone will know you're committed to being here."

"Community patrol? As in staking out bad guys and eating donuts?"

"You might have us confused with movie cops." His mouth twitched. If she didn't know better, she'd swear he was smiling. "We're the eyes and ears for the sheriff's department and help out where we can."

She studied his face, not sure what to make of the offer. Everything Sam told her explained why he'd been withdrawn and reserved around her.

So where does this fit in?

"Is this part of the St. Clair Rejuvenation Committee to help out-of-towners who don't know what they're doing?"

"Yes, it's clearly stated in subsection thirty-nine A. We even throw in a flashlight," he said in a dry voice, before fixing her with a frank stare. "It's been brought to my attention I might've judged you too harshly. Ironic since I spend half my time teaching Kira not to judge people."

His words slid over her. She got the feeling he didn't open up very often. Or admit when he was wrong.

"You really think it will help?"

"Yes."

"Okay." She nodded, not quite sure if she was saying yes to improving her business or to spending time with him. Or perhaps it was both. Either way it was a gift horse.

Whose mouth I'm not going to look in.

"It sounds great. Thank you."

"No problem. I'll pick you up at nine o'clock on Tuesday night. Oh, and by the way." His voice was a low drawl that prickled her skin as his eyes glanced down at the spiky heels. "Try and wear sensible shoes."

Chapter Seven

"Think of your comfort zone as Hell's waiting room. Bad magazines and even worse music. Your job is to get out of there as quickly as possible. And when you find yourself sneaking back in? Well, you know the drill..." **Just Say No**

"So, a little bird told me you were talking to a certain lady bookstore owner last night. In the moonlight. Care to tell me what happened?" Jacob slid the nail gun into his belt the following morning.

Victor's cottage was a hive of activities as hammers and grinders competed with the radio one of the crew had blasting out. They walked away from the din, over to the work truck loaded with timber. A low mist had settled around the property, but by mid-morning the sun would burn it away.

"Sure, I'd love to. Then we can braid each other's hair," Luke growled, not sure who he was more annoyed at. His brother, or himself. Scrap that. Himself.

Offering to help her was a bad idea. And talking about Joanne?

Since when do I do that?

Christ, but he needed to get a grip.

"Sounds kinky," a third person said, and they spun to where Trina was standing, holding up a tray of coffees from Patsy's diner. She favored Jacob, with sandy hair, though her mannerisms were almost identical to their mom's. Not that she'd been old enough to remember much.

"Hey, little sis, when did you get back?" Jacob gave her a bear hug while managing not to spill the drinks.

"Late last night. I thought I'd bring you both a coffee before I see Olive. How is she?"

"Fully recovered and plotting her party. At last count the guest list was at two hundred." Luke gave her a gentle hug.

"And speaking of which, don't forget we have our first rehearsal coming up." Jacob winked with amusement.

It had been a long-standing tradition that each year Luke played Olive a birthday song. But what had started out as a quick serenade around the kitchen table had turned into entertaining an entire party. The more he tried to wriggle out of it, the more everyone insisted he do it. But this year he'd decided his siblings could help out, as payback for the years of teasing.

"Wouldn't miss it for the world," their sister said. "You picked a song yet?"

"Kira's in charge of that. Brace yourself," he said. "How were Stu's folks?

"Great. Spoiled us rotten." She grinned, and the tension left his shoulders. His own marriage had imploded in a spectacular way. Jacob never dated anyone for longer than a month, but their sister had bypassed the family curse and been happily married to the local vet for five years, along with a menagerie of animals.

"And what about Seattle?" Jacob demanded as he plucked one of the coffees from the tray and gave an appreciative sniff. "Clubs? Shenanigans? I'm going to need details."

"I think you're mistaking me for someone else," Trina said before glancing down at the ground, using her sneaker to trace a circle in the dewy grass. "We were only there for Stu's parents' anniversary party. It wasn't like we were out each night on the town."

"O-kay." Jacob blinked before turning to Luke. "Is it just me, or is she acting shifty?"

"It's definitely just you," Trina retorted before using her spare hand to check the time on her cell. "I gotta go, but tell Victor I'll call next week to talk about the painting he commissioned."

"Will do." He took the coffee and walked to the main house, while Jacob headed to the cottage to stud out a wall. Victor was making French toast and watching a Ted Talk on his iPad, while wearing a long silk dressing gown. The man was definitely an enigma.

"Luke, you'll be pleased to know I've narrowed it down to my favorite three. Hungry?"

"I'm good." Luke held up his coffee and sat down on a barstool that flanked the long bench in the kitchen. "And that's good news about the tiles. If you make the final selection, I'll order them tomorrow. By the way, Trina will see you next week about the painting."

Victor's eyes lit up.

Trina's art graced most houses in the area, not because she was a local girl but rather because her work was exceptional, and when she wasn't building up her stock for the tourist season, she took commissions.

"Excellent." Victor slid the French toast onto a plate and smothered it in maple syrup. "Though it'd be a pity to make the final selection before I speak to her. Maybe I should wait until next week?"

Luke clamped down his protest. As project manager it

was his role to keep all the balls in the air, but he'd already done two jobs for Victor. Hurrying him never worked. He'd ask Trina to go around later today. Then, after going over a few more details he left the ex-biker-cum-hairdresser and returned to the cottage.

Jacob and the rest of the crew were hard at work; a buzz of power tools, hammering, and conversation hung in the air, which meant Luke could catch up on paperwork.

Or, I could go over what an idiot move I made last night.

Crap. No. He tried to stop the memory, but like a train on a track it came steaming into the station. What had he been thinking?

But he hadn't been thinking at all.

He'd been suckered in by her vulnerable expression, and his promise to Olive and Kira.

At this rate he'd be helping so much, he might as well be bagging books for her.

Still, it wasn't such a big deal.

He tended to patrol up until twelve, then slept, only responding to callouts, before doing a final round first thing in the morning. Which meant he'd only have to spend three hours with her. *Nothing I can't handle.*

"Earth to Luke." One of his crew coughed. "Victor wants to look at the lighting samples again. You want me to take them over?"

"No. It's okay." Luke shook his head, glad of the excuse to move, since sitting still with his thoughts obviously wasn't a great idea. "I'll do it."

He then gathered up the fixtures and jogged back to where Victor was waiting, all while focusing his mind on what really mattered.

Me and my daughter.

• • •

"Who are you, and what have you done with my friend?" Zoe demanded from the other end of the phone, as Paige tried to decide if a thirty-six-year-old woman could get away with wearing Vans. Normally she would've asked her friend, but it would only take the conversation somewhere she definitely didn't want it to go.

As for asking Audrey, who was sitting in the other room watching the Shopping Channel with the fervor of a four-year-old going to a Minions movie, it wasn't going to happen. Her mother had still been incredibly vague about why she'd come or how long she was planning to stay for.

She'd also taken to ignoring James's calls.

Perhaps we have more in common than I thought?

She kicked them off and settled for a pair of flat black ankle boots she'd bought on a whim and never worn. Then she reached for lipstick. Yes? No?

Definitely no. Lipstick might suggest kissing, and obviously that wasn't going to happen on account of...well... everything. Again, not a conversation she was prepared to have. Not even with herself.

"Nothing. I'm still the same me." Paige grabbed her favorite gray coat and shoved a black beanie into the pocket. "It's just now apparently I'm a 'me' who goes out on community patrol."

"I do believe that's the point I was making." Zoe's voice was dry. "Two months ago, your nighttime activities were drinking cocktails and bitching about Patrick. And now you're going into the wilderness armed only with a flashlight? It makes no—" Zoe sucked in her breath from down the other end of the phone. "Oh. It's a guy. This is about your wild lady oats."

"Absolutely not," Paige said a little too quickly. "It's about making sure I'm part of the community. It'll show I care."

"And do you?"

"I do," Paige responded as she peered out the front window at the ever-changing nightly vista of St. Clair's harbor. "I love it here. I want to make it work. Besides, everyone does extra stuff. My friend Sam's a volunteer firefighter."

"You're not selling the place very well," Zoe retorted, then, as if sensing Paige was about to open her mouth, she added, "Oh, I beg of you, please don't quote that damn book at me."

"I wasn't going to, I swear," she said, missing her friend and her no-holds-barred approach to life. "Zoe, I know you think this whole thing's crazy, but I really am happy."

Her friend sighed. "Okay, well apparently happy's the new black. If that's the case, then go out there and do whatever small town community patrol people do. As for me, I'm going to have a glass of wine and go through the stills from today's photo shoot. Oh, but first, can you please tell me why your hideous ex-boss keeps calling me?"

"Crap." Paige groaned as she recalled the deleted calls and messages. She'd been hoping Ellen would've gotten the hint. She'd forgotten her old boss had the skin of a rhino and the persistence of a dam-building beaver.

"Yeah, crap. I thought this was your year of saying no, so why's she asking me to pass on messages?"

"Because she's impervious to social cues," Paige said. "I'll call her now."

"Thanks," Zoe said. "And don't forget to put your lipstick on."

"It's not that kind of—" she tried to protest, but Zoe just snickered and hung up. She sighed and made the call. Ellen answered on the first ring, which was never a good sign.

"Oh, you're not freaking dead. Where the hell have you been?"

"Um, you do remember I don't work for you anymore,

right?" Paige headed down the stairs to wait. "You can't keep calling me. Or Zoe."

"I wouldn't if you picked up. Now, please stop being a bitch and help me out here. Aimee Watson's refusing to do any press. The publishers are all up in my face because the tour's booked, and we've got four big national interviews lined up. And when I talk to her, she just keeps muttering something about beetroot. What the hell?"

She closed her eyes as Dr. Penny Groves walked through the bookstore wall. She was wearing a surgeon's mask and robe, though it had been bedazzled in a glittering rainbow of rhinestones, so sparkly they could've powered the entire town of St. Clair. For a week.

Really, Paige? This is you saying no?

Stop it, Paige mentally protested while shielding her eyes from the unyielding glare. *This is strategic. If I help her out, then she'll have to stop calling me.*

Oh, is that how it works? Dr. Penny Groves folded her arms, and the light hit the rhinestones, which formed a halo all around her. Before Paige could answer, Ellen coughed.

Paige pushed Dr. Penny Groves from her mind.

Besides, it was all very well for her to be all judgey. She had her life together.

"Can we agree this will be the *last* time you call?"

"Absolutely," Ellen said, though her voice was glib. "What should I do?"

"You should do nothing. Just leave it all to me. I'll call her first thing and smooth it over." Paige said just as the doorbell went.

She flinched. Luke was silhouetted against the glass-fronted door, and her fingers tightened around the handle. In retrospect it would've been better if this had been a daytime activity. Possibly involving masks so she wouldn't be tempted to look at him.

"Are you serious?" Ellen demanded, not hiding her surprise. What did her ex-boss think she'd been doing for the last ten years?

"Yes, I'm serious. But I have to go."

"Fine. Call when it's done," Ellen said, and the line went dead.

Paige glared at the phone before pulling back the door. He was wearing a bright orange High Visibility vest, much like when she first met him, along with the same stony expression. Ten points for guessing who didn't like to be kept waiting.

"Sorry. That was my ex-boss. It's—"

"You don't need to explain." He cut her off with an indifferent shrug, which didn't bode well. She hitched in a breath.

I've worked with all kinds of temperamental authors. I can handle one prickly Community Patrol guy dressed like an Oompa Loompa.

"Fine." She nodded, and he handed her a matching vest.

"I hope orange is your color."

"Actually, I'm more of a fluorescent green girl," she said, as she wriggled to make it fit over her jacket. She was pretty sure she now resembled a marshmallow. A marshmallow that was visible from space. "I take it this is necessary and not a St. Clair hazing ritual."

"Our hazing ritual is a lot more complicated. You have to recite the family history of everyone in town, while drinking tea and looking out the window to see what your neighbors are doing." The hardness left his mouth.

She was going to take it as a win.

"Great. I should be ready in about ten years." She locked the door and followed him to a car that was covered in blue stripes, with Community Patrol plastered along the sides. "What is it that we're really doing?"

"Quote unquote, we're providing a visible presence to let the community know they're safe, and to deter people from doing things they shouldn't be doing." He opened the car door and ushered her in. "There's training involved, but I thought this could be a practice run. See if you like it first."

"Sure." She nodded as he fired up the engine and slowly did a lap along the esplanade that ran the length of the town.

There was a group of high school kids sitting at a bus stop goofing off, but at the sight of the car, they looked up and waved. Not exactly hardcore badasses.

After twenty minutes of driving around he parked and switched off the engine.

He turned to her. "A couple of the restaurants close up about this time. I like to walk around town for half an hour to make sure there's no trouble. You up for it?"

She nodded, and they climbed out of the car.

There were three main streets to St. Clair, and while she'd walked along them during the day, when they'd been bustling with locals, at night it was a different story. Empty and quiet, with faint lights flickering from inside the buildings, and the low murmur of voices.

"I guess this is a change of pace for you," he suddenly said. "You've moved from a city that never sleeps to one that barely opens its eyes."

"Isn't it against the St. Clair Rejuvenation Committee laws to speak badly of the place?" Paige studied his face for signs he was joking.

"Living here doesn't mean I'm blind to its flaws. This town isn't for everyone," he said, his face taking on a stony appearance.

Was he thinking about Joanne?

An uncomfortable silence swelled up between them. This wasn't like the other night. The strange intimacy that had built up around them was gone. Which was a good thing.

What was the point of thinking about something that could never lead anywhere?

Now I just need to remember.

She focused on her footsteps. Tap, crunch, tap, against the pavement.

Soft gusts of wind swirled around them, laden with the faint saltiness that lived in the air. The shops gave away to a cobbled path. She hadn't ventured down it before and let out a gasp as the path opened to a disused marina, eerie in the pale shards of moonlight.

"What is this place?"

"St. Clair's flaws," he answered. "Twenty years ago, there was a fishery here, along with a thriving marina. But when the stocks dried up, the boats went north. No one noticed because there was still a lot of tourist dollars coming in. But then the interstate was diverted, and presto, we were off the map. And sure, we're still a destination town, but it only takes one bad season for things to go belly up. Do you know how it feels to have your fate in someone else's hands?"

Visions flashed through mind, like darting swallows.

Of waiting for her father to come home, for her mom not to be distant and angry all the time. Waiting for Patrick to propose. To reform. To give her the sense of belonging she'd always wanted.

"I do." Her mouth was dry. "What's the plan?"

"We're hoping to start rebuilding soon. We've been replenishing fish levels for the last five years. With fishing, crabbing, and boating charters, we should create a hundred new jobs. We won't just have to rely on tourists." He shrugged as they headed back.

"You really are trying to rejuvenate the town," she said, in awe at his vision. Laney was right. With Luke, it wasn't what he said, it was what he did.

"I am," he said.

Her pulse flickered as his gaze trapped her, forcing her to stare back at him. Her throat tightened, and all the lies she'd been telling herself crumbled.

I should've put lipstick on.

She opened her mouth, but before she could speak the space was filled with a rumbling engine and the low, menacing thud of too much bass on the stereo. It split the night air like an angry predator. Boom. Boom. Boom.

Luke's body transformed in response.

Muscles tightened and coiled, his spine straightened, and his eyes narrowed in concentration. He pivoted while putting a protective hand on her arm, urging her to stay back as a car flashed past, a blur of light with the music streaming out behind it like a bridal veil.

"Shit." He swore under his breath, his phone up by his ear as he waited to be connected. "Ronnie. There's a black Ford heading down to Wilson's Lake. Plate number YGB222. It must've been clocking at least a hundred going through town. Yeah, okay. Bye."

Paige stared at him. "How did you do that? All I got was a smudgy flash."

"Too much practice," he said in a grim voice as they walked back to the car.

"What's next? Breaking up an illegal knitting circle?"

"I'd never take a rookie to something dangerous." The car rumbled to life. "We'll swing by the beaches, making sure there's no bonfires getting out of control. Though, it's quiet this time of year."

They drove away from the main center, the occasional headlights breaking the darkness. Houses melted away as they followed the coast. Every now and then he pulled into one of the small gravel parking lots that dotted the road and peered out.

"Nothing so far," he said, after climbing back in for the

third time.

"That's a good thing, right?" she said as his phone rang.

"I spoke too soon…Hi Mrs. Gilbert. Everything okay?" he said, before his face tightened. "No. Don't you go out. I'm on my way. Yes, I promise. In the meantime, call Mary and ask her to sit with you. No…she won't mind. I'll be in touch."

He put down his phone, the lines around his mouth deepening.

"Trouble?" Paige said, wishing she had a playbook for what his closed expressions meant.

"Hard to say. Mrs. Gilbert's cat, Trevor, is missing. That isn't unusual. I spend half my time climbing up trees after the old boy, but she's convinced she heard a noise as the speeding car went past her house. I said I'd check it out, but first we'll detour into town and drop you off."

"What?" Paige wrinkled her nose before understanding hit her. *He thinks I'm a precious city girl who'll only be in the way.* Meanwhile, a poor woman would be fretting about her cat. She gave a sharp shake of her head. "That doesn't make sense. Especially if it's a detour. Two eyes are better than one."

"I have two eyes."

"I meant sets of eyes, and you know it."

His jaw flickered. "There's a couple of ways this plays out. It's a wasted hour in the undergrowth. Which will be muddy from last night's rain. Or I find Trevor, and—"

"And either way, you'll need a hand. Besides, the longer we sit here talking about it…" She trailed off, and he shrugged.

"Okay, fine." And with that he switched on the engine and pulled back out onto the road.

Chapter Eight

"When the going gets tough, the tough say no." **Just Say No**

This was not the plan. Not even close.

Luke tapped the steering wheel as he pulled up to the section of winding road past Mrs. Gilbert's house. It was almost midnight.

I should be dropping her off and putting this whole night into the delete files in my head. Not asking her to help me search the undergrowth.

Especially so close to a road.

He'd attended his fair share of accidents from tourists who underestimated the speed of the cars.

He sent a quick text message to Mary, the old woman's neighbor, then reached for the flashlights. Dull clouds blocked the moon, while underfoot the ground was soft from the recent rain. Crickets and night insects chirped in an unending chorus.

If Trina had been there, she'd been squeaking and jumping at every sound.

He turned to Paige. The last thing he needed was her getting hysterical.

"Okay. We stick together, and if I stay stop, you stop," he said as a van thundered past on the nearby road, leaving behind a backwind that rocked the patrol car.

"Roger that." Even with the huge coat and High Visibility vest, she was sexy as hell. Her long blonde hair spilled over the collar and down her back, while her eyes were bright against the darkness.

None of which would help find Trevor.

He handed her a flashlight. They flicked them on, and two arcs of brightness radiated out in the darkness. He studied the area, hoping for an annoyed meow. Nothing.

He headed left, his boot sinking in the boggy ground. There was an old path, and after waving the flashlight in slow rotations, he found it. Without questioning, Paige followed. Her breathing was even as they made their way through the low-lying scrub.

"Did you hear that?" Her voice was a whisper.

"No." He matched her tone before he caught the feeble wail. "Yes."

It was louder this time. Definitely a cat.

"It's coming from over there." She used her torch to point, and they threaded their way past clumps of long, muddy grass, until they came to a rusted-out truck that'd been there as long as he could remember.

He raised his torch to scan the area before catching sight of two small eyes peering out from underneath the skeletal body of the ancient vehicle. He stepped closer, but Trevor slunk farther back into the shadows. Not before Luke caught the smear of blood on the fur around the cat's neck.

Crap.

He stepped into the tangled rusty remains of the car, but his hands hit mud as Trevor scrambled over to a crop of rocks.

Luke hurried after him, lowering himself to the ground, but despite stretching his hand out, his shoulder butted the stony ledge.

He swore and tried again, but it was no good.

He dug around in his pocket for his phone to call his sister. Not only was her husband the local vet, but Stu was smaller. It wouldn't be the first time he'd crawled into an awkward spot to rescue an animal.

"Everything okay?" Trina answered, her voice full of sleep.

"Trevor's been hit by a car. I can't get to him, but Stu should be able to. We're just opposite Mrs. Gilbert's house, about half a mile in, near the abandoned truck."

"He'll be there in ten minutes." Trina was wide awake.

"Thanks." Luke finished the call.

Wild berries and vanilla snaked up his nose as Paige joined him, so close their shoulders grazed. A tidal wave of energy washed over him. He swallowed hard and tried to stay focused.

"My brother-in-law will be here soon. He should be able to reach him."

"I can do it faster." She leaned forward, head tilted, as if inspecting the space. Then she dropped to her knees. "I can see him." Her gentle voice was at odds with the muddy ground and the darkness surrounding them.

"Wait. You can't go under there, it's filthy," he said. She gave him a withering look and lowered herself onto her belly. She inched forward, her voice like a lullaby.

"Here I am. Yes, it's okay. Good boy. Oh yes. Well done. Let's get you out of here."

He couldn't do anything but make sure she had enough light as she slowly wriggled into the narrow space. She emerged after several minutes, her arms tightly wrapped around Trevor. The cat let out several pitiful meows, but by the time they were back to the car, he'd calmed down.

Headlights came toward them, and Stu sprang from his Jeep, accompanied by Marc, the other vet from the clinic.

"Trevor, looks like you've really been getting up to mischief tonight," Stu said in a cheerful voice as they carried the cat to the Jeep for a thorough inspection. "He's onto about his eighty-fifth life. There's a large gash, which will need stitching, and some bruises, but he's going to be fine. Marc's calling Mrs. Gilbert now, then we'll patch him up and keep him in overnight."

"Thanks, buddy." Luke waited until Stu had driven away before jogging to where Paige was waiting, half wrapped in a blanket from the trunk of the car.

"You okay?"

"Obviously I'm devastated my lovely new orange vest is ruined." She glanced down at the mud and blood smeared along it, but she was smiling. "I'm fine. Besides, I wasn't the one who was hit by a car. Trevor's the real victim here."

"At least he didn't scratch you, which is his normal trick."

"Maybe I'm a cat whisperer." Her voice was light as she played with the corner of the blanket.

"You did good work. Really good work." The night air hummed with energy, like it was wrapping a circle around where they were standing.

"Oh." Her eyes flickered in surprise. "Well, I might not be great on ladders, but crawling around in the mud is my specialty."

"Obviously." He nodded. It seemed she didn't just have time for his daughter, or for stray pensioners like Smith and Marlon, but it extended to cats as well. It was a powerful combination.

His pulse thrummed, and fire burned in his veins.

Of things long forgotten.

Of things with no name.

Her perfume had faded, leaving behind an intoxicating scent of sea and fresh air, while the mud had dried in primal streaks along her jaw.

She's remarkable.

His heart hammered in response, and the effort of being alone was suddenly like a weight around his neck. So damn heavy.

Her lips were slightly parted, and reason fled as he stepped forward. A moan came from somewhere. Him? Her? He couldn't tell and didn't care.

His mouth found hers.

It was gentle, almost chaste as he kept his hands clamped to his sides. If he touched her, he'd be undone. Yet for all the restraint, blood still pounded in his ears. She pressed closer to him, her mouth never leaving his.

The heat of her skin blazed down his neurons, and his hands slid around her waist.

A soft noise caught in the back of her throat, and her fingers grazed his arms. Her touch was featherlight, sending darting threads of longing through him. Reality blurred, and he dragged his mouth away to explore the curve of her neck, lightly brushing it with his lips.

Her body quivered and pressed against him. She snaked her hands under the bright orange vest, thrusting it away in a fluid motion.

Raw desire pounded in his veins as his hands cupped her face. His mouth found hers again. Another moan, her breath like silk against his lips.

Brrrrrrrrr.

A phone was ringing, but it seemed like a million miles away.

So not answering it.

He kissed her again, but this time she stiffened in his arms and took a shaky step back.

"Is that you or me?" Her voice was husky, as if she'd just woken up.

"Don't care," he murmured and tried to pull her back to him, but she shook her head and gathered up the blanket that'd fallen to the ground.

"It's late. I should probably go home."

And I should probably throw a bucket of cold water over myself.

He took in a deep breath to try and steady himself. It wasn't easy, and he coughed to hide his discomfort.

"Right." He managed to nod as she scrambled into the passenger side of the car. They were silent on the short trip back, and it wasn't until she was safely inside her house that he let out a groan. Hell. His brother had been right all along.

I really need to get laid.

• • •

"I warn you, they swear like troopers, like their men naked, and their jokes inappropriate," a small woman said the following day. Her short silver hair was feathered out around her lined face, while her twinkling emerald eyes matched the greenstone necklace around her neck. "Oh, and if you make the mistake of putting out the good coffee, they'll drink it all. But, if you're prepared to put up with us, we'd love to have our next meeting here, and naturally we'd buy all our books through you."

"Book lovers who swear and drink too much coffee? Sound like my kind of people," Paige said. *And who actually buy things!*

"Wonderful. Oh, and by the way, I'm Olive."

"Olive? As in the famous Gigi?" she said. Despite the lack of sleep, she was full of energy. Okay, she was actually full of caffeine and rum cake, but that was practically the same thing.

"One and the same." Olive patted her hand. "And my fame's nothing compared to yours. My great-granddaughter hardly speaks of anything else. Well, apart from that actor she's all moony-eyed over. Not that I can blame her. He's a looker."

"Yes, he is." Her mouth twitched with amusement. She was starting to understand where Kira got her rapid conversation from.

"What do you say?" Olive nodded her head, as if helping Paige make her decision. Not that it was a hard one.

"Definitely yes." She walked around the counter. "Did Kira tell you about the reading nook?"

"Yes, and it's not just my granddaughter. Myra, Smith, and Marlon have all mentioned you," she said as they settled into two of the pale pink plush reading chairs. "Sounds like you've been a hit with the bingo crowd. Never could stand the game myself."

"I wouldn't say hit," Paige said. None of them bought anything, but since her first encounter with the two old men, they'd started popping in most afternoons, until Myra would appear and shuffle them off into the orange minivan. "But I like them."

"They're a good bunch," Olive agreed, before a curious smile tugged at her mouth. "I heard what happened on patrol last night."

"You did?"

Her breath quickened. Was Olive about to give her a lecture on why she shouldn't have kissed her grandson? Or that kissing a man who thought she was a flight risk was a bad idea? Or—

"How you saved poor Trevor. Tilly Gilbert dotes on the cat. I'm sure you'll be receiving a visit from her soon."

Oh. Right. Trevor.

I knew that.

Of course it wasn't about the kiss. It wasn't like she'd told anyone, and it appeared Luke hadn't, either. Thank goodness for small mercies, because while kissing him had been the thing filthy dreams were made of, the fact she all but threw herself at him wasn't such a highlight.

In her defense, he'd been far too attractive in the moonlight.

A serious set to his brow, and his mouth full and inviting. So she'd kissed him. And it was glorious. Gentle but toe curling. Like chocolate and chili cupcakes. Then his phone had rung, and reality sledgehammered itself into her overheated brain. She was wearing an orange High Visibility vest, covered in mud and cat hair.

He's only helping me fit in.

Hardly code for "kiss me."

Not to mention she hadn't moved here for love, she'd moved here to stop making the same mistakes over and over again.

When I want to say yes, I have to say no.

Which meant Luke Carmichael was a capital NO.

Her thoughts were interrupted by the appearance of a blonde girl, who walked into the store with a swirl of energy crackling and bouncing in her wake.

"Oh, you have it!" She picked up a large art book that'd arrived yesterday and raced over. "Nan, this is the book I've been wanting. I meant to grab it while I was away, but ran out of time. I can't believe it's here. I'm Trina, by the way. Please don't judge me by my idiot brothers. I promise I'm completely sane."

"Apart from hugging books." Olive winked as Trina sat down on a nearby silver leather ottoman. "This one's an artist, in case you couldn't guess."

"It's really nice to meet you," Paige said.

"You, too. Though I feel like we're already friends. Stu told me what a brilliant job you did on Trevor last night. Who, by the way, is much better."

"It was nothing." Paige tried to brush it off. She wasn't used to being the center of attention. "At least it had a happy ending."

Olive's eyes danced with amusement, and Paige and Trina groaned. The older woman was obviously thinking of a double entendre.

"I'd ask you to excuse my grandmother, but there's no point." Trina leaned over and hugged the woman next to her. "What you see is what you get."

"It's a refreshing change." Paige walked to the counter, so Trina could pay for the book.

"I have to prepare Paige for when she meets the rest of the book group." Olive winked as they headed for the door, arms hooked, laughing as they went.

Something lodged in her throat as they left, still chattering like a couple of friends rather than grandmother and granddaughter. Their bond was similar to what Luke and Kira had. *Is that what all the Carmichaels are like?*

She shook the thought away as the door chime went and Nancy walked in with a sketch of her latest tattoo and a request for a book on how to draw dragons.

The rest of the day passed in a pleasant blur of customers all wanting to know more about her rescue mission last night. And this time most of them bought something, giving her a record day. She counted up her takings and put them in the safe under the desk in her office.

Luke had been right. Giving back to the community was working.

She flipped the CLOSED sign and headed to Sam's. The Belles were waiting in the cobbled courtyard that ran the side of the building.

Long wooden tables were scattered around the place, surrounded by hand-chalked menus announcing the specials. Sun umbrellas were nestled against the wall for hotter days, while copper fire pits dotted the space for the cooling weather.

Sam and Laney beckoned her over by holding up a wine bottle.

"I know it's only Wednesday," Laney said by way of explanation. "But your store's been busy. We thought we should celebrate."

"Who knew saving a cat would be the secret to my economic success?" Paige took the offered glass and clinked with her two friends. "Mrs. Gilbert gave me a box of chocolates and a jar of homemade jam."

Laney's eyes widened. "Lucky you. That jam's like gold dust in this town. She only makes a dozen jars a year. Wait until you taste it. Nectar from the gods."

"More importantly, it's like getting the St. Clair seal of approval. No wonder you were busy today," Sam added. "And you still haven't told us what happened last night. How did it go with Luke?"

Well, our mouths are highly compatible.

"It was fine," she said in a casual voice, as if she went out on patrol with gorgeous men every day of the year. No big deal. "He told me about the plans to fix up the old marina. I was impressed."

"You should be. Luke's been the driving force behind the whole scheme," Sam said. Paige wasn't surprised. The more she got to know him, the more she understood just how capable he was.

"And he's not known for letting any women join him on his Tuesday night patrol." Laney leaned forward, eyes gleaming. "Not that they haven't tried. Poor Melanie signed up, thinking she'd get teamed with Luke, and ended up being stuck with Bill Chadwick."

"He has a fondness for pickled garlic," Sam explained. "It took her two months to come up with an ironclad excuse not to do it anymore."

Paige groaned. "I'm guessing my cat-saving heroics won't be getting me into Melanie's good books anytime soon."

Sam patted her hand. "Here's the stupid thing when you grow up in a small town, there are only a certain number of eligible locals, and even if you don't *really* want them, there's a weird territorial thing that comes up. Especially when hormones are ticking. Unless you're me."

Sam hadn't gone into details about her love life, but Paige gathered there had been a bad breakup. One that was still raw. Something she could relate to.

"Besides, if Luke was going to fall for Melanie, surely it would've happened by now," Laney added in a thoughtful voice. "Which means if he asked you to patrol, it's because—"

"He feels sorry for me," Paige cut them off, once again reliving the embarrassment of the kiss. "I'm the city girl who almost fell off a ladder. He's probably keeping an eye on me for public safety reasons."

"I really don't think so." Laney's auburn hair spilled out around her slender shoulders. But before she could continue, Sam's phone buzzed, and her face went pale as she studied the screen.

"Everything okay?" Paige put down her wineglass.

"Principal Watson wants to see me about Cal's behavior." She let out a shallow breath and got to her feet.

"What's he done?" Laney's perpetual smile faded.

"I have no idea, but this is my third visit in as many weeks. At the last meeting there was talk of expelling him." Her mouth was tight with worry. "The only other school in the area is way out of my league."

"It's not going to come to that," Laney said as they carried the glasses back to the kitchen and helped her clean up.

"Let's just hope you're right." Sam gave them both a grateful smile as she locked up the café and headed in the direction of the car.

"Hey," Laney said as Sam's headlights had disappeared. "I'm heading out for pizza with my sister-in-law and her friends. I'd love for you to meet her. I know you'll get on."

"I wish I could," she said truthfully. "But Audrey's gone on a wine tour and is due home in an hour. I said I'd cook."

"Another time, then. Have a fun night." Laney gave her a quick hug and then headed into her store, leaving Paige alone. The dying sun turned the sky into an array of pinks and oranges, while in the distance water lapped against the shore. It was a perfect evening, and she didn't need to go inside and start cooking yet. She headed across the road to the quaint harbor.

Once away from the path, she slipped off her shoes. The damp, dark sand was soft as she walked. The water was cold, but she kept her feet in, as the octogenarians completed their evening swim.

"At this rate, they'll be asking you to join them," a voice said. *Luke.* His own shoes were in his hands, and his work jeans were rolled up to his calves, revealing tanned legs.

He was hot. So very, very hot.

Her mouth went dry.

"Not if they see me swim," she countered, trying to remind herself how to breathe. "What are you doing here?"

"I—" he started and then stopped. "Actually, I've got no idea. I was driving home, and I saw you crossing the road."

"Well, you weren't tempted to run over me, that's promising," she said.

"I wouldn't dare. You're a town hero. I heard you got a jar of Mrs. Gilbert's jam."

"Sam brought me up to speed on what it means. Oh, and I met your grandmother and sister today."

"Sorry if they were being busybodies." He gave her an apologetic smile.

"Not at all. I liked them both a lot. Olive's bringing her book group into the store."

"Yeah, you might not thank her for that. They're so raunchy they can even make Jacob blush. No mean feat." He was at least a foot away, but the heat from his body burned down the side of her arm. He coughed. "About last night—"

The words hung between them.

Reminding Paige of all the reasons why she'd planned to say no to men.

Of why I should've said no to him.

"The mud or the kiss?" She tried not to return his gaze.

He was like a cursed mirror from a fairy story. No good could come from looking in. *Well, not for too long.* She peered up to catch the bemused twist of his mouth.

Boy was it a nice mouth.

"The kiss, Paige. I'm talking about the kiss."

"I know." She dredged up her inner Dr. Penny Groves. "I'm just trying to avoid you talking about the kiss. I should never have thrown myself at you like that." Embarrassment caught in her throat. Saying it out loud didn't make it any easier to accept.

"I don't recall any throwing." His voice was like aged whiskey, smooth and full of heat. She licked her lips and let herself breathe him in. Hints of wood and soap clung to his skin, sending a shiver down her spine. "But my life's complicated. Actually, no, it's not. It's remarkably uncomplicated. I have a daughter. And I know some people can date, but—"

"Please. You don't have to explain. I understand how much Kira means to you," she cut him off. Again, the shame was there. She hated that he had to give her a "but." She'd known from the start how important his daughter was to him. And that was a good thing. She'd grown up with a father who couldn't even be bothered to call on birthdays, let alone put his life on hold for her. "Besides, after what happened with Patrick—"

"Patrick?" His jaw tightened. Obviously, the New York grapevine wasn't as efficient as the St. Clair one. "There's a Patrick?"

"Ex-fiancé." She stared at the pale moon. "Not such a great guy. My whole life was on hold, waiting for him to give me what I wanted. We were engaged until I found him cheating on me. Then, like a thread of a cheap suit, the truth all came out. He'd been sleeping around the entire time."

"Sounds like an asshole." A flash of anger rippled across his face. She swallowed and hugged her arms to her chest, trying to protect herself from falling for his concern.

They're just words. It doesn't mean anything.

"Yeah, he kind of was," she found herself agreeing. "The reason I moved here was to make different decisions, and get different results."

"That's explains the book you've got everyone reading." Molten silver eyes flicked with amusement. She nodded.

"Right now, I have to say no to everything I want to say yes to."

"Which means the kiss itself wasn't what's putting you off."

"Hell no," she said before she could stop herself. *I really need to work on my poker face.* "I mean, it was a good kiss."

"A great kiss, even," he added, his voice low, caressing her skin and doing terrible things to her stomach. *Oh boy.*

"Definitely. And if things were different…"

"Yeah. But they're not." His voice was gruff, as if he was trying to gather up his thoughts. "Perhaps I should borrow the book and get a few tips?"

"I think you'll do just fine. I know it sounds corny, but I'd like to be friends."

"Friends I can do." A smile flashed across his face as he glanced toward the road. "And my first job as a friend is to walk you home."

"Sure." They slowly walked up the path to her front door. Her skin tingled as he tilted his head to one side and said goodnight, but she swallowed it down. Attraction was a short-term thing. But being part of the town, belonging here, that's what she wanted. And as far as she could tell, this was the best way.

Say it enough times and I might even believe it.

Chapter Nine

"We've been sleepwalking through our lives, saying yes to things we don't want. It's time to wake up. A no to someone else is a yes to yourself." **Just Say No**

"Let me get this straight. You said no to kissing but yes to crawling in the mud and rescuing a cat?" Zoe sounded faintly disgusted. "And you're happy about getting a jar of jam?"

"Stop exaggerating. I only said no to the kissing *after* I said yes to it. Besides, I wasn't the only one. Luke had just as many reasons for why it can't happen again."

She adjusted her headset as she walked along the esplanade to the town meeting. The Belles had assured her it'd earn brownie points.

"I'm still not buying it. No man kisses you until your toes curl and then backs off."

Unless they have a fourteen-year old daughter.

And a wife who deserted them.

We made the right decision.

"It's fine. *I'm* fine."

"Please. You're going to a town meeting that'll no doubt discuss goat rotation and hay bale throwing. Sweetheart, you're two interventions away from being fine."

"I'm not quite sure you understand how small towns work. But if you came for a visit, you'd see what it's really like."

"I know what it's *not* like. New York," Zoe retorted, refusing to be drawn into the ongoing campaign. The excuses had ranged from not having a passport, no gumboots, and that she didn't want to get the six million shots necessary to leave her urban jungle. "And I'm serious. You have needs, Paige. Basic primal needs. Tell me the last time you and Patrick—"

"No comment," she quickly interjected. Because if she admitted their sex life had been nonexistent for six months before the breakup, or that it'd been two months since they'd parted ways, she'd be forced to tally up the number of months since she'd—

Nope. Still not going there.

"Fine." Zoe sniffed. "On that note, I'm going to leave you to your interesting discussions on what color to paint the local church."

Paige didn't want to admit that according to Sam and Laney, the color had been picked at the last meeting. Heron blue.

She finished the call and toyed with turning around and heading back to the house. Not because Zoe had put her off, but because she wasn't sure if it was a good idea to leave Audrey on her own. Her mom had come back from the wine tour yesterday in a giddy mood, and while she insisted she wasn't drunk, she did almost end up buying a bright pink patio set for James and Fiona, as an early Christmas present. It had taken all of Paige's efforts to talk her out of it.

James owed her big time.

Then again, stopping her mom from buying weird things online wasn't going to help her business. She put her phone away and kept walking.

The town hall was a quaint wooden building she'd passed numerous times but hadn't been inside. There were rows of chairs with a stage at one end and a long trestle table with tea and coffee at the other.

The majority of people were gathered in small groups, talking to each other, several of whom looked with interest before returning to their conversation.

She wandered farther in, then froze as Melanie's voice drifted over. Her back was turned as she spoke with a red-haired girl in a green dress.

"Please, it's all a con. The only reason she went on patrol was to get into Luke's pants," Melanie said. "She saved Trevor by default, which means it doesn't count."

"Tell me about it. As soon as she realizes he isn't that kind of guy, she'll wriggle out of the job. Mark my words," the redhead said before the conversation took a different track.

Old feelings of discomfort swirled in her belly.

Back from when she and James had met their dad's new wife. The house had been like a foreign land full of unfamiliar furniture and family photos that didn't include her. Memories she couldn't share.

I don't belong here.

But before she could turn and leave, Olive appeared at her side.

"Paige, how lovely to see you."

"Thanks." She swallowed down the flood of unwanted emotions and plastered on a smile. "This is quite a turnout."

"Are you kidding? This is St. Clair's favorite form of entertainment." Trina appeared next to her grandmother. "It's like the stock exchange. Only more ruthless."

"It's true." Olive nudged her to where a couple of elderly

women were engaged in conversation. "To the unassuming eye, Martha and Ronnie Sinclair are just two sisters catching up about the weather, but they're really determining the day for next year's spring gala, which will in turn determine which bride will have to find a new date for their wedding. It will either be Katie Neville or Julie Sampson."

"Classic St. Clair power play. My advice, don't get on their bad side." Trina gave a sage nod and took an envelope out of her bag. "And before I forget, this is an invitation to Olive's eightieth birthday."

"Oh." Paige's throat tightened in surprise. "This is so unexpected. I don't know what to say."

"Say yes." Trina grinned. "Nan throws the best parties in town."

"That's true." Olive's green eyes danced with mischief. "What's the point of getting to my age and not having a little bit of fun? I do hope you can come. It's nothing big or fancy. Just a small crowd of dear friends. Oh, and if your mom's still here, she's more than welcome."

"Thank you," Paige said, not wanting to admit she didn't have a clue if Audrey would still be around, since unlike the Carmichaels, who seemed to know everything about each other, Paige and her mom might as well be strangers.

"Did you give it to her?" Kira appeared from thin air and jumped from one foot to the other.

"I sure did." Trina nodded.

"If you say yes, then you can meet my friends. They're too scared to come into the store in case you get mad at them for talking. As if. Besides, it's not like it's a library," Kira said, the words tumbling out like an avalanche. "Oh, and there's going to be a surprise, but I can't tell you what it is."

"I'd love to come." She opened the envelope. It was on a Sunday afternoon, the week before Halloween. Kira let out a happy squeal and disappeared over to the other side of the hall, where a group of girls her own age waited.

"If only I had half her energy," Trina said as a guy in his fifties tapped the microphone. "Oh, that's the mayor. Looks like it's about to start."

"Over here. We saved you a seat." Sam waved. Laney was next to her, along with Jacob, who was murmuring something in her ear.

"I see you got invited to Olive's party." Laney leaned over just as the mayor coughed and announced the first thing on the agenda.

Blackberry thievery from the bush in the town square.

She could almost hear Zoe's snickering laughter in her head.

Fifteen minutes later she blinked, trying to follow the wide range of topics the town needed to discuss. From fund-raising to moonshine production. There was a continuous dialogue going on between people as each issue was raised. *I'm pretty sure this is what the Stock Exchange looks like at opening bell.*

"Next on the agenda is repairing the bus stop by Second Street."

"I call B.S.," someone shouted out.

Paige's mouth dropped open, and next to her Laney giggled.

"It's not what you think. B.S. stands for Barter System. It can sound a bit like people are speaking in tongues, but it's really just an exchange of goods and services. You'll soon get the hang of it. Oh, here's Luke."

Her stomach contracted as he walked in from a side door. They hadn't spoken since the other evening. Well, not in person. In her head she'd had numerous encounters. Mostly involving the removal of clothing.

But in real life the closest she'd come to him was when he'd waited in his truck to collect Kira. Which was good.

Obviously. Much easier to say no when she didn't have to face him.

A couple of women sighed as he walked to the stage.

She couldn't blame them.

He filled his dark denim jeans in all the right places, while the pale gray sweater turned his eyes into distilled moonlight. How was that possible?

And as for his mouth—

No. On no account look at his mouth.

Hell. What if Melanie and her friend were right? *What if I'm only doing the patrol to spend time with him?*

She pinched herself. Hard.

"You okay?" Sam gave her a curious look, no doubt wondering why a grown woman was pinching herself.

"I thought there was a bug."

"Right." Sam didn't sound convinced.

"Here's the thing," she admitted with a sigh. "I overheard Melanie saying I wasn't serious about the patrol. That I'm only doing it because—"

"Because Luke's hot?" Sam finished off and shrugged. "Just ignore it. They'll get sick of saying it soon."

She was stopped from answering as Luke flicked on a PowerPoint presentation and took the town through the timeline for the new marina. He then moved onto the fund-raiser, The Big Fish, breaking down how people could best help, before wrapping it up. All in less time than it had taken the mayor to discuss moving the WELCOME TO ST. CLAIR sign from three feet in front of the old oak tree to five feet in front of it.

"And one final thing before we close tonight's meeting." The mayor stood back up and glanced to Melanie, who was walking to the stage. "We're short of volunteers for some of our upcoming events. Remember that helping the town is the greatest way to help yourselves, so don't be stingy with your time."

Sam nudged her. "Hey, this is your chance to prove you're here for the long run. I'll let you know which are the best ones to do."

"Okay, sounds great," Paige quickly agreed, dragging her mutinous gaze away from Luke. The busier she was, the less time she'd have to think about things she shouldn't be thinking about. Instead, she'd be promoting her business and finding out just where she belonged in her new hometown.

It was a win-win.

"Thank you." Melanie cleared her throat and stepped up to the microphone. Her long dark hair hung in waves around her shoulders, and her molten chocolate eyes looked larger than ever. "First up, we need two people to join our Carnival Celebration team. Can I please have a show of hands?"

Sam nudged her, and Paige lifted her hand, along with two other people in the room. Melanie immediately pointed at the two people who weren't Paige. "Thanks, Jilly and Ryan. That's wonderful. Now, let's see. We need four people for the Harbor Day committee."

"Oh yes, that's a good one." Sam nudged, and again Paige's arm shot up, along with five other people.

"Wonderful." Melanie purred as she used her pen to point to three old men in the front row, who had a combined age of five hundred and twelve, and then to a young boy who didn't look much older than Kira. "Right, next up we have beautification."

"That's a bit more physical work, but it could still be fun," Sam murmured, though she didn't sound convinced. All the same Paige's hand flew up, hoping for third time lucky, but Melanie just beamed as she allocated it to a couple of German tourists who'd wandered in from the street to see what was happening.

Several heads swiveled to Paige, who still had her arm

up in the air. *Crap.* She lowered it and tried to imagine her cheeks weren't bright red.

Someone needed to invent an earth-swallowing app. Stat.

"Hey, come on, Mel," Jacob called out from two seats down. "Paige wants to help out. She's had her hand up the entire time."

"Oh my goodness." Melanie blinked, as if unable to figure out what had caused such a terrible oversight. "I feel so bad. Okay, what else do we have here…oh yes. We do need someone to help Robert."

A collective murmur went up around the room.

"Say no," Sam hissed under her breath. "No one will judge you."

"Judge me for what? Who's Robert?"

"Not a who, a *what*," Laney whispered. "He's the statue in the town square. The one the pigeons use as target practice. Melanie wants you to volunteer to clean him."

As in clean shit off a statue?

"Unless you don't want to get your hands dirty," Melanie added in a sugary voice. Paige rubbed her chin. Turned out her year of saying no was involving a hell of a lot of yeses.

"I don't mind." She plastered on the same smile she used to get the dreadful YouTube star to sign autographs for the fans who'd lined up for five hours to meet her. "It sounds like it will be lots of fun."

"I'm sure it will be," Melanie said, though her look suggested it'd only be fun if you liked living in hell. With broken air conditioning. And shards of glass for carpet.

Melanie Banks, one. Paige Taylor, minus three hundred and five.

• • •

"Where the hell have you been?" Luke said as his brother

sauntered over. He nodded to the wood that still needed to be cut to length if they wanted to get the decking around the hot tub built before Olive's party in two weeks.

"Just around." Jacob scooped up his work belt and clipped it on. "What's the panic? We have loads of time."

"No. We have today. I've got back-to-back jobs coming up, not to mention the rehearsals so we don't make complete fools of ourselves. It was your idea, remember?"

"I remember," his brother growled, his normal good humor gone.

"What's with you lately?" He frowned.

"Nothing." Jacob busied himself double-checking the measurements. Luke studied his unusually docile brother before shrugging. No point looking a gift horse in the mouth. He handed Jacob the plans and showed him what needed to be done first, before he finished cutting up the wood.

The rest of the morning sped past, and by lunch the framework was finished.

"Thought you could use a break." Olive appeared carrying a tray of homemade hamburgers, while Trina and Stu followed with beers. "How many people will fit into the hot tub? And will we get more in if they're not wearing clothes?"

"Is that a joke?" Stu wrinkled his nose as he handed out the beers. "It sounded like a joke, but I can never be sure."

"Why would I joke?" Olive gave him an innocent smile as she set down the hamburgers and gestured for everyone to dig in.

"Nan, I swear if this party turns into an orgy, I'm going to let you tidy up on your own." Trina sat down on the half-finished deck. "Perhaps we should install surveillance cameras?"

"God, no." Jacob shuddered, taking a deep drink. "Remember last year? Reverend Wilson went streaking across the backyard. What is seen can never be unseen."

"Can't be as bad as watching you chat up every woman who crossed your path," Trina retorted. "You were like a hormonal teenager."

"And your point is?" Jacob gave her an innocent look while Luke took a pull of beer and tried not to think about hormones. Especially the fact his own had been reactivated.

Unrequested, the kiss slammed into his head, but he shut it out.

Get your shit together.

It was just a kiss. And it wasn't just him.

Paige had been quick to agree. Very quick. Which was a good thing, because if she'd given one hint about pursuing it, his well-reasoned arguments would've flown south.

Friends were better. Safer. It was the right decision. Plus, despite how much Paige loved it in St. Clair, he'd overheard her conversation with her ex-boss when he'd collected her for patrol. It didn't sound like she'd cut ties with her old life.

Now I just need to remember that.

"And what the hell got into Melanie the other night?" Trina's voice dragged him back. "I get she's pissed Diana didn't sell her the store, but there was no need to come down on Paige."

"Maybe she's jealous Paige is patrolling with Luke?" Jacob got to his feet and helped himself to a hamburger. "We all know that strange things can happen at night under a St. Clair moon."

"Stop setting me up with everyone," he growled, trying to ignore how close his brother was to the truth.

"Who says we're trying to set you up? This could be for Paige's benefit?" Trina's eyes danced with mischief. "After all, she's gorgeous."

"You think Paige is gorgeous? Should I be worried?" Stu blinked, which resulted in Trina giving him a long, lingering kiss on the mouth. He grinned in response. "Okay, I'm not worried. But you know, if you want to set her up, there's always Marc at the clinic. It's been a year since he moved to St. Clair, and he's desperate to meet someone."

Trina gave her husband a playful pat. "Sweetie, you're so cute, but that'd never work. Marc's a great guy, but he's not right for her. Besides, just because my big brother says he's not interested, doesn't mean it's true."

"Is that so?" Luke's mouth flattened into a straight line that only made his siblings laugh. But before they could needle him further, Trina's phone rang. Her face paled as she studied the screen, and she quickly excused herself. Jacob and Stu followed a few moments later.

"Don't fight it," Olive advised once they were alone. "It will only make it worse. Besides, is it really such a silly idea for you and Paige to date? You're both single."

And I intend on staying that way.

Except while he could ignore Jacob and Trina, it was harder to ignore Olive. She'd virtually raised them. Seen the devastation his mom's betrayal had caused his dad—Olive's only son.

And she'd been there again to help pick up the pieces when Joanne had left town.

"I know they mean well, but I have a lot going on," he said, his voice softer. "Even if I did want a relationship, the timing's bad."

"I know, sweetheart." Olive gave him a gentle smile, as if reminding him she was on his side. "But when is the timing ever good? Have you ever wondered what would happen if you just slowed down and just let things be?"

Things would fall apart.

People would get hurt.

Kira might grow up and decide St. Clair wasn't enough for her.

He toyed with the neck of his beer and swallowed down the familiar panic.

"I need to focus on my daughter," he finally spoke, and Olive patted his hand.

"You do what you think is right," she said as Trina, Jacob, and Stu all reappeared, talking in low voices.

"Sorry about that." Trina studied her shoes.

"Don't be silly," Olive said before frowning. "Everything okay? You look pale."

"I'm fine," Trina said a little too quickly. Luke frowned. Olive was right. Something was definitely going on. Then he shook it off. He had quite enough going on in his own life to worry about someone else's secrets. And with that, he got back to work.

• • •

If mainlining Sam's strawberry shortcake was wrong, Paige didn't want to be right. It had been a busy day paying bills, updating the computer system, and serving a steady stream of customers. She still wasn't making big sales, but at least the store no longer resembled a ghost town, for which she was grateful. It was why she'd decided to celebrate with a slice of heavenly goodness.

She walked out of her small office behind the counter of the bookstore and wiped away the telltale signs of baker's sugar. The store had been closed for an hour, and outside treacle colored leaves dotted the pathway, while heavy black clouds rolled in, bringing with them large raindrops. Any ideas she had of a late afternoon walk fled her mind.

A glass of wine it was, then.

She was just about to lock the door when Audrey pulled up in a taxi.

She had a large scarf covering her head and an umbrella

against the rain.

"Goodness. I thought I'd left this weather behind in Boston." Her mother gave the umbrella a shake and leaned it against the wall by the porch. Rain clung to her long jacket, leaving a silver trail as she stepped in.

"It's certainly coming down in buckets," she said as her mom tugged at the scarf and shook out her hair. Several inches had been cut off the bottom and more body added, causing it to spike out around her face.

Oh, and it was pink.

As in bubblegum pink, with random streaks of purple woven through it.

Paige let out a little gasping noise.

"Does that mean you don't like it?" A flash of hurt crossed Audrey's face.

"What? No, it's just…very pink," Paige croaked, trying to reconcile the woman standing in front of her with the woman who had this morning owned a conservative head of hair. Not that she didn't like the color or style. But it was more something Zoe or one of her friends in New York would do. Not her straitlaced, emotionally frozen mother who didn't even smile at kitten photos.

"I decided it was time for a change."

"Well, you've certainly done that." Was this a midlife crisis? *I'd better Google it when I get a chance.* "Is there a reason you dyed it pink?"

"I didn't know I needed one." Audrey glanced around the store. "I thought you out of everyone would understand."

"I-I do."

"I'm pleased," her mother said, but her voice was tight. "I'm going to have a short rest. If that's okay with you?" This last part was accompanied by an eyebrow raise Paige was *very* familiar with.

She followed her mother up the stairs in ominous silence

and sank down onto the couch. Seconds later her phone rang, and she groaned as James's name flashed up on the screen.

"Seriously, Paige. You let her dye her hair pink?"

"Let her?" Paige whispered. "I had no idea she was going to do it. And how do you know?"

"Because she put it on Snapchat."

"Audrey's on Snapchat?" she yelped, not sure what to make of the entire day. Then another thing occurred to her. James was on Snapchat?

Who are these people?

She swallowed down an ill-humored retort. "I'll talk to her."

"Good. Make sure she goes to the hairdresser and gets it reversed."

"And how do you propose I do that?" Paige said, but James didn't wait for an answer.

She finished the call as Dr. Penny Groves appeared by the window. She was wearing a toga, complete with golden leaves woven around her head.

Haven't you figured out how to say no to your family yet, Paige?

It's a work in progress," she said defensively, to which the imaginary doctor made a clucking noise and flapped her arms like a chicken. Paige picked up a decorative pillow and threw it.

"What's all the racket? I'm trying to rest." Her mother reappeared with a frown on her face.

Paige sighed. What was the point of running away from her problems if they just followed her?

Chapter Ten

"The only thing harder than saying no is actually meaning it." **Just Say No**

"You didn't have to wait outside," Luke said as Paige darted into the car, almost before he'd even come to a stop. The blustery fall weather had finally arrived in St. Clair as the cool night air shrouded her, leaving her eyes bright and the tip of her nose red.

Strands of silky blonde hair fell across her cheek, and it took all his willpower not to lean in and kiss her. *So, yeah. The plan to not think about her is going great.*

"I figured it'd be easier." She shrugged, though her eyes gave her away as she glanced back up to the second floor of her place, where the lights blazed and a Donna Summers song drifted down. He had no idea what her relationship with her mother was, but she obviously didn't want to talk about it. Couldn't blame her for that. "Where to first?"

"Victor's bar. There was an attempted robbery a couple of nights ago."

"Victor the hairdresser?"

"Yeah. This town's a two-for-the-price-of-one setup."

"I've noticed." She fiddled with the seat belt, and he tried not to inhale her floral scent. He failed, and his pulse flickered. He tightened his grip on the steering wheel. He was all too conscious of her sitting next to him, studying her long fingers.

Ten minutes later he pulled up at Cowboy Country Saloon.

Hollywood-style lights surrounded the name, while large cacti grew on each side of the door, and the pale wooden facade was straight from a seventies western movie. For a guy who wanted three bathrooms in his conversion, it was an interesting choice.

There were a few bikes parked outside, all leaning in the same direction, and on the other side of the parking lot were the cowboy trucks. Most of the time the sheriff kept an eye on it, but Toby had called to say they were dealing with an accident on the other side of town. Despite the beat-up appearance there was never much trouble.

She let out a startled noise. "How have I missed this place?"

"Let's just say it's one of the few businesses that doesn't rely on the locals. Bikers use it as a stop through, and cowboys come down from the surrounding ranches. It's a different ecosystem. Would you rather stay in the car?" he said as the door swung open and a blast of honky-tonk music spilled out into the night.

"Hell no." She climbed out of the car with childlike excitement. A reluctant smile tugged at his mouth.

She was nothing like he'd imagined.

Instead of arriving in town with a jaded attitude, she'd been open to everything St. Clair had to offer. And while she said it was to help her business, the inner light that brightened her face told another story.

He followed her in, pleased that despite her navy eyes brimming with curiosity at the table of bikers knocking back shots, and the cowboys gathered around the pool tables at the far end of the place, she wasn't staring at the room like it was filled with purple aliens.

The only giveaway was the soft parting of her mouth as he joined her in the low-lit bar. He brushed his hand against hers and was rewarded by a faint sigh.

I'm playing with fire.

"Still impressed?" he said.

"You have no idea." She shuddered, which sent a hundred volts hammering through his body. *Christ.*

Victor was over by the bar, wearing a neatly pressed pink shirt and a flamboyant tie that looked like it had come straight from the set of *Hello, Dolly!* Luke quirked an appreciative eyebrow. There was a line of people waiting, and it was several minutes before it quieted down.

"Busy night?"

"More like not enough staff. Cheryl's moving to Seattle." Victor pushed back the glasses he'd been using to read a delivery notice.

"Sorry to hear that." He frowned. Cheryl was a local girl who'd been working for Victor for a couple of years. The fact she was leaving town wasn't good news. "Was it because of the attempted break-in?"

"No. She can handle herself just fine. It was a question of cash. Said she could get three times the amount I was paying her. I've only just found a new receptionist at the salon. Who knows how long it will take to find someone for here. At this rate, the only way to keep both places going will be to give haircuts out the back."

"I wouldn't have thought you'd get much client crossover." He nodded at the patrons that either had no hair at all, or

Herculean locks he suspected hadn't seen scissors in years.

"You're right there, son," he said before turning to Paige. "And it's nice to officially meet you."

"You, too," she said as Victor covered her hand in his and kissed her cheek. "I've been meaning to come and get my hair cut."

"You do that. I promise I won't dye it pink. Unless you want me to," he added with a wink, which brought a smile to her mouth. The flash of teeth sent Luke's pulse racing. *Focus.*

"Any problems tonight?" He dragged his gaze away and scanned the room.

He knew a few of the clientele by name, and while they might not be complete angels, most of them stayed out of major trouble.

Victor shook his head. "I told them at the station, it was probably some idiot passing through. All the same I appreciate you both stopping by."

"We'll hang around a bit longer, and then just call if you need a hand."

"Will do," Victor said as a group of women strutted to the bar while eyeing off a cluster of guys in the far corner. "I'll send something non-alcoholic your way."

As they walked across the room, the conversation around them lowered.

"We don't need to stay here too long," he promised as they found a table.

"Hey, if we're here then Trevor must be safely at home and not up a tree somewhere." Her voice was light, but her eyes flickered with uncertainty.

"He's still sidelined from last time," he said as the one remaining waitress brought a tray of cocktails over. He coughed in surprise. It was more of a beer and bourbon crowd.

"Non-alcoholic mojitos. I don't get to try out my skills

very often," she said with a wink before walking away. He passed Paige one of the glasses.

"Thanks. Who knew community patrol would be so diverse?" She idly stirred the drink with a straw.

"Couldn't have you thinking it was all mud crawling." Luke held up the long glass, filled with mint leaves and slices of lime, the clear liquid delicately shaded with yellows and greens. "We have a glamorous side."

"I'm discovering." She took a sip, and her eyes fluttered in appreciation. "Pineapple. Nice."

Luke took a drink and winced. Too sweet for his liking but he forced himself to nod in agreement. "Yeah."

"You're a terrible liar." She laughed, her face lighting up.

"Busted." He grinned and put the drink back down.

"Well, I like it. Much better than the ones my brother made last Christmas. He spent a fortune on the rum as well. Typical James."

She has a brother?

He wasn't sure why it bugged him that he hadn't known that. There was no reason he should've.

"You close?"

"Not really. He's a few years older than me. A lawyer in Boston. Very self-important. We get on okay, but he thinks this is just a phase, and that I should move closer to him. I can look after Audrey and play aunt to the kids." A little sigh escaped her lips. Soft and regretful.

Didn't I think the same thing?

"You don't want to?"

"No. Living too near my brother would be hell. Not all families are as close as yours. I guess I wanted to find my own place." She pushed away the drink. "Just ignore me. It must be the pineapple talking."

He swallowed, guilt pricking his skin.

He'd judged her for wanting to create a better life for

herself. And for working damn hard to make it happen.

Isn't that what I'm trying to do for Kira?

"There's nothing wrong with wanting to belong," he said, his voice low. She was drumming the table with her fingers, like she was nervous. He longed to reach over and touch her. Before he could act on it, the lights darkened, and an old country song came on.

Several couples headed for the small square in the middle of the room. The wooden floorboards were polished from years of spilled drinks.

"Come on, Carmichael," someone yelled out. "Ask your lady to dance."

Luke swung around to see an old school acquaintance who drifted in and out of town depending on his finances.

"Sorry, Joel. I'm on duty," he said, ignoring the fact he'd completely forgotten that.

"All work and no play," another voice called out, and a small chorus of approval rumbled around the room. The chanting increased. Color hit Paige's cheeks, visible even in the low light.

His mouth went dry. *Friends can dance together, right?*

Don't answer that.

"Just ignore them. They'll soon forget we're here."

"We're wearing orange. I doubt anyone's going to forget we're here." She toyed with the stem of her glass before giving a slight shrug. "We could just do it. I mean, being visible to the community is the whole idea, isn't it?"

"Wait? You *want* to dance?" He eyed her, trying to gauge her reaction. It was casual. Unbothered. Which meant he was the only one with fire racing through his veins.

Which is a good thing.

We both agreed.

"Sure, why not?" Again, her voice was light and unaffected. *Hell.* He was damned if he did and damned if he didn't. He plastered on a smile and tried to channel his brother's casual charm. Anything to stop himself from kissing her.

"Paige Taylor, would you care to dance?" He stood and held out his hand.

"I would. Though you'd better have some good moves," she teased as she slid her hand into his. Blood pounded in his temples as a murmur of approval went around the room. Several other couples were already swaying to the music, their hips pressed together.

"Is that a challenge?" he growled, as she stepped into his arms. Heat hurtled through his body despite the layers of clothing. The tang of her shampoo swamped his senses, and the music washed away all the reasons why it was a bad idea. *Oh boy.*

She let out a throaty laugh. "No, I was more concerned I might step on your toes."

"Wouldn't be the first time you've attacked me with footwear," he said.

"Don't remind me." Delicate color swept across her cheeks. "I almost impaled my stiletto into your head. I should come with a warning label."

Hell, yes.

"I'll survive." His hands rested lightly against her back. The oversized protective clothing only emphasized the long lines of her neck. He stepped in time to the beat and tried not to focus on the dip of her throat or the rise and fall of her chest. She matched him, her body swaying against his, sending ripples down his spine.

"I don't doubt it." She tilted her chin, sending blonde hair tumbling over her shoulder in a silken wave. He took another step, and again she followed, the rhythm binding them together. Her fingers tightened around his waist, and her eyes caught his. It would be so easy to—

Brrrring.

He stiffened, and at the same time Paige stepped back from the protective crook of his arm, her shoulders tight, as if she was shrugging armor back on. *Damn phone.*

Jacob's name flashed up on the screen.

As ever, his brother's timing sucked. Then again, judging by the relief on Paige's face, she was probably pleased.

It didn't improve his mood.

"Yeah?" he answered on the third ring.

"Luke, buddy, why aren't you answering your door?" Jacob slurred from the other end.

"I'm out on patrol," he lied, then knitted his brows together. It was obvious his brother had downed a couple of drinks too many. "You okay? What's going on?"

"Nothing. Said she was done with me. Fine. I'm done with her, too," Jacob said cryptically. "Except she took my keys. Can't go to Olive's. Can't go to Trina's. Bit drunk," his brother explained before making a *shhhhh*ing noise, as if it were a big secret.

Luke rubbed the bridge of his nose and glanced around. There was no sign of trouble at the bar, and since dancing with Paige would only lead to the kind of trouble he was determined to avoid, it made sense to leave.

"I'll be there in fifteen minutes. Don't go anywhere."

"'Kay." His brother let out a loud yawn and ended the call.

"Everything okay?" Her arms were wrapped tightly around the orange jacket. Obviously suffering from dancer's remorse.

He nodded. "Yeah. I just got to swing by my place to let Jacob in. He's had a couple too many and forgot I was on patrol. It won't take a minute. Then we can do a final lap of the town before calling it a night."

"No worries." She inched farther away from him. He

made a mental snapshot of her relieved face. If anything would stop him from trying a dumb move again, it would be the colored tinge in her cheeks.

They said a quick goodbye to Victor and exited the bar.

If he wanted to do right by Kira, he needed to stay firmly on the path he'd chosen. Going off track could only lead to disaster. And there'd already been too many disasters in his life. He couldn't afford another one.

. . .

"Paige! You're so pretty. Give me a kiss." Jacob's voice was playful as Luke hauled him up from the deck chair on the front porch of the house. It was a neat two-story wooden house surrounded by small evergreen shrubs and a bright yellow front door.

Kira's favorite color.

He painted it for his daughter. Swoon.

"Please ignore my brother's lack of manners," Luke said in a clipped voice as he half walked, half carried Jacob inside. It was the first thing he'd said since they'd left Victor's bar. Obviously, she wasn't the only one contrite about what had happened on the dance floor.

Almost happened, she corrected, trying to ignore the unsettling heat that still rippled along her back where his hands had been, despite the layers of clothing separating them.

"Consider it ignored." She followed him in. Despite the cooling evening, the house was warm, and the decor was inviting.

"Shhhe's going to regret it, you know," Jacob slurred, and Luke patted him on the shoulder, and they walked through to the kitchen.

"She will. Now, let's get you to bed," he said before

turning to Paige. "I'll take Romeo upstairs, and then we can take off."

"No problem. Though, who's he talking about?" She frowned, since it couldn't have been Laney, who'd been going to spend the evening with her sister-in-law.

"No idea. And considering Jacob's habit of romancing any woman who crosses his path, I wouldn't like to guess," he said before cajoling his younger brother toward the staircase.

Paige pulled out one of the stools tucked under the breakfast bar and sat down.

It was a large open-plan kitchen with wooden floorboards, and there were traces of Kira everywhere. From a handwritten note on the fridge saying *I love you, Daddy* to the cardboard cutout of Trent Burton.

Along the wall was a gallery of photographs, and before she could stop herself, she walked over to inspect them. All different frames filled with shots of Kira as a baby, a toddler, starting school. Photos of Jacob, Trina, and Olive. There were several of a young couple laughing as they stood on the back of the speedboat. His parents? In other shots was a gorgeous blonde-haired woman with a wide smile as a baby Kira sat in her lap.

Joanne.

She caught her breath.

The hurt his ex-wife had caused him had been evident when they'd talked the other night. Seeing her everyday up on his wall must surely be painful. And yet there she was. Paige didn't need to ask why.

Because she was Kira's mom, and his entire focus was on making his daughter happy.

Suddenly, she understood with blinding clarity just why he didn't want to get involved with anyone.

He'd hurt himself before he'd hurt Kira.

Footsteps echoed from the staircase, and she hurried

back to the barstool.

"I don't think he'll be stirring until tomorrow," Luke said as he stepped back into the room, his ashen eyes studying her. "You okay?"

"Yup." She got to her feet and walked to the door, suddenly eager to get out of his house, and away from all the things she couldn't have.

She didn't belong there, and the sooner she remembered that, the better.

• • •

"This is going to blow Gigi's mind." Kira clapped her hands as she finished listening to the recording of the song, yet again. Jacob, Trina, and Stu had left the house half an hour ago, and while they weren't quite ready for a nationwide sellout stadium tour, they were tight enough for the party.

"It's sure going to blow something." Luke strummed a few notes on his guitar before putting it back in the stand. Still, his daughter was right. It didn't matter what they sang, Olive would love it because that's just who she was.

"I still think we should wear costumes." Kira fixed him with a solemn stare.

"No costumes. Halloween isn't for another week." He shook his head. He might not be able to deny her song choice, but no way was he dressing up.

"Relax, Dad. I'm just teasing." She reached for a shopping bag. "Besides, I already know what I'm wearing. Trina got these for me in Seattle."

"Why does that not surprise me?" His sister and daughter shared a special bond and a mutual love of clothing and purses. Not that he could blame Trina. The whole family was putty in his daughter's hand. They were probably lucky her sweet nature meant she didn't go puppet master on them.

"Come on, then. You'd better let me see."

She didn't need to be told twice as she reverently lifted out a pair of pale-pink jeans and a white sweater with pastel stars on it. She sucked in a breath. "Do you like them?"

What he actually liked was the way her face lit up as she waited for an answer. His chest expanded.

"Yeah, I do," he agreed. A smile spread across her face as she carefully put her haul back in the bag, though her mouth had taken on a pensive line. "Hey, you okay?"

"Sure." She nodded a bit too quickly and then sighed. "Maybe."

"Spill. What's going on?" He leaned forward.

"Have you ever had a crush on someone?" she asked.

"You mean apart from Bond girls?" he said, trying to keep his voice light, but on the inside his stomach twisted. She'd be fifteen next year, and he was uncomfortably aware that not only was she gorgeous and smart, but she'd been paying more attention to her clothes and hair. *I'm so not ready for this.* "Why? Do you have a crush on someone?"

"Maybe," she said in a noncommittal voice. "I just wanted to know what you're meant to do if you like someone."

Luke stiffened.

If it's me, I have a conversation and decide to only be friends.

If it's you, you cut the no-good creep out of your life and don't talk to any males until you're at least thirty. Make that thirty-five.

"I guess it depends how much you like them," he said in an even voice, trying not to sound like a crazed father *or* like someone who was out of their depth. *Or like a hypocrite.*

"Well, I kind of like him a lot. I mean, Cal's just so funny and cool."

"Cal?" The name was out of his mouth before he could stop it. "As in Cal Harris?"

He'd gone to school with Sam's sister, Vivian, and it was no secret she'd fallen on hard times, which was why the boy was living back in St. Clair. And stirring up a shit storm of trouble at the school if rumors were to be believed.

"That's right." Kira nodded before fixing him with a measured glare. "And don't say anything about how bad he is. None of it's his fault. Besides, Uncle Jacob told me some of the things you did at school."

"Oh, did he?" Luke ran a hand through his hair and tried to figure out what he was most pissed about. Jacob squealing on him, or him turning into the kind of father he swore he'd never be.

"Are you mad?" she asked in a cautious voice.

Hell. There's my answer. Reason number two it is.

"Definitely not mad. Though you're not allowed to date until sixteen. And either way he'll be having a good long chat with me first," he said, trying to keep the panic out of his voice, while hating the idea they'd already moved into this territory. He caught her hand and swallowed. "Why didn't you tell me about Cal sooner?"

She shrugged. "I guess because you're not into that kind of thing. And you've been grumpy lately."

"I have?" His whole body stiffened. *Grumpy?* "Since when?"

"Since forever," she said before her face filled with alarm. "But I still love you. And you know, you *have* sounded a bit happier lately. The other day I heard you humming."

"And humming is good?"

"Well, duh. Everyone knows you don't hum when you're grumpy. According to Jacob that's what you used to be like."

He was saved from answering when Kira's phone beeped with an incoming text. She showed him a screen full of emoticons, before replying to her friends in what he could only guess was yet more emoticons.

He headed for the kitchen, where the remnants of dinner were on display. He quickly scraped the plates and loaded up the dishwasher. His mind whirling.

All this time he thought he was doing the right thing by not getting romantically involved.

Or, as Kira so eloquently put it, not being *into that kind of thing.*

But apparently staying away from relationships was making him grumpy. *So grumpy that my fourteen-year-old kid figured it out.* Worse. She hadn't wanted to tell him about her first crush.

Shit.

Guilt lodged in his throat. He'd watched his own father crumple and spiral after his marriage ended and promised he wouldn't be that person.

Couldn't be that person.

Kira deserved better. Now he just needed to figure out how to balance being a good parent and an actual human being.

Chapter Eleven

"To fully love yourself, first you must love your no." **Just Say No**

So it had all come down to this.

Paige readjusted the facemask and stared at the concrete statue in the middle of the town square. Robert Joseph Vance had been a pioneer who'd built the first public bar in St. Clair, not to mention starting the fire service after his first bar burned down. But the local pigeons regarded him in only one light. As something to be coated in crap.

It was obviously a challenge they took seriously.

Sam and Laney had suggested she do it on Sunday afternoon because most of the town would be at an annual sandcastle building competition thirty miles up the coast. It was a small consolation. She twisted the hose and directed the spray of water to Robert's head.

A putrid aroma of rotten eggs lifted into the air, carried by the fall breeze as droplets of water fell down over the statue like a melting candle.

Several pigeons took exception to the activity. They swooped to a nearby bench to watch her progress, cooing and rustling their wing feathers at her efforts.

"Stop it," she instructed them from beneath the mask. "This is all your fault."

Is it, though? Dr. Penny Groves appeared, wearing a dark navy evening dress with a glittering necklace around her throat. Her face was puckered in annoyance, as if Paige had interrupted her on a night out.

Have you ever wondered if you're blaming the wrong people?

They're birds, not people. She turned off the hose and frowned. *And whose side are you on?*

I'm on your future self's side. The doctor held up a compact mirror and began to expertly apply siren-red lipstick. Hmm. It was actually a cute color. *You're trying too hard.*

Wait. What does that even mean? I thought I was meant to be trying hard. She picked up the bucket of water and an industrial cleaning cloth as Dr. Penny Groves tucked away her compact and lipstick and disappeared, leaving only the pigeons. *Hey, no. Come back. I don't understand. How can I start a new life if I don't keep saying no?*

There was no reply.

She plunged the cloth into the water and scrubbed. That was the problem with having an imaginary conversation. The person in question could just leave cryptic messages and scamper away without a care in the world. She was probably laughing about it right now.

Besides, it made no sense.

It was six weeks since she'd moved to St. Clair, and while the business wasn't making megabucks, it was slowly ticking over. Everything she was doing was working. She attacked Robert's right knee. The grayish white mess slowly dissolved to reveal gunmetal concrete.

See, even this was turning out okay.

Seconds later there was a rustle of feathers as a group of pigeons flashed past her. Then, much like a squadron of jets letting off bombs, the birds collectively blanketed everything in their path with crap. Including Robert, who was once again dripping with smudgy white guano.

Paige gritted her teeth. It was going to be a long day.

• • •

Five hours later it was done. And while Robert had a new lease on life, she hadn't come out as well. Her leg muscles were cramped, and her shoulders ached from the repetitive scrubbing. Everything hurt.

All she wanted was a shower to remove the acidic tang clinging to her entire body. Her nose twitched. Actually, make that three showers.

Still, it proved her future self was wrong.

If she hadn't tried hard to clean the statue, it wouldn't be gleaming in the sinking afternoon sun as cars flooded back into the town from the sandcastle competition. And while in theory she wanted people to know she was an active part of the community, she didn't want them to see her stinking of bird crap, wearing baggy white overalls, with grime all over her face and hair.

She gathered up her cleaning gear and turned to the bench where a group of pigeons were standing on something green.

"No. Go away. Stop it, stop it!" She dropped the gear in her hands and waved them off. There was a chorus of guttural cooing as they took flight, leaving behind the remains of what had once been a very cute purse.

She'd bought it last year after a particularly tough week, convinced the green leather and heavy gold hardware detail would help her feel better. And it had.

Until now.

She retrieved her gloves and tentatively lifted it up. It was completely ruined, but she still needed to get her keys and phone. She reluctantly tipped it upside down. Lipstick, receipts, earbuds, and her phone all tumbled out, along with a pair of sunglasses covered in the gluggy crap.

But no keys.

How can there be no keys?

She gave it another shake, then checked her pockets. Still no sign of them. The pigeons chortled from the safety of Robert's shoulders.

"Please tell me that you didn't steal my keys." She stared at them.

The pigeons cooed some more as she retraced her steps, searching the grass in the hope they might turn up. They didn't.

Shit.

She rolled her shoulders and tried to stay calm. Good news was her store was only ten blocks away, and since Audrey was there, she'd be able to get in and retrieve her spare car keys.

She pushed away a loose strand of hair, heaved up the cleaning equipment, and gave the pigeons one final glare before walking away.

Ten minutes later she arrived at the bookstore to find it locked up tighter than a coffin. Audrey hadn't mentioned she was going out. Then again, that didn't mean much. She called her mother, but it went through to the answering service. Damn. She peered around before catching sight of Sam's café sign swinging in the breeze. Cal. The evil genius who'd already broken into her place once before.

But after ringing the bell five times with no success, she sighed. There was only one other option. Break in. Hysterical laughter caught in her throat, but she swallowed it down and assessed the building.

There was a small window at the back. If she could get it open she might be able to wriggle in. Thankfully it wasn't that high, which meant she didn't need the ladder. A trash can should do it. She dragged it over and examined the window. It was tiny, but she should be able to fit. The trash can wobbled as she climbed onto it, but after the ladder incident, the usual panic didn't rise up to her throat. Progress.

She stood up on her tiptoes to test the window, but it didn't budge.

She licked her lips.

She could wait until Sam and Cal got home, or she could find a rock and break the window. At least she now knew how to replace the glass, thanks to YouTube. There was an old brick next to a potted plant. She lifted it behind her head and threw.

Glass shattered down, leaving jagged edges that clung to the frame like teeth.

She'd just climbed back onto the trash can when a familiar voice floated toward her from the pavement. Luke.

Out of all the people she didn't want to see right now, he was top of the list. Still, just because she'd heard him didn't mean he'd know she was there. After all, she was in the safety of her backyard, and daylight was lowering like a theater curtain, not to mention the fence between the yard and the pavement that ran alongside the building.

She sucked in a breath and dared to peer over the fence. He was walking toward the esplanade, his phone to his ear.

She closed her eyes and pressed her body into the wall, trying to pretend she wasn't on a trash can surrounded by broken glass and stinking of pigeon.

I'm invisible. I'm invisible. I'm invisible, she chanted, her eyes still closed, because everyone knew it was more likely to work that way.

"You know I can see you, right?"

So much for that plan.

"Let's just hope you can't smell me." She reluctantly opened her eyes to face her fate. She immediately regretted it.

His hair was damp, his jeans fresh, and sweet Lord, but his long-sleeved T-shirt was hugging his torso. She sighed and awkwardly climbed down from the trash can, glass crunching under her boots.

"I've smelled worse." He shrugged, a bemused smile tugging at his mouth. "You really like climbing things, don't you?"

"And you really like catching me at terrible times," she responded.

"Everyone has a talent." His smile lingered. "Need a hand?"

"Actually, I need a spare key. Or a time machine. Either would work right now."

"Sorry, I just got rid of my last time machine. Kept trying to take me back to a really bad concert I went to as a teenager." He leaned against the side of the house, arms folded. "I take it you've lost your keys."

"You say lost, I say stolen," she muttered before realizing it probably wasn't a good idea to share her pigeon conspiracy. Not if she wanted to appear sane. "Long story but I don't think they're going to reappear anytime soon. My car's still at the town square, and I have no idea where my mother is. Hence the broken window. I was just about to clear the glass and climb in."

He looked at the window and back at her. "I hate to tell you this, but unless you're secretly Fagan and have a collection of undersized urchins at your disposal, I'm not sure you'll fit."

She wasn't sure whether to be impressed by the Dickens

reference or dismayed she'd broken a window for no reason. "Are you sure?"

"Yeah," he agreed, once again looking at the tiny space before dragging his phone from his pocket. He dialed a number. "Hey, Len. Mind swinging by the bookstore? Paige is locked out."

She gulped. "Len, as in the window guy I didn't use? He's the local locksmith?"

"One in the same. But don't worry. He doesn't hold a grudge." He put his phone away.

"What are the chances of him telling people what I look like?"

"You're pretty safe," he assured her, and true to his word, when Len drove up, he barely blinked at Paige's outfit.

He spent five minutes with his tools before opening up the front door and another half an hour replacing her lock in case the crazy pigeons gave the keys to a deranged stalker. Personally, she wouldn't put it past them.

Once it was done, she stepped inside, hoping that the aroma of books would wash the pigeon horrors away. She went to pay him, before remembering her purse had been the victim of a terrible crime.

"Er, can I give you a check after I decontaminate my purse?" she said, heading to the back office, but Len merely shrugged and packed away his tools.

"Tomorrow," was all he said before disappearing back to his car.

"He's not much of a talker," Luke said.

"Who needs words when you can open doors. And thanks for your help. I hope it didn't ruin your plans."

"No problem. Kira's sleeping over at Trina's. I was just doing a quick patrol to keep any eye on things."

"Well, now you can add good Samaritan to your evening plans," Paige said, painfully aware of the stench coming from her clothing. "I guess I'd better do my bit for air pollution and get out of this gear."

"Tell you what, you get a shower and I'll board up the window for you."

"You don't have to do that," she said.

"I know, but I figured since we're trying this friend thing out for size, it'd be a good place to start."

She clamped down on her lower lip.

She should do as the book said. *Just say no.* After all, it wasn't his problem. But if the window was boarded, it was one less thing she had to do before burying herself in body wash. A fresh layer of putrid scent rose up from her overalls, and just like that, body wash won.

"Okay, thanks."

She waited until he'd gone to the shed to retrieve the same board that'd been used for the last broken window before jogging upstairs.

There was no sign of Audrey, but her presence was everywhere, from the neatly folded laundry to the jigsaw puzzle that had taken over Paige's only table. To the left of the puzzle was a note poking out from under a candle. She snatched it up.

Have gone to Seattle.
Back Wednesday.
Audrey

She stared at her mom's neat handwriting, no clue as to why she'd gone on a eight hour round trip to Seattle. Or why she hadn't said anything sooner. Then again, nothing about her behavior made sense. Not the hair color, the excessive Shopping Channel purchases, or the vagueness.

Paige put the note down and headed to the bathroom, dragging off all her clothes. The steaming hot water prickled her skin as it sluiced away the layers of stench. In the end she washed her hair three times before toweling herself off.

A faint padding noise told her Luke was moving around the living room.

He was still there?

Don't get too excited. Last time he saw you, you smelled of pigeon poo. He's only here as a friend.

All the same she dragged a comb through her hair. If she styled it, he might think she wanted something. *Hell, I might think I want something.* She left it to dry naturally while dressing in yoga pants and a plain T-shirt that had seen better days.

As a reminder not to throw myself at anyone. Especially unavailable men.

She opened the bathroom door to be greeted to a mouth-watering smell of curry. Her gaze drifted to the table, which had been set for one in the small space left by the jigsaw.

"I boarded up the window, then saw your spare keys on the table. I figured I'd pick up your car and get some food in. Not sure if you've had Patsy's curry before, but it's the best," he said by way of an explanation as he got to his feet. "I'll get out of your hair."

"Why are you doing all this?" She joined him at the top of the stairs. Her skin prickled as she breathed in the heady scent of pine and soap. Mistake. She took a small step back.

"Because I know what a lousy job it is. I got stuck with it once when I was sixteen," he said in a light voice, though, as his eyes drifted down to her T-shirt, they flickered. Her breathing quickened.

"No way," she croaked, trying to focus on his words and not his mouth.

"Yup. Olive caught me carving my initials into the church pew, and as my punishment she offered up my services."

"Let me guess, it was B.S.?" Her voice was thin as she became achingly aware of just how long it had been since she'd had sex.

Her nipples hardened against the thin fabric. This was torture. Plain and simple.

"Pretty much. You're the only person in the history of St. Clair who's agreed for no reason," he said, studying her face. "Unless you *did* have a reason?"

"No." She tried not to think about how gorgeous he'd looked at the town meeting the other night. Of how gorgeous he looked now. *Of how irrational I am around him.* "I figured it'd help the store. And keep me busy."

"Busy from what?" His voice was lower now, and it sent another ripple of longing through her, warming her bones.

"According to my friend, Zoe, I've neglected certain things. Of the—um—physical kind. I'm trying to keep busy to avoid—thinking about that sort of stuff." Humiliation jostled with the building heat in her body. She tried her best to tip a mental bucket of cold water over it. "And now you think I'm crazy. I mean, we had the talk, right?"

"Right." His voice dropped, and his breathing increased. Time stopped, the world faded, and her mouth went dry. *Was he feeling it too?*

There were so many reasons why it was a bad idea.

She was meant to be saying no to men. No to complications.

Stop trying so hard. Dr. Penny Groves's advice rang out in her ear as Luke's finger trailed up her arm. Her skin heated, and desire pooled low down.

"Tell me what you want, Paige?" His voice was chocolate-coated sin, all warm and dangerous, and before she could stop herself, she stepped into him. Smashing through the wall of no's that had been lying between them.

His body was hard, and she hitched a breath. *I'm on fire.*

He let out a moan as his arms snaked around her, holding her tight as his mouth searched out hers.

Their first kiss has been sweet, warm and full of promise,

but this kiss was different. An earth-shaking tornado, dragging her into a vortex. His mouth was hot against hers, hungry, intense, and demanding.

"I want this." She shifted enough to answer him as her hands tugged to remove his T-shirt. His torso was still tanned from the late summer. Her knees knocked as she shakily ran a finger along his skin. He planted hot kisses along her jaw and lifted her own T-shirt off, as his eyes drank her in.

"I want this, too." Then his mouth was back on hers as he picked her up and walked in the direction of the bedroom. Somewhere along the way her yoga pants fell to the floor, quickly followed by his jeans. As he joined her on the bed, all reason fled her mind, and it was just the two of them.

Chapter Twelve

"No is your inner GPS. Yes is the crazy voice trying to tell you to turn headfirst into oncoming traffic." **Just Say No**

Paige let out a contented sigh and was about to go back to sleep when an unfamiliar noise drifted in from her kitchen. *Probably just mice*, she decided before stiffening. *Wait. I don't have mice. More to the point, I don't want mice.* She wriggled into a sitting position as her sleepy mind shifted back into her body, which was still tingly from—

"Morning." Luke walked into the bedroom. His jeans were slung low on his hips, and his chest was bare.

Sex. I had sex. With Luke.

She tugged the sheet up to hide her own nakedness. He was balancing a tray with two cups and her mom's old teapot she'd kept despite never using. A quick glance at her phone told her it was six in the morning.

"Sleep well?" His voice was a long drawl that turned her insides to mush. She gripped the sheet. His hair was tousled, and the faint beginnings of blue-gray stubble accentuated his silvery eyes. He unleashed a dimple that was almost her undoing.

"Um, yes," she said before wrinkling her nose. "I guess this is where we do the day-after talk. It's been a while since I've had one. I'm not sure of the protocol."

Amusement danced in his eyes. "There's a protocol?"

"You know what I mean. Where we talk about how it was lovely, but a mistake, and that it can never happen again."

"Oh." He lowered the tray onto the cabinet and sat. His weight caused the mattress to sag as he trailed a finger along her leg still covered by the sheet. "Right, protocol. How about this?"

He leaned forward and cupped her chin. Butterflies pounded against her rib cage demanding to be released as his mouth found hers.

"Okay, that works." She tried to untangle herself from the desire rampaging through her body. To be detached. To think logically. It was difficult when his scent was filling her nostrils. "W-what happens now?"

"I know what I want to happen," he said as his finger inched along her thigh. He kissed her again, and the sheet fell away. He sucked in a breath as he seemed to drink her in. Exhilaration flooded her senses.

"I meant after today," she managed to say as he planted a series of kisses down her neck. Her body arched of its own accord, and her reason started to flee. "I don't want to make a mess of things. So many people in this town still look at me like I'm an alien. I'm pretty sure if they knew about... well...this, my face would appear on a Wanted poster. Crimes against St. Clair's favorite son."

"You're overestimating my popularity." He drew away, his gaze never leaving hers. "Is this your way of saying no?"

Yes. I mean no. I mean I don't know.

She sucked in a shaky breath. "It's my way of saying we

both have a lot going on. You have a daughter. An amazing daughter, and I have my life to rebuild. What if this screws everything up?"

"Apparently, I'm screwing up regardless of what I do." He leaned back and rubbed his chin. His eyes darkened.

"What are you talking about?" She instinctively leaned forward and trailed a finger along his jaw, the rough stubble doing wicked things to her stomach. "Is this about Kira?"

"She told me about her crush." He closed his eyes, and a shadow crossed his face.

"You didn't know?" she said, before instantly regretting it.

"No, but I'm guessing you did."

"Sometimes it's easy to talk to a stranger," Paige said, hating the hurt in his voice. "And I know you might be concerned about Cal, but from what Sam's said, he's a good kid. I really don't think you have anything to worry about. My first crush was on a senior who had six piercings and a spider tattoo on his neck. These things burn themselves out."

"I know she's going to have a million crushes. It was more that she thought I wouldn't be interested because I'm not into...well, I'm not into—"

"Oh." Paige's pulse quickened. "Oh."

"Yeah." His mouth turned into a rueful smile. "I guess you're not the only one who's been saying no to things lately."

What's he telling me?

That he wants *this?*

She sucked in her breath. Luke had even more on the line than she did. This was his town, where his daughter lived. If it fell apart—

She cut herself off.

Stop trying so hard.

"What would it even look like?" she dared to ask, her voice not much above a whisper as her hand reached for his.

They were brown and strong, and a tremor of longing ran through her.

"I have no idea. All I know is I have to think about my daughter," he said, though his fingers tightened around hers, filling her with warmth.

"It's one of the things I admire the most about you," she said before shyly tracing a line down her chest. "Well, that and your hot body."

"Hot body?" A playful smile twitched at his lips. "Now I'm almost wishing I could do Jacob's party trick. It involves moving his pecs."

Paige smothered a horrified laugh. "Please tell me he doesn't."

"Oh, he does." He kissed her again. This time harder. Hungrier. Her body melted into him. "I hear what you're saying. What if we just take things slow? And keep it to ourselves until we know if there's something here."

"I can live with that," she said as he joined her back in the bed. *If this is what slow looks like, I can get used to it.*

• • •

"I think I'm in the wrong business." Laney poured out the last of the wine. Despite the cooling weather, they'd decided to sit by the water on a large picnic blanket with an equally large picnic hamper Sam had filled with her delicious cooking. The sun dipped low, and night insects serenaded them in the dying light, as coppery leaves drifted past them in the breeze.

Paige blinked. "What do you mean? You love being a florist."

"I do." Laney nodded. "But at the end of the day all I feel is tired, not glowing and smiling like you are."

"I'm not glowing and smiling," Paige protested as she hid her face behind her wineglass. *Stop thinking about sex.*

Especially sex with Luke. Because, apparently, she had a tell. A really big freaking tell. "How did the sandcastle building go?"

"Well, let's see. Laney flirted up a storm with Jacob, then Cal disappeared for half an hour, and I found him hacking into someone's wireless network."

"We weren't that bad." A delicate blush rose up on Laney's face. "And even though I know it's just harmless fun, I'd forgotten how nice it is to be the center of someone's attention. Does that even make sense?"

Hell, yes.

Flirting. Having sex. All things designed to give a girl a warm glow.

She licked her lips.

"To each their own." Sam shrugged before turning to her. "And you still haven't told us about your date with Robert? I can't believe you cleaned him."

"It wasn't bad," Paige said truthfully, still consumed by the aftertaste of Luke's mouth on hers, the burn he'd left behind on her chin, and the possessive way he'd claimed her.

"She's doing it again," Laney pointed out.

"I swear it's nothing." She crossed her fingers. Despite how close she'd grown to the Belles, this wasn't something she wanted to share.

You want to have your chocolate chip cupcakes with vanilla frosting and eat them, too. Dr. Penny Groves appeared to the left of Laney's head.

Luke isn't a cupcake of any description, Paige retorted. *Besides, I thought you'd be happy. I'm not trying too hard,* and *I'm still focused on my business.*

Oh, Paige. You're so funny, the author chided.

There's nothing funny about it. It's perfect.

"Well, whatever it is, keep doing it." Laney leaned forward, blocking Dr. Penny Groves from view. "Because you seem really happy. And like Dr. Penny Groves says, 'your true *no's* will lead to happiness.'"

I did say that, didn't I? The imaginary author reappeared over Laney's shoulder, a preening smile on her ruby-red lips. She really did have a great lipstick collection.

"Here's hoping." Sam drained her wine and got to her feet. "Because I need to go see Cal's headmaster again. I'm starting to think he'll give me a stamp card. My tenth visit will be free."

"Hang in there." Laney stood and hugged her. "You're doing a great job with him."

"I sure wish it felt a bit better," Sam sighed as the three girls packed away the hamper and said good night.

The pungent aroma of garlic clung in the air as she walked into the upstairs apartment, along with a fusion of herbs and spices. Further proof her mother was home were the numerous shopping bags that littered the floor.

"You're back?" Paige couldn't help but state the obvious as she walked into the kitchen. Audrey's pink hair was spiked out, softening the lines on her face. Making her look younger. Happier.

"A half hour ago," her mother affirmed while neatly chopping vegetables. "I saw you across the road by the water, but I didn't want to disturb you and your friends. You hungry?"

"No." Paige shook her head and frowned. "How come you didn't mention you were planning a trip to Seattle?"

"It was a last-minute decision." Audrey busied herself stirring the vegetables before adding a splash of soy sauce.

"Did you have a good time?"

"It was lovely," her mother said, then turned up the volume on the news story she'd been listening to. Paige gave up. Besides, not only did she have accounts to do, but there was a text message from Luke which she wanted to reply to in the privacy of her own room.

· · ·

A ringing buzzed in Paige's head. She reached for her phone and answered without looking. "Hello?" she grumbled.

"Great news."

"Ellen?" Paige rubbed her eyes awake. Then she caught sight of the time. Six a.m. In the freaking morning. "What's going on?"

"I'll tell you what's going on. We're about to start working with the hottest new fantasy author in the world. This book's going to blow *Lord of the Rings* out of the water."

"And you're telling me this why?" She reluctantly stood up and stretched, not bothering to mention it would take a rocket launcher to blow LotR out of the way. Knowing she'd have bags under her eyes from lack of sleep, she avoided the mirror and walked into the kitchen to make a coffee.

"Because it's time for you to come back," Ellen said in surprise. "What other reason could I possibly be calling for?"

Paige stopped and blinked. "How about the fact I don't work for you anymore. I left seven weeks ago, remember? Bought a bookstore. Moved across the country. Ringing any bells?"

"Um, yes. But it's just a phase. And I can appreciate that. I had my own phase back in '98. Er, I mean 2008. Anyway, I went to Ibiza for three months. Lived on a diet of cocktails and cute waiters. Actually, there was even a cute waitress in there."

"I really hope there's a point to this." Paige shut her eyes and tried to erase the images from her mind.

"The point is, it was a phase, Paige. You get it out of your system and then come back. That's what I'm saying. It's time to come home."

"Goodbye, Ellen." She fumbled for the percolator as her cell phone rang again, with her brother's ringtone.

Were they part of some evil morning-loving tag team?

"This is unacceptable," James said by way of a greeting. "You both have to come to Thanksgiving. Otherwise, what will people think?"

"Honestly, I have no idea." She awkwardly managed to fill the percolator while the phone was nestled under her chin. The sooner she got caffeine into her system, the easier this conversation would be. "They're your friends, not mine."

"The pair of you are as bad as each other," he retorted. "Poor Fi's trying to juggle all of her family without this extra worry about her seating arrangements. Any more than thirty people, then she needs to use a different dinner service."

She bit back a reply about the true spirit of Thanksgiving. After all, she couldn't even get her mom to tell her how she was spending her days and nights. Let alone organize a dinner for thirty people. Not to mention that she'd already explained why she couldn't make it back.

A sliver of guilt chewed in her stomach.

Despite their strained relationship she'd always gone for Thanksgiving and Christmas. But this year it wasn't just the distance, it was that she wanted to be in her new home.

To start new traditions.

With new people.

Sam had invited her to spend the day with her and Cal, and jokingly called it a Waifs and Strays meal.

Her brother's cough roused her, and she forced herself to focus.

"I'll ask her again when she comes in."

"And that's another thing, why isn't she answering my calls? Are you sure she's even staying there?"

Paige glanced around the small living space. Boxes from her mother's latest Shopping Channel binge were piled next to the table, along with a tray of root vegetables a strange man had dropped off the previous day, and a brochure for hiking the Camino Trail in Spain.

"Oh yes. She's here all right."

And getting more mysterious by the minute.

• • •

By four in the afternoon Paige was yawning. Ellen had sent several more text messages explaining just why she had to move back to New York, while James had taken to sending photos of the two competing dinner services. It was a reality TV show in the making. She yawned again and was just debating whether to start unpacking a box of books when the door chimes jangled, and Luke walked in.

Her entire body heated up.

"Hope I'm not interrupting."

Never.

"No, it wasn't important," she said. It was the first time she'd seen him since he'd left her bed, and the twin emotions of desire and shyness battled in her chest. "H-how are you?"

"Better," he said, his eyes catching hers, and despite a pile of books between them, her panic lessened. "Definitely better."

"That's a very good answer." She returned his smile as Kira raced over from the shelves she'd been dusting. Her eyes gleamed, obviously at the sound of her father's voice. Another pang caught in Paige's throat as the young girl gave him a fierce hug.

The bond they shared was special all right.

She tried to dredge up a memory of when she'd been like that with either of her parents. All she got was chirping crickets.

"Guess what," Kira said in her normal rapid-fire way. "I

met Paige's mom, Audrey. And don't worry, she said I could call her Audrey. Anyway, she has pink hair. Can I get mine dyed, too?"

Confusion fanned out across his face. "Pink hair? Is that even a thing?"

"You need to keep up, Dad." Kira gave him a world-weary eye roll.

"Obviously," he said in a dry voice as he fished in his pocket for his car keys. Then he turned to Paige. "If you want to skip tonight's patrol, that's fine."

"Skip it?" Paige said, trying to hide her disappointment. "Er, I mean, I don't want to let the town down."

His eyes studied hers, boring into her skin. "Okay, I'll pick you up at nine."

"Great." Paige nodded, her mood lifting. "I'll see you then. And sorry about the pink hair."

"Just give me a heads-up if your mom gets any tattoos I need to worry about."

"I'm pretty sure you're safe," Paige said, though when Audrey walked into the store ten minutes later, she wasn't so certain.

Her mom was wearing a mossy green fishing jacket, complete with lures and flies. In her hand was a large bag from Bernie's convenience store, which also sold tackle and bait. Apparently, a lot of it, considering the size of the bag.

"Um, hi." She widened her eyes.

"Hello, darling. Stop looking at me like I have something on my face. It's just a fishing outfit." She put down her bags to inspect another pile of boxes that had arrived during the day.

"I didn't have you pegged as a fishing person."

"Just because I've never tried doesn't mean I won't like it. Besides, I saw there's a competition coming up. The Big Fish. It sounds fun."

"Right." She blinked. She'd go along to it because Luke

had organized it to raise money for the marina. But as for it sounding like fun?

"One needs to keep an open mind. Now, if you'll excuse me I'm going to take these boxes upstairs."

"James called again. He needs to know if you're going back to Boston for Thanksgiving. He's already booked a ticket for your flight and said it won't be the same without you there."

"Let me guess, the dinner service?"

"You knew?"

Her mother shrugged. "Fiona might have mentioned it once or twice. I'll make up my mind after the fishing competition."

Then without another word Audrey walked to the stairs that led to the apartment above while Paige rubbed her brow. She was never going to understand her mother.

• • •

"Ah, the Carmichael brothers. Aren't you both just a sight for sore eyes?" Patsy sashayed to the counter to retrieve the pies for Olive's party that afternoon. In true St. Clair style, the catering list had been given to Patsy and Sam, who'd split it up between them based on what suited them best.

"Not looking too bad yourself," Jacob countered with a wink as he glanced around the diner. "How's business?"

"Can't complain." She reached for the coffeepot. "You boys like a cup before you head off?"

"Sorry." Luke peeled off some notes to pay. "The to-do list is growing by the minute, but we'll see you at the party."

"Wouldn't miss it for the world." Her eyes narrowed with laser focus. "You look different. Are you seeing someone?"

"I wish," Jacob answered on his behalf. "Unfortunately, my brother's sworn off women for the next five years. At least."

"Hmmm," Patsy said by way of an answer before drifting down to the far end of the counter. Luke let out a breath. The last person in the world he wanted to know about Paige was his brother. With Patsy not far behind.

"You know," his brother drawled as Luke swung a hard left and they headed to Olive's bungalow. "Whatever you're thinking about must be pretty good because I've had Imagine Dragons on for the last five minutes, and you haven't told me to turn it off once."

"Just going through the list." Luke swallowed down his smile and kept his voice gruff. It seemed to keep Jacob happy. Which was good. He could hardly explain it to himself. Especially the part where seeing Paige was in direct conflict with the promise he made to always put his daughter first.

Like hell if he was going to explain it to anyone else.

Chapter Thirteen

"Repeat after me, people. No." **Just Say No**

"I thought this was meant to be a small party?" Paige craned her neck as she stood next to Sam and Laney in Olive's bungalow. There were groups of people squeezed into every corner, and the outside deck was just as busy. Somewhere a splash of water, followed by a round of laughter, suggested the hot tub was full. The only person she couldn't find was Luke. Not that she was looking.

Okay, not much.

"I guess small's a relative term," Sam said with a shrug. "Last year it was double the size, and they had to rent out the town square. Then again, you're probably pleased you're nowhere near Robert today."

"You know it," Paige agreed, forcing herself not to smile too much. But she was smiling on the inside.

"Your mom seems to be enjoying herself." Laney glanced over to where Audrey was happily chatting to Mrs. Gilbert. As for how they knew each other, she had no idea.

Then again, her mother was quickly becoming an enigma.

Paige thought for sure Audrey wouldn't want to come to the party. But she'd instantly agreed and even donned a pale gray dress with a scooped neck and strands of shimmering pearls that accentuated her hair. She suspected both items were hot off the Shopping Channel.

"How long's she staying?" Sam asked before her attentions shifted at the arrival of an old guy wearing a white Stetson. "Oh, I need to see a man about a horse."

"Is that literal or code for something else?" Paige blinked.

"Literal. Sam rode lots as a kid and is considering buying old Jim's mare," Laney explained as Jacob appeared and dragged her away under the guise of a floral emergency.

Okay, so *that* was code. But before she could compose her face to let the world know that she was fine—*fine*—standing at a party on her own, Trina and Stu appeared.

"There you are. We have strict instructions to bring you over to Olive so she can thank you for the darling book you gave her."

"I'm not sure that's how I'd describe a Kama Sutra coloring book," Stu said.

"Her words not mine," Trina said. "And well done. Nan has no time for people who give her socks or lavender-scented drawer liners. Those things are for old people."

"I'm glad she liked it." Paige let out a relieved breath. She'd actually tossed up whether to give something sensible like stationery, but after the coloring book had literally fallen off the shelf while she'd wandered the store, it seemed wrong to ignore fate.

Still, it was nice to know fate hadn't just been messing with her. And hopefully it wasn't obvious she'd actually practiced a couple of the moves the previous week with Luke.

"Understatement." Trina navigated her way through the crowd to a resplendent Olive. A powder-blue silk kimono was draped over her shoulders, partially covering the white trousers and blouse she had on underneath. The outfit was completed with layers of crystals that caught the light as she moved. Her smile amped up at the sight of them.

"Oh, my sweet girl, aren't you an angel. Thank you for my book." Olive dragged her into an embrace. Her arms were strong, despite her age, and her floral perfume wove a web of comfort and safety through Paige's body.

Her throat tightened as something shifted in the pit of her stomach. The Carmichaels were so unlike her own family she wasn't even sure what to do with the emotions streaming through her.

"Nan, don't forget she needs to breathe," Trina scolded, but with a laugh in her voice.

"Nonsense, you can never have enough hugs." Olive was unapologetic as she slowly released her.

"They're pretty good hugs," she agreed, not that she had much to go on. Her family weren't exactly huggers. Rather, they specialized in reserved indifference to each other. *And if I'd given my mom or brother a Kama Sutra coloring book, the only thing I would've gotten was frostbite.* She caught another flash of pink hair in the distance and frowned. *Then again, who knows what Audrey likes these days?*

"See? Now make sure you have fun." Olive squeezed her hand before being carried off by the woman from the post office.

"She likes you," Trina said as Stu reappeared holding a tray of drinks.

"This wine is from a fresh bottle. My advice—don't drink the punch. There's enough vodka in there to fuel a Russian poker game for a month. Plus, it's blue. No one wants a blue drink."

"Thanks." She took the proffered glass as Jacob appeared and whispered in his sister's ear.

Trina flashed an apologetic frown. "There's a minor food emergency. I'll be back."

"No problem. I can keep Paige company." Stu kissed his wife, then waited until she was out of earshot. "And as for the wine, don't thank me, thank Marc. You remember him, don't you? Great guy. And he's amazing with animals, which I always think is the best way to judge a person."

"S-sure. I remember." Paige wrinkled her nose in confusion as Stu nodded for the other vet to join them. She inwardly groaned.

It was a setup.

"Hey, Paige." Marc was with them in a flash. The other night she hadn't noticed much more than that he was tall with very white teeth. But now, under the party lights, those things were accompanied by spiked caramel hair, warm brown eyes, and a broad chest. Good with animals *and* he worked out. He was in his mid-thirties, and as far as she could tell, there was only one thing wrong with him.

He wasn't Luke.

"Hi. Um, it's great to see you again. I heard Trevor's doing just fine."

"Sure is. I swear he's had more stitches than a baseball." He flashed the perfect teeth, and Stu beamed, as if he'd just been awarded an Order of Cupid medal. "How are you settling into St. Clair? I know it took me awhile to find my feet."

"Er, buddy. I wouldn't go that far," Stu interrupted and patted Marc on the shoulder. He then gave Paige a wise smile. "This guy's so modest. He moved here from Reno and within a week had been invited to join two racquetball teams."

"Cool." She wasn't quite sure how to respond to that information, but was saved by the return of Trina, who immediately flashed Paige an apologetic smile, as if to say, "Sorry, but this is what happens when I leave him to his own devices."

"I hate to be a spoilsport, but I need to borrow both of these strapping guys to help with the barbeque." Trina briskly linked arms with both the men.

"That's Jacob's domain," Stu protested before catching his wife's pointed stare. "Oh, right. Barbeque."

Paige didn't know whether to be amused or relieved as they were dragged away.

"You're here." Kira bounded up, followed by two other girls. They were all matching in jeans and colored T-shirts and were giggling from a shared joke. "Are you having fun?"

"Yes," she said. The bungalow was heaving with people, their voices rising into the air like exotic birds. "Olive sure knows how to throw a party."

"Yep." Kira beamed. "And the police haven't even arrived yet, which means Jacob owes me ten dollars. He thought we'd get the first warning by four, but I said it wouldn't be until after dad starts playing. If they do, I get an extra ten bucks."

"Playing?"

"Guitar," one of Kira's friends piped up. "And he sings. It's all old stuff, but he's still pretty good."

Wait. Luke played guitar? And sang old stuff?

Why didn't I know this?

Then she caught herself. *Because we only just met, that's why.*

"He hates playing in public, but Gigi always tells him it's the only present she wants," Kira explained, her green eyes earnest. "And this year I'm helping. I've been sworn to secrecy over the song."

"She hasn't even told us," the second friend complained before narrowing her eyes in Paige's direction. "Do you know?"

"Hello, Hailey. How would it be a secret if I told people what it was?" Kira folded her arms and poked out her lower lip.

"I don't know anything about it," Paige said, bemused by the conversation.

"Okay, just had to check because I know you two are tight," Hailey said before pointing to the corner of the patio where Luke was plugging a guitar into an amplifier. "Hey, your dad's setting up now."

"Oh yay, I'd better get ready." Kira and her friends raced through the crowd, their hair streaming out behind them as they went.

Paige put her empty glass down at the bar and squeezed out to the patio. *I'm only being supportive.*

The late afternoon sun was dipping, and the faint chill was held at bay by the large fire pit farther down the garden that several men had taken ownership of.

Luke was wearing his regular uniform of jeans and a sweater, and his dark hair was tousled. On anyone else it might have looked styled, but she suspected he'd just run a hand through it. His eyes were narrowed in concentration as he tuned his guitar. Then he glanced over and dipped his head in acknowledgment.

Her mouth went dry, and heat spread.

Olive walked toward him and lovingly put an around his broad shoulder. Considering what Kira said, Paige wondered if it was to stop him running away. Olive certainly was strong enough to manage it. Laney and Sam reappeared just as Olive reached for the microphone Luke had set up.

"Thanks for coming. It's lovely to be with so many old friends, and new ones, too," she added with a wink as she glanced to Paige. "As you can see, my grandson's kindly agreed to keep us entertained. Thank you, dear boy."

Luke took the microphone from her and planted a kiss on her cheek. "I learned long ago that saying no to Olive wasn't an option. She has a bigger heart than anyone I've ever met. Not to mention a knack for getting her own way." This earned him a laugh, and he waited until everyone was quiet before strumming his hands down the strings. "I wanted to celebrate her eightieth birthday in true Olive style, but I'm going to need a bit of help. Trina, Jacob, Kira, Stu. You're all required."

As they materialized on the stage, Olive's mouth dropped in surprise. By this time the entire party had converged onto the patio as Luke and his makeshift band turned away from the audience.

Silence cocooned the space, only broken when Jacob turned around, sounding out a beat on the drum. *Boom. Boom. Boom.* A low murmur of primal excitement spread through the crowd like an unlit fire waiting for a spark as Trina, Stu, and Kira turned one at a time.

Luke was last to spin around, as his fingers ran up and down the neck of the guitar. He then gave his grandmother a rueful smile before launching into "Shake It Off" by Taylor Swift.

The entire patio roared in delight, filling the air with a thudding pulse. To the left of the makeshift stage Olive and her friends began a raunchy dance routine that had people clapping and singing even louder.

But all she could focus on was Luke.

His voice was raspy, but every note was full of unwavering strength, wrapped up in a promise that he'd take everyone joyously through to the end of the journey.

She swayed with the crowd as Luke and his family played for the woman they all adored. It was like walking through a secret door into a brand-new land.

A land I don't want to leave.

Finally, the song was over, but the noise didn't die down until the sound of sirens wailed in the distance. Kira immediately punched her arm into the air and turned to

Jacob, who pulled a face, no doubt at having to pay out an extra ten bucks to his clever niece.

Despite the noise and chaos, Luke wrapped Olive in a hug, leaving no one in doubt that he'd meant every word he'd said about how much he loved her.

Emotion caught in her throat as Jacob, Kira, and Trina joined them, laughing and teasing her about the dance moves.

What was it like to be part of something like that?

Her mouth tightened, and while Sam and Laney raced over to congratulate them on the song, Paige slipped down to a quiet part of the garden. She was too hot, too overwhelmed by the tight family unit.

"You look like you could use a drink." Melanie appeared at her side holding two glasses of wine. She was wearing a pale-pink dress that perfectly suited the long dark hair curling down her back.

"Sure it isn't poison?" Paige said, but took the drink all the same.

"I never like to go the obvious route." A smile twitched on her full lips.

"I noticed," Paige said, holding up her fingers, which were still red and wrinkled from all the scrubbing. "Death by pigeon's a lot more original."

"I do what I can." Melanie shrugged as her gaze drifted to the Carmichaels, who were still up on the patio, laughing with one another. "They're quite a family, aren't they?"

"They sure are." Paige slugged back her wine and nodded.

"Can I give you some advice, Paige Taylor?" Melanie turned back, her Bambi eyes wide.

"You know you don't have to use my full name, right?" she said, but Melanie just ran a thoughtful finger down her wineglass, collecting the watery beads into a trail.

"Cleaning a statue and going out on patrol once a week aren't enough to fit into this town. The real trick to St. Clair is about staying here when the staying's tough. Can you do that?"

Paige studied Melanie's beautiful face and caught the tension around her mouth. The slight tilt of disappointment, a hint of bitterness. Understanding hit her.

"Is that what happened to you? You tried to leave but couldn't?"

The other woman closed her eyes and was quiet. "My mom got sick, so I stayed. And I've built a life for myself here. Not the one I'd dreamed about, but I've tried to make it good." Then she opened her eyes as if recollecting where she was and *whom* she was with. "It could've been better if you hadn't come along and stolen my bookstore out from underneath me."

"About that. I'm really sorry. I had—"

"Save it." Melanie shook her head. "It's done now. Besides, when you leave I'll still be here, check in hand."

"And what if I don't leave? Have you thought about that?"

"Nope." She drained her glass and narrowed her eyes. "They all leave. This town's cracked better people than you, Paige Taylor."

Again with the name.

Then she winced. Melanie was obviously referring to Luke's ex-wife. Joanne. Trina had said they'd been friends. Part of her longed to ask what she was like, but the part that'd done a course in sanity training stopped her.

"Perhaps I'll surprise you?"

"I highly doubt it. You might as well cut your losses sooner rather than later."

Paige opened her mouth to protest, but before she could, Melanie lifted up her nose and walked back into the throng of people.

"Let me guess, Mel was giving you one of her famous pep talks?"

Her stomach contracted, and goose bumps dotted her arm. *Luke.*

"She'd make a killing on the after-dinner circuit," she said, and wrinkled her nose. "I don't think my statue-cleaning abilities won her over."

"Is that what you were hoping for?" He sat down on a bench underneath the shade of a low-hanging willow. Soft light infused the leaves, like a magical veil.

"No." She pushed aside a long lazy branch to join him on the bench. "Okay, a little bit. I'm a reformed people-pleaser. Well, almost reformed. Anyway, that was quite the performance. I didn't have you pegged as a Taylor Swift fan."

"There'd be a reason for that—though, don't tell my daughter—she'd slay me." His silver eyes flickered.

He's happy.

"Kira told me you have one veto a year where she was concerned. You could've used it on the song." Paige tightened her hand around the glass stem to stop herself from running a finger along his thigh.

His laugh was a rumble. "Is there anything my daughter hasn't told you?"

"Don't worry, her secret-keeping ability is coming along nicely. I had no idea you were going to all perform together."

"I hope you're using the word 'perform' very loosely," he said.

"Definitely not. It was amazing. How long have you been playing for?"

He shrugged and studied his fingers. "After my dad died, I found his old guitar when we were cleaning the place out. I was fourteen, I guess. Kira's age. Olive didn't have the money to pay for lessons but suggested I start raking up Mr. Green's leaves. He lived next door and was a recluse, but at night I'd hear him playing some crazy-ass riffs. Eventually he offered to teach me."

B.S. was far reaching.

He looked across the fence line, as if memories were trying to climb over it. The light in his eyes dimmed, and instinctively her finger reached out and brushed his hand. A nuclear blast spread through her body, and she went to pull away, but his hand tightened around hers. She didn't dare move.

"I'm sorry about your dad. Is your mom still alive?"

A shadow flickered across his face, and his gaze fixed on something in the distance. "I keep forgetting you're not from here. She left town when I was ten. Fell for a hotshot lawyer and ran off with him. She never came back."

Pain lodged in her throat.

Seemed they had a bit more in common than they knew.

"My dad walked out when I was six, and I can count on one hand the times I saw him after that," she admitted, not sure why she was telling him. Was it to take away the pain in his eyes and let him know he wasn't alone? Or because she wanted to give something back to him in exchange for letting her into this world of his?

"Is this where the people-pleasing came from?" His gaze was now fixed firmly on her, his hand still holding hers. Emotion rippled through her.

"So my brother would have me believe. Then again, my father didn't cut him out, so he didn't have to work so hard."

"Shit." Luke's jaw slackened. "Your old man kept seeing your brother but not you?"

"Pretty much." She forced herself to nod as the words hung in the air like a thundercloud. She swallowed.

"Did you ever confront him about it?"

She shook her head. "Sometimes I wish I'd pushed him more. Demanded to know, but I never did. He had his reasons, made his choice. And I guess in a way it helped me make my choices." Memories clambered to the surface, but she swallowed them down.

"You're pretty remarkable."

Warmth skittered along her skin. "Thank you. Like you said, it happened a long time ago. But that's why I want this new life to work."

"I do get it. That's how I feel about Kira. I couldn't stop Joanne from leaving, or my mom for that matter, but I sure as hell can make sure her life's as perfect as possible from now on."

"Does she ever—" She stopped. Not sure if she was straying into dangerous territory. "Sorry, forget it."

"It's okay. It's actually nice to talk to someone who can relate," he said. "When she was younger she couldn't understand why she didn't have a mom to take her to school. She was worried she'd done something wrong. The last few years she's hardly mentioned her, but I'm sure she still thinks about her. I still feel helpless."

"Kira adores you for it."

"I hope so." He ran a hand through his hair. "Though it's definitely more challenging as she gets older."

"Is that why I saw you talking to Cal before?"

A rueful smile tugged at his mouth. "It was a pretty one-sided conversation, but he was okay. Sam tells me underneath all the emo grouching, he's smart, as in go to MIT smart."

Paige didn't bother to add that his lock picking skills were second to none. "Good for you. You know you can't tell Kira any of this?"

He burst out laughing. "You understand my daughter well!"

"Hey, you two. What are you doing over here?" Kira appeared, eating a huge slice of the cake Sam had spent last night making. Paige went to let go of his hand, but he lingered, his fingers tightening around hers.

Molten heat raced through her entire body.

How could that *be such a turn-on?*

"Discussing your dad's rock star moves," Paige said as a joke, before wincing as she caught the double meaning. "And yours. You were pretty amazing up there."

"I know, right," Kira agreed, displaying her chocolate-smeared teeth. "Dad, Jacob wants you to get more ice. He sounded cranky."

"Probably because he's had to do work," Luke quipped as he got to his feet. Paige quickly followed, and the three of them wandered back to the party, where Olive was showing everyone her Kama Sutra coloring book.

It was still going strong, but by nine, Paige was ready to crash. If she wanted to stay in St. Clair, she really needed to work on her stamina.

After saying her goodbyes she went in search of Audrey. A handful of times during the party, the pink hair bobbed up then disappeared again, but now there was no sign of her. And she wasn't answering her phone.

The party had spilled out onto the street, and she threaded her way through the scattered groups of people, hovering around their cars, half-heartedly attempting to leave. Still nothing. She reached the end of the street and was just about to turn around and try the other side when a familiar laugh hit her ears.

It was coming from a large black Ford. She moved closer and was treated to a flash of pink hair through the half-open window.

"Audrey?" Her brows pinched together as she walked over, only to discover her mother wasn't alone in the car. She was sitting in the lap of a large man wearing an apricot silk shirt. "Victor?"

The pair stiffened and turned. Her mother's normally immaculate lipstick was smudged, and at least half of it had made its way over to Victor's mouth. And her eyes—well, there was no other word for it. They were brighter than the moon.

Paige tilted her head.

Nope. Still made no sense.

Her mom was making out. With Victor.

She rubbed her brow.

"It's not what you think." Her mother extracted herself from his lap with surprising grace, and the pair of them climbed out of the car. As Victor's fingers threaded through hers, she began to laugh. "Actually, it's exactly what you think."

"Okay." She nodded, pleased someone knew what she was thinking.

Victor appeared to sense it was unfamiliar territory as he held Audrey's hand up to his mouth and pressed a kiss to it.

"I'm going to leave you two to chat. But I won't be far, and don't forget you owe me dinner for doubting my dance moves."

Color flooded her mother's face as she kissed the hairdresser/ex-biker/bar owner and told him she was like a Lannister. The debt would be paid.

Paige shut her eyes. Apparently, her mother was dating, gambling, and making *Game of Thrones* references.

"You should know Victor and I are seeing each other," Audrey said, once he'd faded into one of the small groups dotting the sidewalk. Well, as much as a six-foot-two guy wearing an apricot silk shirt could fade.

"Okay. There's that." She dumbly nodded and leaned against the side of the Ford. Her mom did the same. Even with the rumpled clothing, smudgy makeup, and pink hair, she managed to look dignified. "Why didn't you say anything? Why were you so secretive?"

"I'm not really sure. I guess just wanted to enjoy the moment. To be carried away in the excitement."

Paige rubbed her chin, desperately searching for something to latch onto. For it to make sense. But it was so out of character. So far removed from the woman who'd raised her. She might well have been speaking in Klingon.

"Is that what you've been doing for the last year?"

"What do you mean?" Her mom's voice was sharp.

"I mean you've been acting…differently. First the cruise, then moving to Boston. And then you show up *out of the blue* with no explanation. James and I are both worried. And while yes, I know his concern is mainly about his Thanksgiving seating plan, he still cares. And now you're suddenly dating Victor?"

And making out in the front seat?

Her mom studied her fingers as the fixed, unflinching mask Paige had grown up with crumpled away.

"I'll tell you what's going on, honey. I'm tired of waiting for my life to come back to me. I stayed in New York for thirty years, just in case your father realized what a mistake he'd made. For him to give me what he'd promised."

Sadness clung to the words, filling the space with a familiar loneliness and longing that had marked her childhood. The air squeezed from her chest as her mind scrambled to process it.

Have we been feeling the same way all this time?

"You stayed for thirty years, just in case?"

A pained sigh escaped her mom's mouth. "When you say it out loud I know it's silly. I just thought that's what a good wife was meant to do. Because—"

"You'd said yes to him." She finished the sentence, understanding her mother for the first time. All the coldness. The bitterness. *It wasn't at me.*

Her mom had been trying to make sense of the unwanted situation she'd found herself in.

Audrey's lower lip trembled. "I feel so foolish. When he

died, it was like being woken up after a really long sleep."

"That's why you booked the cruise?"

"I wanted to kick-start my new life. You were right. Going on a cruise after not dating was a bit…overwhelming. When I got back the anger continued. I wasn't sure who I was mad at. Your father. The universe. Or myself. I just knew I needed to do something. Which is why I sold the house and moved to Boston. Did you think I was deserting you?"

Paige shook her head. "I did wonder if you were having a breakdown because you were acting so strangely."

"Let's just say I was out of practice at knowing what it was I really wanted. I've been trying different things on for size. To see what fits."

"Like ordering all those things from the Shopping Channel? Getting your hair dyed pink and going to Seattle," she said as something formed in her throat. She had no idea that Audrey had been lost for so long.

"Yes. It was actually the hair that changed everything. I met Victor, and we had an instant connection. Like nothing I'd ever experienced with your father. It was like we'd been waiting to step back into each other's lives. But Victor told me how small the town is and how much people like to gossip. That's why we decided to go away. To see what would happen."

From the smile on her mother's face and the smudged lipstick, Paige was pretty sure how that turned out.

"I'm sorry I didn't tell you," her mom added. "I just wasn't sure where to start. We've never been that kind of family. I blame myself for that, too. Perhaps if that book of yours had been written twenty years ago, I wouldn't have wasted my life."

Paige's hands began to shake. Like the universe was being unraveled and stitched back together, in front of her eyes. Instinctively she reached for Audrey's hand. Her mother hesitated before awkwardly squeezing her fingers.

"You haven't wasted your life. I mean, there's us."

"Yes. Though James is turning out just like his father." Audrey wrinkled her nose, more like her old self. "Is that terrible to say about my son?"

"Only if you're a saint. Thanksgiving is about all I can deal with," she confided, before recalling she hadn't even agreed to go. *Perhaps every second Thanksgiving?*

"But you always looked like you were having fun."

"So did you," Paige pointed out.

"I guess we have more in common than we thought." Her mom tightened her grip on Paige's fingers. She returned the pressure.

"I'm still not sure I understand. I mean, when you arrived here, you were—"

"Cold? Distant? Here's the thing, darling. While I desperately wanted a new life, I also realized how much of a burden I'd been on you. All those years of you running around after me, and now I was landing on your doorstep trying to figure out who I was? I didn't want you to think I was in the way."

Paige swallowed down her guilt. "You're not in the way."

"Thank you."

The music from the party spilled back out into the night along with the chatter of voices from people making their farewells and heading home. Silence sat between them as Paige tried to readjust her thinking. For so long their relationship had been strained, and awkward, and nothing like the loving moms from books and movies. Then again, at least Audrey had stayed, unlike her father.

Unbidden, Melanie's words flooded her mind.

To stay when the staying's tough.

"What are you going to do now?" Paige asked. "Are you going to move here?"

"Would you hate that?" Her mom's voice was tinged with uncertainty.

"No, I wouldn't hate that. This place has a way of getting under your skin."

"That it does. Actually, Victor's offered me a job as well."

A job?

"You mean as a hairdresser?"

"Goodness no. Don't you remember that one time I was so broke I thought it would be good to save money by cutting our hair?"

"Ah yes, the great matching bangs saga," Paige said, not sure who was more traumatized, her or James? Then she frowned. Funny. She'd remembered the cuts but not the fact her mom had done it to save money.

"It wasn't my greatest idea," she admitted with a rueful smile. "I'm going to help out at the bar until he finds someone else."

"You're going to work in a biker bar?"

"Don't be a prude. Besides, they're all very nice young men, they just need to watch their language," her mom said in such an Audrey-like voice that Paige burst out laughing.

"You're really fitting in here."

"Aren't you?"

Luke flashed into her mind. The heat of his lips on hers. The warmth of his family. The way the whole town moved as one, like a shoal of fish making their way through the tide, keeping each other safe. A smile slid onto her face as the low yellow moon peeped out from behind lumbering clouds.

"I hope so," she said. "I really do."

Chapter Fourteen

"Yes is a Casanova. A beautiful but flawed lover who will whisper sweet words in your ear before disappearing the next morning without even leaving a note. Your no will stay with you in the cold hard light of the dawn." **Just Say No**

"Hey, watch out, Miley's in the house," one of his crew shouted as Luke climbed out of his work truck on Monday morning.

"I think you mean Taylor," a second voice said, accompanied by some air guitar, which earned a chortle of laughter. Luke was tempted to leave the box of donuts on the seat. Unfortunately, builders were like truffle hounds, and their noses twitched as they jogged toward him. He relented and handed the box to Jacob, who shot him a wink.

"Thanks, J-Lo."

"Yes, you're all very funny," Luke retorted. Not that he was surprised, since it's what happened every year after he sang for Olive.

Next year I'm buying her a gift card.

He wouldn't, but it was nice to dream.

He nodded for Jacob to accompany him as he inspected the site. He'd been held up over a building permit for another job, and his brother had stepped in to cover. He'd also asked him to follow up with Victor on the tile choice.

"I've got the two Tonys finishing off the loft bedroom, and the two Richies are studding out the bathroom wall. Bad news is Victor's gone underground. I think he's ghosting us." Jacob bit into a jam-filled donut, sending a dust shower of baker's sugar down his face.

"I'm not sure someone who owns two businesses and three dogs can ghost themselves away." Luke nodded to the house, where the ex-biker was standing on his patio filling his bird feeder. "Especially when he wears pink silk robes."

"In my defense, I had a very late night." Jacob gave him a rueful smile as he finished the donut. "I might not be operating at one hundred percent. I swear for Olive's eighty-first I'm only going to drink lemonade."

"No, you won't."

Jacob let out a sigh as he wiped his mouth. "You're right, I won't. Still, I wish my head wasn't pounding."

"Probably didn't help you were flirting with every girl in sight."

"Not *every* girl," Jacob leered. "Paige only had eyes for—"

"Don't go there," Luke growled. "Now, let's go over today's schedule one more time, and then I need to see Victor."

Jacob opened his mouth before shrugging. "Fine, you're the boss. But a word of advice. Liking someone *isn't* the end of the world."

"I could say the same for you. You were spending a lot of time with Laney. Anything you want to tell me?" Luke retorted, not really expecting his brother to bite. To his surprise Jacob's face colored.

His brother hadn't confided in Luke about the mysterious "she" from the other night. He just hoped if it was Laney Mitchell, that Jacob wouldn't play his normal tricks on her. She might not be St. Clair born and bred, but her husband, Simon, had been, and the entire town had a soft spot for the kindhearted widow.

"Back to work it is." Jacob gave him a friendly slap on the back before walking away. Luke blinked. He had no idea why his brother had gone shy, but he was grateful for it.

Being quizzed about last night was the last thing he wanted.

By his brother *or* himself.

Getting to know Paige felt right. And he was tired of things feeling wrong.

It had been ten years since Joanne had left, and even though he'd had the occasional one-night stand, somewhere deep down the gold band that'd once sat on his finger still burned with a fiery presence.

Until now.

I like her.

And she understands about Kira.

No doubt from what had happened with her own father.

Annoyance flared. No one deserved that. To be dismissed as if they were no longer important. Then again, perhaps that's what had given her the tenacity he admired? The determination to stand on her own two feet—even if it was often in inappropriate footwear. A smiled tugged at his mouth, and he had to force it down.

Three small dogs raced toward him as he reached the house, tongues hanging as they sniffed and prodded at his leg. He patted them before stepping into the kitchen, where Victor was carefully lifting up a delicate teapot and letting a stream of pale-green liquid fall into a china cup.

"Ah, Luke. Care to join me? It's designed to cleanse the liver." He nodded to a second cup.

He shook his head. "Any chance it's designed to help you pick your tiles?"

Victor waved a tattooed hand at him. "I swear it's not my fault. I'm still waiting for Trina to discuss her artwork. Your sister's an elusive thing at times."

Luke frowned. He'd spoken to Trina the other day and asked her to put Victor at the top of her list.

"Any chance you could pick the tiles first and then get Trina to paint something that matched?"

"Dear boy, do you really want me to answer that?"

"Yes," he said, but wasn't surprised when the guy just laughed and took a delicate sip of tea. In his giant hand, the cup was like one of Kira's old doll sets. "Okay, I'll talk to my sister. There's a big job coming up over in Tucker's Bay, and once the guys start, we won't get them back for months."

"I have the utmost faith in you," Victor assured him in a serene voice, and Luke had to content himself with going over the landscaping plans. He was just packing them away when a woman with pink hair walked into the kitchen.

Paige's mom?

She was dressed in a silk dressing gown similar to the one Victor was wearing, her bare feet, and a wide smile. He swallowed his surprise and stood up.

"I won't intrude any longer," he quickly said, though it didn't appear anyone had heard, as the couple embraced each other, oblivious to his presence.

Okay, hadn't seen that one coming.

He patted the dogs, who were still hovering at his heels, and jogged to the cottage. He received another encore of jokes for his trouble as he checked that everyone was on track. Despite the clear blue sky, rain had been forecast, and as he gave Jacob extra instructions, his stomach growled.

He glanced at the empty donut tray. He hadn't eaten since yesterday. He had a meeting for the Big Fish in an hour, which meant just enough time to swing by Patsy's and grab breakfast.

The place was bustling with morning diners when he walked in ten minutes later, and he nodded to a couple of locals at the long counter that ran the length of the place. Steam rose up from the grills out back, and his nostrils twitched as bacon infused the air.

"Hey there. That was quite a show you put on yesterday." Patsy appeared behind the counter, notepad in hand. "I'm thinking Dolly Parton would be great for next year."

"We'll see," he said in a noncommittal voice. "I'll have a chicken on rye and a large coffee to go."

"Let me guess? No time to sit?" Patsy jotted down the order and passed over the docket to the cook.

"Am I that obvious?"

"Yes." She fixed him with the same stare that'd brought many a badly behaved customer to their knees. "You know, Luke, one of these days all this running around will catch up with you."

"I'll take that under advisement."

"Make it sooner rather than later." She bustled off to fix his coffee and plate up an order of pie. While he was waiting, he called his sister, but it went straight to voicemail. He left a message, then replied to a couple of emails.

Outside, the sky had darkened, and the predicted rain pelted down onto the diner. It was followed by a jagged flash of lightning and a rumble of thunder. Luke let out a relieved sigh that they'd finished the roof last week.

"Chicken and rye, plus one coffee to go." She reappeared with his order.

"Thanks, Patsy."

"For the food or the lecture?"

"Both," he said, which earned him a laugh as he fished out some money as Paige walked in the door.

Her blonde hair was plastered against her skull from the rain, but her cheeks were bright. She'd obviously been wise enough to stay away from Olive's lethal punch last night.

Oh, and she was hot as all hell in a pair of black jeans and a fitted sweater that hugged her chest thanks to the unexpected downpour. His pulse quickened, and he dragged his gaze upward.

"Hey." Her brows lifted, and a delicate flush crept up her neck, like she was uncertain how to act around him. "I didn't expect to see you here."

"Breakfast." He held up the takeout bag. "What brings you to this neck of the woods?"

"I'm here to pick up an order. Sam assures me if I want to impress Olive's book club today I need Patsy's salted choc-chip cookies." She gave him a shy smile that made him ache to drag the wet sweater off and breathe in the scent of her body. He shifted slightly and tried to control his thoughts.

"That's because Sam knows what she's talking about." Patsy appeared with a carrier bag that contained a large white box. She passed it over but shook her head as Paige went to open her purse. "No, no, no. Clock this up as B.S. I have Christmas shopping to do."

"Okay, great." Paige nodded her head, but it wasn't until Patsy had shown a new group of diners to a table that she let out a squeal. "Did I just get accepted into the system?"

"Welcome to St. Clair. Your secret decoder ring should arrive this week." His mouth twitched at her excitement as they headed outside. Rain pelted against the concrete like bullets while thunder continued to rumble in the distance. He glanced around the parking lot. "Where's your car?"

"I walked." She stared at the rain, as if hoping that would make it go away. "It was such a nice morning. I'd better call an Uber unless I want to host my first book club looking like a drowned rat."

He considered explaining Uber hadn't hit the town yet, or that the sole cab driver tended to have a morning nap from nine until ten, then dismissed it. It might dull down her excitement of being a B.S. member.

"I'll give you a lift."

"I don't want you to go out of your way."

"It's not. I've just come from Victor's, and now I'm running errands," he said. At the mention of the ex-biker's name her face whitened. "I take it you know."

"She told me yesterday. Well, actually I found them making out in his truck, which is almost the same thing."

"Don't let the tattoos fool you. He's a good guy, if you're worried."

"I'm not. I mean, it's fast, but she's ridiculously happy. It's the most we've talked in years. Dating obviously suits her."

"That's good," he said as a group of people walked into the diner. They stepped away from the entrance as the rain continued to fall. "We'd better make a run for it."

They were both panting by the time they climbed into the cab, and a strange energy danced between them. Like a shared secret. Which was stupid. It was rain, not an alchemist gathering the secrets of the universe. The windows steamed from the moisture clinging to them. He flicked on the wipers and drove the short journey back to her store.

Rain sluiced against his skin as he took the cookies and followed her up to the door, where she fumbled with the keys. Strands of damp hair pressed against the nape of her neck, and droplets of water clung to her lashes.

I want her.

Not just because she was hot—though damn she was hot. But because she had fight in her. *Fall down seven times, stand up eight.* Who else would've faced up to Melanie at the meeting? Or actually cleaned the damn statue? Or given his kid a job just because she recognized a fellow reader?

He followed her in and shut the door behind them. There was still fifteen minutes until the store opened. The effort of not touching her was too much.

He pulled her closer, and she trembled in his arms. He cupped her face. Her wet skin was warm and her mouth half open.

"Hey." An explosion caught in his throat as his mouth found hers.

"Hey," she replied.

Her nipples were hard under her rain-slicked sweater, and his hand slid along her body. Heat burned his skin as he dragged the wet sweater off to reveal a white lace bra nestled against her pale skin. Fireworks exploded in his chest. The bra fell to the ground, followed by his own shirt until they were skin on skin.

She let out a groan as her eyes found his.

She's right here with me.

He dragged her closer, his gaze never leaving hers.

"Hello?" There was a sharp rap on the glass door at the front of the store, and Paige sprang out of his arms at the sound of his grandmother's voice.

Christ.

They both froze.

"Shit." She looked at him, her full mouth wide and her dark blue eyes smudged with mascara. "It's Olive. She must've come early for the book club."

"Screw the book club," Luke growled, but he stepped away. He dragged his shirt back on and zipped up his jeans, wishing he could zip up his libido.

I should get a medal. Or be declared a living saint.

"Oh God. What will she think of me?" Paige retrieved the discarded sweater and scrambled to the mirror and rubbed her face to smooth out her rain-soaked makeup.

"She'll think you got caught in the rain." Luke crossed toward her and swiveled her around to face him. "Go upstairs and get dry, I'll let her in."

She opened her mouth as if to protest, but before she could, he brushed his mouth against hers. More heat. *Christ.* He broke the kiss, and when she stepped away the panic in her eyes had lessened.

"Thank you." Then without another word she hurried away. He walked to the front of the store to let in his grandmother, who wasn't at all surprised.

"Whatever you're thinking, don't," he warned.

"I don't know what you're talking about." Olive patted his arm. "Now I need to get set up before the ladies arrive. Is Paige here?"

"She got caught in that downpour, I drove her home from Patsy's. She'll be down in a minute."

"If you say so, dear."

He opened his mouth before deciding it was best to pick his battles, and this was one he wasn't going to win, so he said a quick goodbye and hurried out of there before the rest of the book club arrived and started to ask even more questions.

• • •

"Mrs. Raine?" Paige raised an eyebrow as the elderly woman settled down in one of the wooden chairs, while Olive marshaled in the rest of the Fifty Shades of Grey Rinse. "I thought you and your husband only read John Grisham?"

"A woman's allowed a little mystery." The elderly woman winked and lifted a paperback out of her knitting bag. "This is a good one. A reverse harem where the girl gets all of the guys. You can borrow it if you want."

"Not before me," another woman exclaimed as she sat

down next to Mrs. Raine and then gave Paige an apologetic smile. "Sorry, this has been on my wish list for ages."

"Be my guest," Paige said, quickly taking the opportunity to leave the conversation. She had enough problems trying to navigate things with one guy, let alone a harem of them.

She busied herself pouring hot drinks and offering up the cookies along with the muffins and finger sandwiches she'd made earlier.

Before she'd been distracted by Luke.

Stop it, she instructed as her body tingled in response. She tried to push down the heat of his mouth on hers. His hands burning into her skin, while his eyes seemed to drink her in like she was special. Precious.

Again with the stop it.

She shook away the sensations.

What she did with Luke was one thing, but running her business was something else.

Something she needed to focus on.

"Aren't you an angel," Olive said as she took a cup of coffee. "Why don't you sit down and join us?"

"We don't bite." A second woman gave her a warm smile. She was in her mid-sixties with rainbow-colored hair and a playful gleam. "Unlike some of the characters we read about. Paige, tell us a bit about yourself?"

"There's not much to tell. I'm from New York and worked in publishing." *Which basically meant I ran around like a headless chicken for my ungrateful boss.* "Then after reading a book, I decided to move here."

"An epiphany!" The woman grinned in delight. "Let me guess, it was *Fifty Shades of Grey*, and when you read it you just knew it was time for you to explore the parts of you that had been repressed?"

"Actually, it was a self-help book," she corrected. "It was all about the power of saying no to people."

"Oh." The woman's face fell. "Well, that doesn't sound like much fun."

Olive laughed. "It's okay, Ronnie, remember she's younger than us, she might not have been as repressed."

"Good point." Ronnie perked up and gave Paige a hopeful smile. "Perhaps next time you'll tell us what your favorite passage is."

"From a book," someone chimed in, and everyone laughed. Paige smiled and once again edged her way out of the conversation.

I'm not sure the world's ready for the women in the store to be more unrepressed.

• • •

"And then he had the nerve to tell me I was too good for him," Zoe raged the following evening as Paige stared in the mirror, trying to decide if the orange visibility vest looked better open or closed. "Of course I'm too good for him, but what happened to my right to decide if I wanted to date down or not? I swear there's no decent men left in New York."

"Hey, I'm not the one still living there." Paige settled on leaving it open, so a hint of her shirt was revealed, along with her favorite lacy bra.

I'm only wearing it because it's laundry night, not because I want to sleep with him after our patrol's finished.

"Yes, but I refuse to be fickle and leave when the going gets tough. As Emma Thompson says in *Love Actually*, 'true love lasts a lifetime.' Anyway, none of this would've happened if you hadn't left. You would've taken one look at Roger and warned me not to go out with him."

"If you knew not to go out with him, then why did you?"

"Because I'm trying not to be so judgey. Besides, how was I to know he had a personality defect? Not to mention hairy eyebrows. Would a little wax have killed him?"

Paige resisted the urge to smile as Luke's truck pulled up outside the store. "Zo, I have to go."

"Yeah, yeah." Her friend let out a dramatic sigh. "You need to fight evil with your new lover."

"We don't fight evil. We're a community patrol. And he's not my new lover," she protested before catching herself. *Or is he?*

"Save your breath," Zoe said. "You can fool everyone else, but you can't fool me. You slept with Gas Station Guy, and now you're hoping it will happen again. I bet you're wearing that blue lacy bra and matching panties. Which, for the record, I totally approve."

"What—" Paige glanced down at the blue lace peeking out from the top of her shirt. Damn, her friend was good. "How did you know?"

"A magician never reveals her secrets. Now go and have some dirty sex and tell me all about it tomorrow."

"Pass. But all the same I love you. And hang in there. Prince Charming's just around the corner," she said as Luke's silhouette appeared in the glass door. Her pulse hammered.

Zoe offered up a cynical snort, and Paige tugged a jacket over her shirt, self-conscious about the bra, before opening the door.

Cool air rushed in to greet her, but she hardly noticed as Luke stood on the doorstep. His molten ash eyes glowed in the moonlight.

"Hey. You're drier than last time I saw you. How did book club go?"

"Well, I'm no longer an erotic fiction virgin," she said, his gaze still on her, like he was fully focused on what she was saying. It was a heady experience, especially since Patrick never had a conversation unless he was also holding his phone. "Olive has some *colorful* friends. They took turns reading their favorite passages."

"Pick up anything interesting?" His voice was a low rumble as his eyes narrowed in on the peek of lace below her shirt and jacket.

Longing swirled through her core, wild and burning. She sucked in a breath only to catch his scent on the night air. Wood and soap and honesty.

"I guess it depends on your definition of interesting," she managed to croak as he took a slow step forward, his mouth slightly parted. Her body tingled. "A-aren't we meant to be patrolling?"

"Two-for-one tacos doesn't stop for another half hour. But if you don't want to…" He trailed off, his dark eyes fixed firmly on her mouth. She caught her breath.

"Oh, I want to." Paige took a wobbly step back into the store until they were both inside. He shut the door and instantly found her mouth with his.

His breath was hot against her skin, igniting her entire body.

She tore at the brightly colored vests, desperate to be closer to him. Sparks slammed into her as he lifted her up, and she wrapped her legs around his waist. They crashed into the wall, but she hardly noticed, too caught up in the press of his mouth on hers. Perhaps it really was okay to have the occasional yes?

Chapter Fifteen

"The new you might make other people uncomfortable. Prepare for waves." **Just Say No.**

"That was some party." Smith shook his head to say no to the second cookie Paige had offered him.

"Really? I thought last year's was better. There was a lot more frolicking." Marlon frowned while at the same time taking the cookie in question and slipping it into his pocket.

"Frolicking?" She blinked. "As in—"

"Yes," Smith cut in before Marlon could answer. "Whatever you're thinking, double it. I wasn't involved."

"I was." Marlon beamed as he slurped his coffee and picked up the book of limericks Paige had given him. Neither of the men had spent a dime since their first visit, but she enjoyed their company and found their encyclopedic knowledge of all things St. Clair fascinating.

Their visit was brought to an end by the appearance of Myra, who herded them out to the minivan. "Sorry," she mouthed to Paige as they left a trail of cookie crumbs behind them. She'd just finished cleaning up the mess when the bell above the door jingled and Melanie stalked into the store, eyes blazing.

"Hi there." Paige mustered up a smile, while checking the other woman wasn't carrying a baseball bat or sharp weapon. Melanie didn't reply as she snatched up a copy of *Just Say No* and waved it in the air.

"Answer me this, Paige Taylor. Why are men so terrible? I mean, what the hell makes them think I don't have feelings?"

"Perhaps they're projecting?" she offered as Melanie walked over to the counter and slapped the book down, sending a bundle of packing slips fluttering into the air before scattering out on the floor.

"Or perhaps the universe doesn't want me to be happy? After all, I wanted the bookstore and instead *you* got it. And now—" A strangled sigh escaped her throat. "And now I am bitching about the guy who ruined my life *to the woman who ruined my life*."

"Okay, first, I'm really sorry I outbid you on the store. I had no idea anyone else was even interested. And, as for the guy—if you're talking about Luke—"

"I only *wish* I was talking about Luke. What's wrong with me?"

Paige blinked. "Wait? You don't hate me because of Luke?"

"Don't get me wrong. I have plenty of reasons to hate you, but he isn't one of them. Unfortunately. My life would've been easier if I'd fallen for the decent Carmichael brother instead of the immature—oh, shit." Her hand flew to her mouth.

"You're talking about Jacob?" Paige once again wondered if she'd wandered into an alternate reality. "*Jacob* Jacob?"

"Yes, Paige Taylor. I'm talking about *Jacob* Jacob. Is that really so hard to believe?"

"That's not what I meant. It's just you look like a model, and seem like a really nice person—well, when you want to be. And Jacob's—"

"Silly? Immature? Thoughtless?"

"He's been flirting like crazy with Laney," she said in a pained voice.

At the mention of Laney's name, Melanie's face darkened.

"Trust me, we've had words about that. According to him she's just a friend, though I'm not sure she saw it that way." She stretched her neck and peered at the ceiling, as if it would somehow give her answers. Apparently, it didn't. "I know exactly what kind of guy he is, and yet I keep falling for him over and over again."

"You're the 'she'!" Paige said and then regretted it as Melanie's eyes narrowed.

"What did he tell you?" Melanie trained the full force of her laser focus on her. Paige buckled under it.

"Not much, I swear. One night on patrol, we had to detour to Luke's house because Jacob turned up drunk. He kept saying 'she' had his apartment keys."

"I had his car keys in case he did anything moronic like driving." Melanie folded her arms, her ire increasing. "Tell me, Paige Taylor. If I buy this book, can you guarantee it'll help me say no next time he tries to seduce me?"

"I wish I could," she said truthfully, recalling what it had been like with Patrick. How he'd sucked her back in every time she started to question their relationship. The helplessness of wanting one thing and saying yes to the very thing that'd guarantee she wouldn't get it.

Of having no control.

Of not belonging.

The other woman let out a bitter snort. "I knew I shouldn't have come here. I mean, there's desperate and then there's desperate."

Paige gritted her teeth and reminded herself Melanie was in pain.

"No one can guarantee anything." She took the book and flipped to Chapter Nine. "But if you really want to stop seeing him, this is the place to start. Tell you what, take it home, and if it doesn't help, you have my permission to throw it against the wall. It might make you feel better. But if it does help, come back and pay."

Melanie's shoulders dropped, as if the fight was going, and she reluctantly picked up the open book. "'*How to say what you mean and mean what you say—five steps to owning your no and reclaiming your life,*'" she read out before frowning. "Seriously, you believe this shit?"

"What have you got to lose?"

"Don't get me started." She tucked the book under her arm. "Oh, and I saw your mother now works at Victor's as well as dating him. Any other family members I need to know about?"

"You're safe." Paige shook her head, confident her Boston lawyer brother wouldn't be moving there anytime soon.

"Humph." Melanie snorted by way of a thank you before marching out of the store. Paige wanted to pinch herself. Two months ago, *she'd* been Melanie. Stuck in a relationship with Patrick and desperately looking for something to help guide her out of it. *Just Say No* had been that something. And now, here she was with everything she'd ever wanted.

As she got back to shelving new arrivals, she began to hum. Life really didn't get much better than this.

• • •

"Dad, are you even listening?" Kira demanded from over by his office door. His throat tightened, and he lifted his hands into the air. His daughter's eyes gleamed with mischief.

"Sweet. That means you now owe me fifty-three dollars."

"You seem very happy you've caught me not listening to you fifty-three times." Luke added another buck into the large jar on the shelf by his desk.

He'd started the system a couple of years ago when he'd realized lying to his daughter didn't help anything. Instead he admitted if he'd zoned out or if he'd made a questionable decision.

"You still listen more than Hailey's parents. Or Maxie's." She shrugged. "Besides, the money will pay for a new Trent Burton T-shirt. Oh, and I got twenty bucks from Uncle Jacob."

"As long as it's going to a good cause." He rolled his eyes and pretended to groan, before giving her his full attention. "What were you saying, kiddo?"

"I was asking if you liked my new lip gloss. Auntie Trina gave it to me." She held up a tube that looked like all her other lip glosses.

"It's nice." He nodded, the faint color barely visible on Kira's mouth. He hated the idea of her wearing makeup, but Olive and Trina assured him denying a fourteen-year-old girl her lip gloss would seriously dent their otherwise great relationship. Then he frowned. "When did you see your aunt?"

He'd been trying to get hold of his sister for the last two days to discuss Victor, but she hadn't returned any of his calls.

"At Gigi's. Then she and Jacob went to Carriage to talk about something."

I bet they did.

They'd both been cagey for the last couple of weeks, more since Olive's party. Had they noticed him talking to Paige and done the math? Or seen them at the bookstore together?

Annoyance flooded through his veins. How many times had he told his siblings to stay out of his love life? And that was before he'd even *had* a love life.

I'm not ready to share this.

Especially not with St. Clair. He'd seen it before. Half the town would be planning the wedding, and the other half would be betting on how long it would last.

"Oh, really." Luke pushed away from his office desk.

"If you're going to Carriage, can I study with Hailey at the library?" She gave him a hopeful smile.

He didn't like her going out on a weeknight, even if it was just to the library. But he didn't need his brother and sister getting involved in his business. He gave a sharp nod of his head.

"Okay, just this one time. I'll drop you there now and will pick you up in ninety minutes."

Her face brightened. "Awesome, you're the best, Dad." She hugged him before darting off to round up her schoolbooks and put on yet more gloss. Ten minutes later he dropped her outside St. Clair's library that doubled as a post office, then walked the short distance to Carriage.

Jazz music played in the background, and the low murmur of voices and chinking of glasses filtered out around him. Jacob normally sat at the bar, where he was sure to be seen, but there was no sign of his brother or sister. He scanned the room, his gaze falling on Paige, who was sharing a meal with Audrey and Victor.

She glanced over. He gave her a faint nod and commanded himself not to look at the hollow of her throat. Or imagine the heat of her skin against his mouth.

"Can you believe her mom's dating Victor?" Melanie appeared at his side, making Luke wish he'd just stayed home and finished off his paperwork. "You meeting anyone, or do you want a drink?"

"Sorry, Mel. I'm looking for Jacob and Trina. You seen them?"

"They're over there." Her eyes narrowed as she glared at a booth in the corner.

"What's he done now?" Luke sighed.

"Let's see. He's been flirting with Laney George like there's no tomorrow, and then I caught him almost having phone sex with some poor soul. The guy has no shame."

"Tell me about it." He scanned the booths before picking out his brother's head. Then he frowned. "Are you okay?"

"No, but I will be." She let out a long sigh and turned to signal she was done talking about it. He muttered a quick goodbye and stalked over. Trina's jaw was tight, while Jacob had a pensive expression in his eyes.

"What are you doing here?" Trina was the first to notice him. "I thought you and Kira were hanging out tonight."

"Plans changed." Luke slid into the booth and folded his arms. "What's going on?"

"Nothing." Trina shook her head a little too quickly. He narrowed his eyes. He'd assumed that they were scheming to set him up, but the way they were both avoiding his gaze suggested something else.

"Okay, spill."

It was Jacob who crumbled first. "We have news, but you're not going to like it."

"What happened to not telling him?" Trina hissed.

"You know I'm no good in situations like this," Jacob protested. "Besides, if you don't tell him, imagine how much worse it will be when—"

"Okay, fine." Trina swiveled to face him. "I saw Joanne in Seattle. She's living in Portland but traveled up to see me."

The jazz music stopped.

The bar faded away.

There were no more voices.

No more sounds of glasses being raised.

Just silence. It buzzed in his ear, darting under his skin

like an insect, as Trina's words revolved around his head.

"I know you're angry," she said in a rush, while glaring at Jacob. "You have every right to be, but hear me out. She saw on social media Stu and I were going to be in town for his folks' anniversary and turned up at the house. I couldn't very well ignore her."

"She wants to speak to you," Jacob said, his voice unnaturally quiet. "To say sorry."

Sorry?

Luke closed his eyes.

It had been ten years since she'd walked out on Kira. On him. Ten years since she'd told him, tears streaming down her face, that small town living was killing her. That she couldn't stay. That she needed to clear her head.

And I was fool enough to believe her.

But instead of coming back to him and their four-year-old daughter, she'd booked a one-way ticket to Africa to volunteer in a hospital. The frantic phone calls, emails, and text messages he'd sent were all ignored, and in the end, it was Joanne's sister who'd contacted him to say that she was sorry. Jo wasn't coming back. That as much as she loved them, she just couldn't be the mother or wife they needed. She was doing it for the best.

"She's back in the country for good, Luke. And she's engaged to a nice guy. And—" Trina sucked in a breath. "She wants to discuss having visitation rights to Kira."

The chair fell backward as he stood up. Blood pounded. He was too mad to speak. Too mad to stay. He turned on his heel and walked out of the bar to collect his daughter.

Kira. Whom he'd raised on his own for the last ten years, because her mother ran out on them. And if Joanne thought she could step back into their lives, then she had another think coming. That was for damn sure.

...

"She's dating an ex-biker? This is completely unacceptable."

"Actually, it's none of our business." Paige walked around the store, checking that the windows were locked. She always shut early on a Saturday, and if she had to listen to James list all the reasons why it didn't suit him or Fiona for Audrey to date, she might as well get some work done.

"You'd say that," he retorted. "Because you're content to drift through life not caring what people think."

"According to Dr. Penny Groves, managing other people's expectations is the surest way to go crazy."

"Obviously this friend of yours hasn't tried to run a law firm in Boston," was the tart response. She shut her eyes. Arguing with her brother was a futile activity.

Besides, regardless of his reservations, he hadn't seen the way Audrey's mouth melted when Victor had gently brushed the pink hair away from her eyes. The way his whole body turned toward her when she spoke.

Her mom was right. Whatever was happening between them was serious.

"Sorry, James. I've got to close the store."

Her brother grunted and finished the call as Kira darted over to the window and pressed her nose against it.

"Are you looking for your dad?" Paige joined her, because...well, because it was Luke and she couldn't quite help it.

Audrey wasn't the only one falling hard.

"No. I'm hoping Cal might go by. I heard someone at school saying he has to work at Sam's café to help pay for the things he broke in the science lab. Not that it was his fault. He was trying to do an experiment and it backfired."

"Oh," Paige mouthed, hoping for Sam's sake it was true.

"There he is!" Kira let out an excited squeal as Cal

wandered out to the front of the café and lifted up the chalkboard menu that had fallen over in the wind. He righted it, then slouched back inside. "Did I tell you I almost spoke to him at the library the other night?"

"No. What happened?" Paige asked with interest. Kira had been keeping her updated on her crush, but to her knowledge it had all been played out from a distance.

"He walked in and sat down next to me and Hailey. Can you believe it? At. The. Same. Table! I almost said hi, but... well...then I chickened out. Do you think I should put more lip gloss on?"

"For him to not see you through the store window?" she said as her phone beeped.

Luke.

She blinked. She hadn't spoken to him since their patrol on Tuesday night, but she'd thought about him once or twice. Okay, fine, six billion times a day.

"Hey," she answered as Kira went back to her window staring, clutching at her book like a life ring. "Everything okay? I'm just about to lock up if you're on the way over."

"There's a problem." His voice was strained and distant. "I'm tied up with a last-minute job and won't be back until later. Olive and Trina are out, and I haven't been able to track down Jacob. I was hoping you could ask Sam to keep an eye on Kira for me. Just until I find Jacob. I tried calling him, but no answer."

"I will. Though you know I'd be happy to do it."

There was a pause.

"I couldn't ask you to help like that. You might have plans with your mom."

I'm pretty sure Audrey's plans all involve Victor, and if I think too much about it, I might get icked out.

"No. I was just going to pay bills."

"I'm not sure."

This time the pause was longer. And surrounded by question marks. She could almost picture his brows knitted together, as if searching for a way to let her down lightly. Her chest tightened, and she tugged at the collar of her shirt.

He doesn't trust me with his kid.

Had she imagined what had been growing between them?

"If you'd rather I ask Sam, I totally don't mind." It came out as a squeak as she valiantly tried to swallow down the hurt.

"I know who Kira would prefer, if you're really okay with it."

"Absolutely. Do you want to speak to her?" The tightness in her chest lessened.

"I'm in a hurry. Just give her my love. And, thanks."

"You're welcome," she said, but he'd already finished the call.

"Was that my dad?" Kira asked with interest.

She nodded. "He's running late, and he can't track down Jacob, so you have the pleasure of hanging out with me for a couple of hours."

"Seriously? That's awesome. We could sort out some more books. Or work on your blog. Or—"

"I have a better idea. What about we go and have some lunch. At Sam's café." She glanced over to where Cal was half-heartedly busing the tables in the courtyard.

The young girl's mouth dropped open, and her eyes bulged, while a series of expressions darted across her face.

"Are you serious? Because if I went there on my own, or with Hailey and Maxie, he might think we were stalking him. But if I went there with someone as—"

"Please choose your next words carefully."

She suppressed a giggle. "I was going to say 'cool,' not 'old.' You know, you're just like my Aunt Trina."

"I'll take that as a compliment." She retrieved her coat

and purse from the office, while Kira methodically added an extra layer of transparent lip gloss to her mouth before doing a complicated dance routine.

"Ah, it's the ladies who lunch." Sam led them through the crowded café to an empty table in the courtyard. "It's been crazy today. Cal, you remember Paige, and you know Kira."

Cal, who'd been hunched over a table, stacking plates and coffee cups into the wide plastic tray with the speed of a snail, offered a vague grunt. It could've been hello, or an eye roll with verbal accompaniment. It really was too close to call.

Once they were gone, Kira leaned over, her face glowing.

"Did you hear that? He said hello to me. Okay, it might have been to both of us, but that still counts, right?"

"Absolutely." She bit back an amused smile. It didn't take them long to scan the menu, and she left Kira to text her friends with the latest Cal update while she went to order.

"Everything okay?" Sam glanced over to where Kira was giggling at something one of her friends must've written.

"Yes, Luke's just been held up, and the rest of the Carmichaels are busy. How's it going with you? Kira said Cal had a problem at school."

"You say problem, they say explosion." Sam glanced over to where Cal was leaning against a wall, his head nodding along to the music that was obviously coming out of his ear buds. "I think we can safely say I'm no longer 'Cool Aunt Sam.' At least I managed to keep him from getting expelled."

"Hey, you're doing an amazing job."

"Sure wish it felt like that." Sam finished making the drinks. Kira was glowing when she got back to the table.

"Wow, someone's plugged you into a power socket." Paige passed a gigantic hot chocolate covered in cream and marshmallows, while setting her own coffee down.

"That's because I'm happy." Kira plucked one of the marshmallows out and chewed it, cream and chocolate covering her mouth. "While you were at the counter, Cal looked over at me three times. Three! Plus, there's even more news."

"More news than three glances?" Paige hid her amusement and took a sip of her coffee.

"Look! Meg Mitchell's just tweeted!" Kira held up her phone. "She's doing a book signing in Seattle, and Trent Burton's going to be there, too. It's to promote the movie."

"O-kay," Paige said, not quite sure how a book signing three hundred miles away was big news. "You might have to help me out here."

"Don't you get it?" Kira bounced in the chair so much that the table jiggled. "You could invite Meg Mitchell and Trent Burton to come here. To St. Clair. I mean, that's what you did in your old job, wasn't it?"

Paige opened her mouth and then closed it again, uncertain how to explain that most tours were paid for by publishers and only went to the bigger stores, where there were more people to reach.

"Technically," she answered. "But I'm not sure I could make that happen."

"So you won't try?" Kira's face dropped.

No. It had to be no. But the woebegone expression across the table was hard to ignore. Memories of her own childhood flooded in. And though Kira was surrounded by love, she still lost herself in the world of books and believed in the magic that came with it.

I don't want to be the person who takes it away.

"I'm not promising anything, *but* my old boss owes me a favor. Several, actually. I'll see what I can do."

She picked up her phone and called. Ellen didn't answer, so she sent her a text with the request and added a note in her calendar to follow up tomorrow.

"And?" Kira said with puppy-like eagerness.

"I've asked her, but like I said, there's no guarantee. Okay?"

"Okay."

Thankfully, the conversation was cut short by the return of Cal, who sauntered over and set down two plates in front of them.

"Here's your food," he muttered before dropping his shoulders and wandering away. If slouching was a job requirement, he would've been employee of the month. However, Kira thoroughly approved, and the rest of the meal was spent talking about books and movies as they split one of Sam's amazing red velvet cupcakes. It was almost two o'clock when Olive and Trina appeared in the courtyard.

Kira was immediately up on her feet and hugging them both.

"Paige, thank you for taking care of her," Trina said. "Nan and I were halfway to Holland Bay when he called."

"Please, it saved me from doing bookkeeping. Though I'm not sure I'll be able to move for the rest of the day after that dessert." She got to her feet, and they headed out as Kira chatted to her grandmother and aunt about what they'd done. The two women were totally engrossed in what she was saying. A sliver of something pressed down on her throat.

The thing she'd always wanted.

A sense of belonging.

Of fitting in.

It was strange Luke's ex-wife had been part of this and walked away. Then she caught herself. As Dr. Penny Groves always said.

Don't judge others unless you want others to judge you.

• • •

Luke stared at the house in front of him.

It was an arts and craft bungalow with stone pillars leading up to the porch and wooden walls. An extension had been added at some stage, probably to help house a growing family. And now it belonged to Joanne and her new fiancé, who were back in the country. Living in Portland.

He longed to just turn around and make the hundred-and-thirty-mile trip back to St. Clair. The only thing stopping him was it might encourage his ex-wife to turn up at the house unannounced. After the divorce she'd signed away her parental rights. It had been the last time they'd spoken.

The last time he thought they'd *ever* speak. After all, he'd spent years convincing her to be part of Kira's life, and she'd refused. Stating over and over again it was for the best.

He rubbed his hand along the stubble on his jaw. He'd been sitting out in the truck for two hours, trying to decide if he should go in.

A good parent does what's best for their child. Olive had always told him that. Even when his mother had walked out and not come back.

What was best for Kira?

When she was younger, she'd often asked why Joanne had to work overseas to help all the sick kids, when she could be in St. Clair. It had ripped holes in his chest to hear that. He'd always told her it was because those kids didn't have any parents, that's why she'd gone to help them. He'd sworn he'd never leave her, and the last few years Kira had never even mentioned her mom, which he'd assumed meant the pain had gone.

When I was her age did I want my mom back?

Oh, hell.

His fingers closed around the handle, and he climbed out.

The front door opened before he was even up the path, and Joanne appeared. She'd obviously been watching him from the window the entire time. Her hair was longer now, her face drawn, and she was wearing a baggy white shirt and a pair of jeans, while her hands were tightly laced together.

She's scared.

"You got out of the car," she said in a faltering voice as tears streamed down her face. She brushed them aside and managed a smile. "Thank you."

He stopped at the bottom step, his indecision replaced by the slow anger that'd smoldered under his skin for the last ten years.

"I'm only here because of my daughter." Even to his own ears, his voice was harsh, but it had to be.

Kira had suffered too much when she was younger—the nightmares and tears and confusion as to where her mom was. The worry it had been something she'd done. That she wasn't good enough.

It was his job to make sure it didn't happen again.

"W-would you like to come in? Owen's here, but if you'd rather he left for a few minutes, that's okay."

Luke shook his head. "There's nothing we can't discuss in front of him."

"That's fair," she said as he followed her inside.

The house was nice. Wooden floorboards, white walls with huge photographs of the African savanna, and a long gray couch. Once the door was closed Owen joined them. He was tall with an angular face and wire glasses. There was a serious expression around his mouth, and he was the last kind of guy he thought Joanne would've fallen for.

Then again, what the hell do I know about what she likes?

After a tense introduction, and Luke's refusal of anything to eat or drink, they awkwardly sat down around the table. Tension hung in the air, thick as soup.

Joanne was the first to speak. "I'm sorry I went behind your back to see Trina. I wasn't sure what else to do."

"You mean apart from walking out on us ten years ago,"

he retorted before he could stop himself. Owen immediately bristled, but Joanne put a calming hand on his arm.

"Hey, it's okay. Luke's only telling it like it is."

"No, he's telling it from his side of the story. Jo, it's time you told him yours."

Luke stiffened. "Nothing will change the fact my daughter's grown up without a mother."

This time Joanne let out a little sob, but she sucked it back in. Her face was pale, and she falteringly began.

"Before I moved to St. Clair, while I was still at med school, I suffered from a bout of depression. It was a dark time. I barely left my room, barely ate, barely did anything but listen to the hammering thoughts that were in my mind all the time. A friend noticed and convinced me to get treatment. It wasn't easy, but as the meds started to work, slivers of sunshine and color crept back into my life. Two years after I graduated, I got the job in St. Clair and met you."

The room was silent as Luke tried to reconcile the woman he'd first met with someone unable to leave her room. He couldn't do it. Joanne had been adventurous, energetic. Full of life. Once she'd challenged him to swim the length of the bay, and he'd had his ass handed to him. Then there was the time she'd stayed up all night watching old black-and-white movies because she loved them. Or when she'd had her long hair cut so it could be donated for a wig.

He glanced up. Joanne and Owen were both trying to gauge his reaction.

"I truly thought those dark days were all in the past. That my perfect life would be just as advertised. That I'd be happy. And I was, Luke."

"If that's true, then why am I only hearing about this now?" The words tore at his throat. She bowed her head and let out a shuddering sob.

"I was ashamed. I was the town GP. I didn't want them

to know the truth about me. I didn't want *anyone* to know the truth. And then I got pregnant. I was ecstatic, and while there were times when dark clouds were surrounding me like vultures, I only had to look at you, and they'd disappear. You were in love with Kira, even before she was born. It was like the stars and planets had aligned. The world made sense. You were strong, and I figured that'd get us all through it."

"Through what?" Despite himself, Luke leaned forward and unclenched his fingers, which had been in two tight balls.

"The blackness. By the time Kira was four months old, I knew I had postnatal depression." Her voice was bleak.

He recoiled as a fist slammed into his gut, sucking the air from his chest. Noise ricocheted in his ears. A low buzz, drowning everything else out.

All this time, there was a name for what had happened to his life?

Something to explain why the fabric of his world had ripped, with such a jagged edge it was impossible to stitch back together?

And she'd never said a fucking word.

He stood up so fast the table shook. He didn't care. He needed to move. To try and rid his body of the excess energy building up inside him. The noise faded, and he returned to the seat.

Joanne had shrunk toward Owen, who had a protective arm around her shoulder. This was obviously a well-trodden path between them. Unlike for Luke, who felt like he'd woken up in a foreign country with no way home.

As if sensing it was safe to speak again, Joanne coughed. "I know I should've told you. Should've told someone. But it snuck up on me like a thief, and by the time I realized, I was consumed by it. And arrogant enough to think I could fix it myself. I just kept functioning. But the self-medicating didn't work, and eventually all I could think about was the ways I might accidentally hurt my daughter. Kira. Who I loved more than anything. I had to take myself away from her. To keep her safe."

He shut his eyes.

He'd spent his life trying to figure out what could make a person leave their child. Why his mother left. Why Joanne left. But he'd never been able to come up with an explanation.

The anger drained away, and he lifted his head up to stare at the ceiling.

"Why now?" He returned her gaze. "You've had ten years to tell me."

"She's had ten years to recover," Owen said.

"It's taken a long time to get my depression under control," Joanne said, untangling Owen's arm from her shoulder, as if to say she could stand on her own now. "Even longer to get over the shame of abandoning Kira. And you. It's been overwhelming. All-encompassing for such a long time." She paused and sucked in a breath. "I'm not asking you to forgive me. That's out of my control. But I am asking to see her. Luke, I know this is a lot to take in."

It was. Ten years of pain to try and untangle. It wasn't like Olive's skeins of wool that could just be unwound and turned into a new ball. He stood up again and this time walked to the door. Then he turned and took a deep breath.

"You're asking the wrong person. It's not my decision, it's Kira's. And if I agree to talk to her about this, you *have* to respect her decision."

"Thank you," she whispered, once again sagging against Owen's shoulders. Like the weight of the conversation was too much for her.

He needed to get out of there. Get some fresh air. Try and figure out how to make sense of what Joanne had said. Try and figure out how to make sure Kira didn't get hurt all over again.

Chapter Sixteen

"The problem with starting a new life is your old life doesn't always get the message. This is when it helps to really know your no." **Just Say No**

"This one time at school, Georgia Griffith handed out free cookies, and everyone took them because hello, free cookies," Kira said with a wave of her arms. "And they were the good cookies, too. The kind you only buy at Thanksgiving or Christmas. You know, with the caramel in the middle and chocolate on the top."

"Okay. Not quite sure if that's a yes or no for ice cream." Luke held up the tub of Pralines and Cream to his daughter, who was sitting on the kitchen counter, her legs dangling over the side, resting on the back of a chair.

"I want the ice cream, but I also want to know what's going on."

"Not sure I follow?"

"When Georgia handed out the cookies it was because she wanted everyone to vote for her as class president. *And we never have ice-cream on a Monday night.* Besides, why aren't you in your study working on the Big Fish?" The last part was said with a flourish, much like a closing argument in court.

Damn, she's smart.

He put the ice cream back into the freezer and nodded for her to join him at the kitchen table. The red-and-white Formica top was chipped, and the surrounding chrome had seen better days, but he'd never been able to part with it, no matter how much Joanne had teased him.

He clenched his jaw.

He hadn't slept a wink since Saturday.

Nor had he answered his sister's phone calls or his brother's text messages. What was the point? Even surrounded by his family, his town, the people who'd known him his entire life, he was raising a daughter alone. And as much as he'd wanted the village to support him, it was a solo job. All up to him. Which was why he'd spent so much time weighing up his decisions. To make sure he didn't screw it up. Like his mom had. Like Joanne had.

Correction. Like I thought *she had.*

Despite his anger, he'd been forced to accept there was more to her desertion than he'd known. Another side to the story. One Kira had a right to know.

"We need to talk."

"Talk about what?"

Talk about the things I've been avoiding. About how you might get hurt. About how our lives might change.

He took a deep breath, wishing there was an easy way to say it.

"Your mom's back from overseas, sweetheart. She wants to see you."

His daughter's mouth dropped open, but no sound came out as she sat, statue still. Silence stretched out between them as color leached from her face. Pain shattered in his chest. She normally spoke at a million miles an hour, while constantly moving. This wasn't who she was.

"I told her it wasn't up to me. It's your decision."

"Why?" Her eyes met his, swirling, like moss caught in the current.

"Why does she want to see you?" Luke rubbed his jaw. It was Joanne's story to tell, and no matter how many mixed emotions still raced through him, he couldn't quite bring himself to betray her. "Because she loves you."

"No, she doesn't." The chair went crashing to the floor as she stood up. Her small hands were balled into fists, and the sickly pallor of her skin blossomed with red. "You don't believe it, why should I?"

"Kira?" He stiffened at her uncharacteristic outburst. "That's not true. And I know this is a surprise. Trust me—"

"No." She shook her head as she stepped away from the fallen chair. "I don't want to talk about it." Then without another word she stormed out of the room and down the hall. The slamming door echoed throughout the house.

He ran a hand through his hair, a tight lump in his throat.

Even though she'd never had a tantrum before, he'd witnessed enough of his sister's teenage blowouts to know she'd need time to cool down. Which left him stuck where he was, unable to help the person he loved most in the world.

• • •

"You know you're going to have to talk to me eventually," Jacob said by way of greeting when Luke opened the door. He thrust some beers at him and walked in. "I figured we'd get it over and done with. On a scale of one to ten, how mad are you?"

"Eighty-five and counting," Luke retorted, but all the

same he shut the door and handed one of the beers to his brother.

"I can work with that." Jacob shrugged and twisted off the cap. "You were one hundred and twenty that time I borrowed your bike and crashed it."

"You say borrowed, I say stolen." He joined Jacob on the couch.

"So...you talked to Kira yet?"

"Yeah. It went as well as could be expected." He rubbed his jaw to ease away the frustration and tension. It didn't work. Kira had eventually come out of her room, her face tear stained, but the anger had subsided enough for them to talk through her options. Together. Just like they'd always done.

"I see." Jacob nodded before turning to him, guilt in his eyes. "We should've told you. I'm sorry. We wanted to, we just weren't—"

"It was a shit situation. I get it," Luke cut him short.

"We're cool?" Jacob's eyes seemed to be searching his face for clues.

"Yeah." Luke held his beer up, and they both took a long drink. But even though the lines around Jacob's mouth had lessened, his shoulders were still tight, and his neck was strained. "Is something going on with you?"

A montage of emotions rippled across his brother's normally relaxed face as he let out a shuddering breath. "I really screwed up, Luke."

"Screwed up how?" he said in surprise, not at the confession, but at the rawness of his voice. His brother normally treated everything in his life with amusement, before shrugging it off like a jacket he no longer needed. Regret wasn't part of his vocabulary.

"With Melanie."

Melanie Banks?

He was rendered silent. *Was Mel the "she" from the other*

night? He raked a hand through his hair, trying to make sense of it. None was forthcoming. Especially considering her reaction every time she mentioned Jacob's name. Then again, there was often a fine line between love and hate.

"Want to talk me through it?"

"What's the point?" Jacob angrily put his beer down and folded his arms. "I messed it all up. What's done is done."

Luke blinked. "Since when does Jacob Carmichael admit defeat?"

His brother gave a flicker of a smile before closing his eyes and shaking his head. "All those other times don't count. I mean, they were just for fun. But this is different—"

"You really like her?"

"I'm crazy about her. Problem is first I thought we were just messing around. Having fun. Plus, she was hot and cold. I figured she thought it was funny when I flirted with other people."

"Laney." Luke let out a long whistle, and Jacob's face filled with misery.

"Yeah. And before you start, I've apologized to her, and we're all good. I didn't mean anything by it. But now Melanie's got this damn book and keeps quoting stupid passages at me. They don't even make any sense. How am I meant to compete with that?"

He knew the book.

Olive and her friends had started reading it, and Paige had confided it was the reason she'd moved to St. Clair in the first place. Not that he understood it.

They were just words.

He knew firsthand that words didn't mean anything. It was action that counted. A smile spread across his mouth. If there was one thing his brother was good at, it was taking action and making noise.

"What's so funny?" Jacob stirred himself from his

gloomy contemplation. "Because I'm suffering here."

"I know. That's the problem." Luke put down his beer and gave his brother a friendly slap on the shoulder. "Since when do you play by anyone else's rules? If you like Melanie, then figure out another way to let her know."

"Like what?" His brother leaned forward, eyes curious.

"I have no idea. But weren't you the guy who drove two hundred miles to impress that French backpacker you were seeing last year?"

"Well, yeah. Said she liked tulips, and not even Laney could get any in. I figured it would be romantic, and boy was I—" Jacob stopped as understanding hit him. "You, my friend, are a genius! Like I always say—go big or go home."

Luke was pretty sure his brother never said that, but was relieved to see the gleam back in his eyes. "You got this."

"Thanks." Jacob's expression went serious again. "So do you, big brother. Kira's lucky to have you as a dad."

He nodded as the pair of them finished their beers. Seemed like they were both figuring out how to do things right.

• • •

Paige wasn't a morning person, but years of having to get up early enough to fight through the New York subways had taught her to go through the motions. And, since she had enough paperwork to sink the Titanic waiting in the small office, she resisted the urge to ignore her alarm.

She stifled a yawn, and like a zombie, she shuffled her way to the kitchen and the lifeline she called coffee. Her nose twitched as the burned, nutty aroma of her favorite grind greeted her. Along with the irresistible siren-like call of sizzling bacon.

Her eyelids peeled back.

Victor was working the grill in her tiny kitchen like a *MasterChef* contestant, while her mom was laughing at something he said. They both looked guilty as Paige walked in.

"Did we wake you? Victor wanted to come by and cook breakfast."

"It's okay." She gratefully took the coffee her mother handed her. "I've got a list a mile long to get through, which meant staying up late to finish a book probably wasn't such a great idea."

Or fantasizing about Luke.

She hadn't spoken to him since Saturday, but it hadn't stopped her imagination from getting very graphic.

Her mom exchanged a look with Victor, who coughed. "So, I need to go buy milk," he said before turning everything off, thoroughly kissing Audrey on the mouth, and disappearing downstairs.

"Okay, what's going on?" She narrowed her eyes.

Her mom walked over to one of the chairs. "There's something I wanted to talk to you about."

"Does it involve the new gym set I saw you looking at on the Shopping Channel the other day?"

Her mom coughed. "Not exactly. Victor asked me to move in with him. I know it's fast, and I want to make sure you don't have a problem with it."

Paige blinked.

Her mom had managed to go from a man who kept her waiting for thirty years to one who moved at lightning speed. And it was obvious by the beaming smile which one suited her better. Not that James would see it that way. Then again, it wasn't James's life, it was Audrey's. *And I've never seen her happier.*

"I don't, as long as you're sure this is what you want."

"It is." Audrey reached for her hand.

"Then I really am happy for you both. I might not have

much experience in the father figure department, but I think he's—" She broke off as her mom let out a sob. "What is it? What's wrong? I thought this was a happy moment."

"It is." Her mom blew her nose and tried to shake away the tears. "But there's something I should've told you a long time ago."

"Told me what?"

Her mom took a deep breath and turned to her, eyes the color of denim. "Your father was a jealous man, and before you were born he was convinced I was having an affair with one of the doctors at work."

The room began to tilt. "What?"

"I wasn't. Not even close. We weren't even on a first name basis, but your father never believed me. And after you were born, he was convinced—"

"That I wasn't his." The words came out in a rush.

Like a missing part of a puzzle she'd spent a lifetime searching for had been found. All the times he'd ignored her, dismissed her, favored James. There was a reason for it.

An actual reason.

Audrey nodded. "I thought if I took a DNA test it would convince him, but he still wouldn't believe me."

"Why didn't you tell me?"

"I didn't know how...and because I was ashamed. Ashamed I couldn't convince him otherwise. Ashamed I could still want him in my life despite how he acted." Her face crumpled. "I haven't been the best mother, and I'm so sorry."

Tears pricked in the corner of Paige's eyes as something tore through her chest. She wrapped her arms around her ribs but couldn't stop the pent-up emotions racing through her. Anger at her lost childhood, relief it hadn't all been in her head, confusion as to what it all meant. And tiredness, from carrying it around for so many years.

"I'm glad I know the truth," she said.

"Me, too." Audrey took a shuddering breath, as if trying to control herself. "If you need time…I understand."

Paige studied her mother's face. It had always been the same. Pinched, firm, unyielding. But over the years tiny lines had gathered around her mouth and the corners of her eyes. *None of us are getting any younger.*

She shook her head and shyly reached for her mom's hand. "I think we've wasted enough time, don't you?"

"Thank you, sweetheart." Audrey's fingers tightened around hers. They stayed that way until Victor made a coughing noise from the top of the staircase.

"It's okay," Audrey said in an unsteady voice. "It's safe to come in."

"You sure? I can always go back out."

Paige wiped away the tears and shook her head. "It's fine. Plus, you can't tease me with bacon and then not finish cooking."

"She's right. Us Taylors like our breakfast," Audrey seconded as he walked back in and hugged them both, before returning to the kitchen.

After they'd all finished eating, Paige grabbed a quick shower and headed downstairs to attack the most pressing things on her list. Her mind continued to replay her relationship with her father, but the pain had gone. If her mom hadn't been able to change his mind, there was nothing Paige could've done.

By the time she'd opened the doors, her lack of sleep was catching up with her, but she pushed it aside with the help of more coffee.

She reached for her phone and hit her ex-boss's number. She'd spent the better part of the week fruitlessly trying to get in contact with Meg Mitchell's publicist before accepting it was time to bite the bullet. That had been yesterday. This time Ellen actually answered.

"Hey, I'm pleased to get through. Did you listen to my messages?"

"No. That's what assistants are for," she said in a quelling voice. Paige gritted her teeth.

"Do you know who the publicist is for Meg Mitchell? I'm hoping to convince them to send her to my store for a signing."

Her ex-boss burst out into rapid-fire laughter. It went on for quite some time.

"My therapist was right. Humor really is good for the soul. If I'd known you were so funny, I wouldn't have fired you."

"You didn't fire me, I quit. And I'm not joking."

"Sweetie, you live in the middle of nowhere. Why would the hottest YA author in the world want to traipse over to that dreadful place?"

"Because it's not dreadful. It'll have novelty value."

And I have a fourteen-year-old girl desperate for it to happen.

"If you think for one moment I'm going to be the fool who suggests something like that, then you're crazy."

"Please, could you just help me out?"

There was silence, then Ellen let out a pained sigh. "Fine. Call Tiffany Attwood, but I swear if you mention my name you'll regret it. And when are you going to forget about this bookstore and come back?"

"We've been through this."

"Exactly," her boss said before the line went dead.

She swore at her phone before going in search for the publicist's contact details. As expected, she didn't answer her phone to an unknown number. Paige fired off an impressive email, filled with all the charming and novel reasons why a signing at such a small store could actually be a great thing. Then she crossed her fingers and hit send

An email pinged back almost immediately.

It was polite and filled with all the words Paige once used, but in a nutshell, it was a resounding no. With chocolate sprinkles on top. No wonder Ellen had been amused. Was it so bad she'd been hoping for a miracle? After all, the last two months had shown that the most unlikely things were possible.

Finding a place where she belonged.

Meeting a man who did wicked things to her pulse.

Falling for his family almost as much as she'd fallen for him.

She called the publicist to give it one last shot, but this time she didn't even warrant the flowery language. It was just a straight no. Damn. She rubbed her chin. Now she had to figure out a way to break the bad news.

• • •

"Hey." Kira poked her head into the office later that afternoon. Normally her cheeks were rosy, thanks to her habit of running from school to the bookstore, but today they were drawn and pale. "Have you heard back?"

Her body tensed. As much as she wanted to lie and protect her, it never worked.

"I'm sorry. It's not going to happen."

"Oh." The color faded from her mossy eyes, and her mouth trembled as she hugged the *Desert Witches of Numara* close to her chest. "That's okay."

Paige bit her lip. "I really wish I had a different answer for you. But hey, the first day the movie comes out we could go together. My treat. As much popcorn as you can eat."

"That'd be really cool." Kira smiled, though it didn't reach her eyes. After a short silence, the young girl coughed, her face solemn. "Can I ask you something?"

"Of course."

"What was it like growing up with your mom?" Kira asked. Paige stiffened. It wasn't the question she'd been expecting, though it wasn't difficult to figure out why Kira was asking. Growing up without a mom, even when she was surrounded by a family who loved her? *Some hurts never go away.*

"We didn't always get on, but she tried her best," Paige answered. "She was pretty sad about my dad leaving. She wanted him to come back."

"Did you?" Her eyes were wide, and Paige stiffened.

Did I?

It was a question she'd never dared ask herself, because if it'd happened, her whole life might've been different. *My family might've been different.* Then again, now she knew the truth, if he'd stayed, things could've been worse.

"It's complicated. I was mad at him. Really mad. But he was still my dad. The thing is he never wanted to come back, which took the decision out of my hands."

Kira was silent, as if considering the words. "What did you do?"

"I focused on the things I could control. Like doing well in school and working a part-time job, just like you. Oh, and I read a lot of books," she said truthfully. Kira's face had taken on a waxy hue. "Hey, are you okay? You look a little pale. I could call your dad to pick you up if you want."

"No. I'm fine." She pushed a book back in place and started to straighten everything up, just like she did most days.

She opened her mouth to reply, but before she could, James's ringtone sang out. As ever, his timing was the worst.

"Tell me if you change your mind," she quickly said before answering his call and wishing yet again she'd managed to get that extra cup of coffee. It was turning out to be a very long day.

Chapter Seventeen

"Saying yes to things you don't want is like looking at a menu and ordering a bowl of rusty nails with a side serving of broken glass. Saying no will reclaim your life and let you order all the dessert you want." **Just Say No**

"It's a perfect day for fishing," Audrey declared—a vision in khaki clothing and pink hair—as they walked to the car. Paige wasn't quite sure her mom knew what constituted a good fishing day, but it was true the November sky was pale shades of blue, dripping and melting into each other, while the breeze had dropped, turning the weather mild, despite the carpet of golden brown leaves.

"It certainly is beautiful," she agreed, glancing back at the CLOSED sign on the door. Laney and Sam had assured her there was no point staying open on a Saturday when everyone would be down at the old marina taking part.

They were right. The normally empty parking lot was filled with vehicles. Marc, the vet, was wearing a High Visibility vest and inexpertly directing traffic farther up the road. She followed the trail of cars snaking in front of her.

All these people had turned up to support Luke's vision for the town.

To support him.

She eventually found a spot and helped Audrey carry the ludicrously long fishing pole and new tackle box as they followed the crowd of people to the sign-in tent. Several other tents had been set up with food, drinks, and souvenirs to help increase the donations.

A few people nodded and smiled as they walked past. She returned the greetings, but her eyes continued to search for one in particular.

There he was.

Sunglasses covered his eyes, and strands of dark hair carelessly fell across his forehead as he chatted with several volunteers all wearing bright purple sweaters with the competition logo printed on the front. As she got closer, he lifted up the glasses, silver eyes twinkling.

"Oh my." Audrey sighed. "He really is very good looking. No wonder you like him."

"W-why would you say that?" Despite their growing bond, she hadn't mentioned her fledgling relationship to anyone.

"Let's just say I recognize the symptoms." Her mom gave her a gentle smile, then took a piece of paper out of her pocket. "If you don't mind, could you give him this? It's the tile and fixture selection he's been waiting on. Victor sat down last night to do them."

"I had a very good incentive." Victor emerged from the crowd, his wide smile leaving her in no doubt just what the incentive was. He promptly took the fishing rod and tackle box and wrapped Audrey up in a giant hug.

Paige decided to leave them to it.

"You made it. I hope you brought your sea legs," Luke

said when she reached him. His shoulder brushed hers, sending a trail of flames racing down her arm. She swallowed to cover the effect he had on her. And to stop herself from doing anything too scandalous in public.

"I can't say I did." She glanced at the rows of small boats all lined against the shore waiting to take everyone out. No one had said anything about boats. Then again, she should've guessed. After all, that was how to get to the fish. She glanced at his clipboard. "I don't suppose you need any more volunteers. Preferably with things that don't involve floating on water?"

"That can be arranged," he said. "Besides, you've suffered enough by cleaning Robert. I suppose we should go easy on new recruits."

"It wasn't all bad," she said, longing to step into his arms. Press her mouth to the shadowy curve of his neck. To ignite the heat between them. "By the way, Audrey wanted me to give you this."

His had grazed hers as she passed the list over, and a smile played around his mouth. *It's not just me.*

"Clearly I can't underestimate the Taylor women. Audrey's a miracle worker." He unfolded the paper and let out a long whistle.

"I'm guessing you don't want to know the secret to her success," Paige teased.

"Unless you want to replicate it." His eyes gleamed with amusement, sending an avalanche of illicit thoughts crashing through her.

"What did you have in mind?" she whispered, as the heat between them increased, dragging her closer, like a physical, tangible thing.

"Well, let's see," he said, his voice low, like a caress against her skin. She shivered in anticipation. "First we could—"

"Luke. We have a problem." Stu appeared, followed by

several locals all bickering about the use of illegal flies. He gave an apologetic smile before clapping his brother-in-law on the back.

"No problems, only solutions," he said in a bright voice, before his gaze caught hers. "Can we put this *conversation* on hold?"

She nodded, not trusting herself to speak.

"If you need a minute, I can wait," Stu said, not seeming to read the subtext. Which was probably a good thing.

"No, you stay. I'll go help Olive, and...I'll see you later?"

"You better believe it," he said, and with a brush of his hand on her arm, he was gone. Paige tried to calm herself down before heading to the sign-in booth and got to work.

The day was a blur of activity, and it wasn't until the prize giving was about to start that her stomach growled. There was no sign of Luke, but the barbeque tent where Sam and Patsy were working the grills was still going strong. Tangy spices drifted over, turning her tastes buds into a quivering mess.

She smiled to some customers as she went, threading her way past several parked trucks that belonged to the volunteers.

"Hey." Melanie appeared in front of her. Her glossy brown hair was hanging down her back as if she'd just walked out of Victor's salon rather than spent the day in a boat catching fish. She didn't appear to be armed and dangerous.

"Hi." She returned the greeting cautiously, still not quite sure where they stood.

"Relax, I'm not here to bite your head off. Even though this is Luke's event, I'm the head of St. Clair's Volunteer Association. I wanted to say thanks for your hard work today. And for cleaning Robert. There's beer and burgers in the main tent after it's all finished. You should come."

"Oh." She widened her eyes. "Sure. That sounds great."

"Don't look so surprised. I'm not always a bitch," Melanie

said with a rueful smile. "And thanks for not mentioning what I told you to anyone."

"No worries," she said before wrinkling her nose. "Though, how do you know I didn't?"

"This is St. Clair. If you'd let the cat out of the bag, I would've heard."

"Did the book help?" Paige asked, trying not to stare at Luke, who'd just emerged from the judging tent. Somewhere along the way he'd obtained a pink cap with a unicorn on it. There were a few fishing rods in one hand, several purses draped over his shoulder, and a couple of stuffed animals under his other arm.

He was a walking lost property.

And boy did he look good doing it.

"Hell, yes. I've been Jacob Carmichael-free for seven days now." She held up her hands in victory, before seeming to notice the direction of Paige's gaze. "Looks like I'm not the only one dealing with a Carmichael. Anything you want to tell me?"

Heat sizzled her skin, but she quickly shook her head. She wasn't ready to share it without anyone yet. *Not until we know what it is.*

"Nope."

"Hmmm." Melanie didn't appear convinced, but before she could probe, Luke strode toward the makeshift stage, stopping only to deposit the lost items with Olive, who was at a nearby table. Up on the stage was a collection of trophies, glistening in the afternoon sun.

"Okay," he said by way of greeting as he stepped up to the microphone. "Let's hand out the prizes. First up we have—"

"Before you start, I have something I want to say," Jacob cut in as he strode onto the stage and plucked the microphone from the stand. The jovial expression he normally wore was gone, and his eyes were dark and serious. Paige gulped, and next to her Melanie stiffened.

"What the hell?" the other girl muttered as Jacob scanned the crowd before signaling in on her. The crowd went silent, all watching as Luke shot his brother a questioning stare, but Jacob seemed to dismiss it with a shake of his head.

"You see, folks, I screwed up. Big time. I know I've screwed up before, and hell, I probably will again. But this time the difference is I know what I did and I'm damn sorry about it."

"Jacob, are you sure?" Luke hissed, but it was picked up by the microphone for everyone to hear.

"Yes, brother. I'm sure," Jacob said as he pointed his finger to where Paige and Melanie were standing. "Mel. I'm sorry. Forgive me. This is for you."

Then, without another word he launched into song.

His voice was a nice tenor, warm with lots of strength, and the crowd swayed back and forth to the melody.

"Without you, time makes no sense. Without you, my life's incomplete. Without you, I'm not myself."

Paige had never heard the song before, but it was clear from Melanie's face that she knew it. As did most of the audience, who sang along on the chorus. And when it was finished, everyone broke into rapturous applause.

The only person who wasn't clapping was Melanie.

"You okay?" Paige murmured as the crowd parted for Jacob to walk toward her, a hopeful gleam in his eyes.

"Not even a little bit," Melanie growled. "How could he do this to me?"

Then without another word, she turned and ran. Paige gulped as Jacob's face flickered with pain, while everyone stared at him. The cat was definitely out of the bag now.

• • •

"It wasn't that bad," Luke said, and it was true. His brother had a great voice, and he'd sung a song that the whole town knew because it had been written by a St. Clair local back in the fifties, and then been a surprise national hit when a country singer had done a cover of it.

"You obviously weren't listening." Jacob let out a strangled groan in response. "That's it. I'm done with love."

"No, you're not." Trina appeared in the corner of the sponsor's tent and gave him a hug. "It's your first time out in the ring, you just lost your bearings."

"Lost my bearings?" Jacob blinked. "I crashed and burned. It was carnage. I mean, everyone saw me. More to the point, everyone saw Melanie ice me. She just turned and left."

"So what?" Trina shrugged. "Everyone saw you that time you made out with Jennie Tobias in tenth grade while you were wearing a chicken costume. You didn't care about that."

"It's different."

"No, it's not. Now get your stuff and come with me."

"Um, no. I have beer to drink. Sorrows to drown."

Trina shook her head. "That's where you're wrong. You're coming home with us, where you and Stu will do manly things, like finish building my pizza oven. Oh, and Luke, I know you've got to finish up here, but can Kira sleep over? I kind of promised her a night of girly movies and pedicures."

"Did you ask him?" Kira bounded up, as if on cue.

"I did." Trina nodded, and Kira turned to him, her eyes widening like a puppy dog looking for a new toy.

"Can I, Dad? Please, please, please."

He tilted his head, uncertain. Ever since he'd told his daughter about Joanne, he'd been on tenterhooks, searching for clues of how she was coping. Determined to spend as much time with her as she needed. But as she danced from foot to foot, her hands clasped together in a pleading motion, his worry lessened.

And admit it. You want to spend time with Paige.

Correction. You want to drag her into bed and rip off her clothing.

He swallowed. His plans to take it slowly turned to ash every time he was near her.

Like earlier. When all he'd wanted to do was lose himself in her mouth, regardless of the fact they were surrounded by the entire town.

"Sure." He nodded before turning to Trina. "You think you can handle both of them? I know Kira won't be a problem, but this one—"

"Hey, I'm right here," Jacob protested before letting out a strangled sigh. "And I warn you, Trina, if I can't have booze, I'll have to eat my feelings with cookie dough."

"That I can do," she said before they all made their goodbyes and headed out of the tent. He began to stack the chairs when Paige walked over, balancing two hot dogs.

Her blonde hair was hanging over one shoulder in a heavy braid, and her mouth was soft. Like she'd been laughing. His appetite increased, but it wasn't for food.

"Hey," she said. "I wasn't sure if you'd eaten."

"I haven't," he said, taking the food and resisting the urge to plant a row of kisses along her jaw and down to the porcelain arch of her throat. It was getting harder to resist the pull. "I saw you going after Melanie. How's she doing?"

A frowned swept across her face. "I couldn't catch her. She's a fast runner. How's Jacob?"

"He's convinced it's the end of the world, but Trina thinks it'll be the making of him. Usually, he's the one running away. Right now, Stu's keeping him busy building a pizza oven."

"Poor guy. Putting yourself out there is hard."

He ran a hand through his hair. "Yeah, I probably didn't help. I told him to go big. I just didn't expect him to go *that* big."

"I thought it was sweet."

"I'm not sure sweet's what he was going for," Luke said, suddenly not wanting to talk about his brother. Or anything else. He stepped closer to her. Hints of vanilla still clung to her, along with sunscreen. He trailed a finger along her arm. She shivered in response, her mouth parting. "I've had enough of this place for one day. Want to get out of here?"

"What did you have in mind?"

"We could go back to my place."

Uncertainty flickered in her eyes. Vulnerability. She studied her shoes, refusing to look up at him. "What about Kira? Won't that—"

"She's staying with Trina for the night."

"Oh." It was almost like a sigh, and when she looked up at him, the uncertainty had gone, and a shy smile played at her lips. "In that case, I thought you'd never ask."

· · ·

Paige stirred as unfamiliar cotton sheets brushed her skin. Next to her, Luke's breathing was soft and even. *I'm in his house. In his bed.* Unbidden, Jacob's grand gesture to Melanie crashed into her mind. If it had been Luke doing it to her, would she have run or stayed?

Stayed.

A smile crept onto her mouth as her hands slid across his bare flesh. The warmth of his skin caused her pulse to quicken.

What had she been scared of?

Luke wasn't Patrick.

Wasn't her father.

"Morning," he murmured and twisted to face her. His gray eyes were hooded, groggy with sleep, but a hint of a smile danced on his lips.

"Morning," she whispered back as his hand caught hers, dragging her toward him. Heat pulsed between them, broken only by the dull buzz of his phone. Indecision skittered across his face before he elbowed himself up.

"I'd better get it," he said before fumbling for the handset. "Trina, hey. Everything—wait…slow down. I can't understand what you're saying."

His face turned a sickly green color, and his silver eyes darkened. The warm heat pooling in her body abruptly faded, like a switch had been flicked off.

His panic was palpable, like a banging drum that echoed out. Her own heart pounded in response.

"What's going on? Are you okay?"

"Kira's missing. Trina went to wake her for breakfast, but she was gone." The words were ripped from his throat. Dark, raw, and jagged.

A thousand questions flooded her mind, but she dismissed them all. There was only one thing that mattered.

"What do you need me to do?" She forced her voice to stay calm. To not make his agony even worse. But the dark shadows scratching at his face told her it was too late. His daughter was missing.

His worst nightmare had come to life.

"Can you think of anything she said to you in the last couple of days? Any indication she might want to run away?" He climbed from the bed, stepping into yesterday's clothes.

"Run away?" Her brows furrowed together as she stood up and searched for her own clothes. "She might just be with one of her friends. Hailey or Maxie."

"Trina's already spoken to them. She's not there, and neither of the girls have heard from her." He swallowed, his shoulders stiff and jaw clenched. It was like he was going into battle.

"Joanne's back in the country and wants to see her again. Kira didn't take the news well."

His ex-wife was back in touch?

And he didn't say a word.

He began to prowl, as if there were a feral animal inside, trying to escape.

"If you can think of anything. Please, Paige."

"I really don't—" She let out a gasp. "The other day she was asking me about what it was like growing up, and did I miss my dad. I just thought it was to help her make sense of not having her mom in her life."

"What did you tell her?"

"Not much. Just that there were things I couldn't control, so I focused on things I could control. Like doing well in school. Are you sure she's run away?"

"Trina found a note saying not to worry," he said, his voice filled with anguish. "I never should've let her stay over. I never should've—"

He didn't say the words, but he didn't need to. Paige could fill in the blanks.

He never should've let himself get distracted.

Luke stalked to one side and dragged his phone up to his ear. He made call after call, his jaw clenched, muscles bunched. Once he was finished, he stalked back.

"I've just spoken to the sheriff. Normally they wouldn't do a missing person's report, but they're putting everyone on it. I need to find my daughter, and I need to find her now."

Chapter Eighteen

"Sometimes your no likes to hide in plain sight. And sometimes it likes to bury itself under a mound of crap. It's time to start digging." **Just Say No**

Luke stalked along the rocky shore of the harbor, sweat gathering on his forehead while the threatened rain began in earnest.

Somewhere behind him, Jacob was smoothly talking to the volunteers, keeping everything calm and under control. Not that Luke cared. *Please be safe.* It'd been the only thing keeping him sane in the last hour as the entire town stepped in to find his daughter. The note she'd scrawled blazed across his eyes, leaving him dizzy, like he'd been punched.

I'm okay. Don't worry.

And the change jar he kept for her was empty, along with money she'd been saving to buy more books.

His phone buzzed, sending his heart racing as he stared at the screen. Not Kira. Joanne. He'd called earlier, but there hadn't been an answer, and he'd been forced to leave a message.

"I'm on my way," were her first words.

"No," he snapped, before he could stop himself. He winced. "Sorry. That came out wrong. But you need to stay there just in case she's headed to Portland."

"But how would she even know where I lived?" Her voice was tight, and shaking.

How do kids know anything?

"If she wanted to find your address, she could," he simply said. A small sob came from the other end of the call, gathering momentum like a breached dam.

"Find her, Luke. Please. I know I don't deserve to have the right to care, but please, find her."

His anger evaporated as the rain pounded against his skin.

The overwhelming sense of hopelessness hammering at his skull from the moment he'd discovered Kira was missing didn't let up. Was this what Joanne had been going through for ten years?

"I swear I will. Just keep your phone nearby, I'll stay in touch."

"Thank you," she whispered. He finished the call and glanced at Jacob, who was busy giving directions to everyone. When his younger brother wanted to, he could be quite the man. He started jogging to the far end of the shore when his phone buzzed again.

It was Sam.

"Hey." His voice was curt.

"Luke. It's okay. She's safe. I know where she is," she said in a rush.

She was safe? Found? Okay?

A surging wave of relief slammed into his chest. Shaking his throat. Sending his pulse into an excitable frenzy.

He leaned forward to steady himself. To push away the black, numbing pain that had been filling his body.

She was safe.

"Where is she? Tell me everything." His voice was a growl as he pressed the phone to his ear.

"She's at Patterson Falls bus depot."

"What the hell?" The words exploded out of him. "That's fifty miles away. How do you know she's there?"

"Cal's with her. And before you go berserk, he caught her climbing onto a bus headed for Seattle. I don't know any details apart from the fact he convinced her to get off at Patterson Falls. He texted me as soon as he could."

"I'm leaving now. Sam, thank you. And can you please let Trina, Jacob, and Olive know."

Then, without waiting for a reply, he sprinted the rest of the way to his truck and slammed it into gear. He needed to get to his daughter as fast as he could.

. . .

After what seemed like an eternity, the bus station came into view. The rain had turned to drizzle, and through the misty window a tiny figure was visible. His jaw loosened.

Kira. There she was. Her caramel hair pulled back in a ponytail and her favorite purse hanging from her shoulder. Next to her was Cal. An unmoving statue, glaring at anyone who even looked their way. Paige had been right about the kid.

He crushed the thought down.

No more thinking about Paige. No more thinking about anything that wasn't his daughter. He spun into the parking lot and slammed to a stop. Kira's eyes widened as he climbed out, and for just a second, she looked unsure before she came flying into his arms, sobbing.

"Don't be mad. I didn't mean to make you mad. I just wanted to focus on something I could control." The crying got louder as he tightened his arms around her. "I wanted to get my book signed."

His jaw flickered.

On the frantic drive over, Sam had gleaned more information and relayed it back to him. Kira had been heading to Seattle to meet her favorite author. Something she'd decided to do after discovering Paige couldn't get the author to come to St. Clair.

He swallowed it down. Whatever reason she'd hopped on the bus was a conversation for another day.

"Hey, I'm not mad," he soothed her. Just like he'd done so many times over the years. "All I care about is you. I've been going out of my mind."

She finally stopped crying and wriggled back. Her faced was tear stained. "B-but I left a note."

"A note that didn't make sense," Cal spoke for the first time. His voice was surprisingly musical. Underneath the hoodie, his blue eyes were alert, in sharp contrast with his hunched shoulders. Then, as if realizing he was being scrutinized, he shrugged. "Sorry. But she told me what she wrote, and I figured you'd be freaking out."

Understatement.

Luke was pretty sure he'd gained about ten years worth of gray hairs. He held out his hand to Cal. "Thanks for taking care of her."

"No biggie. Seemed like the right thing to do."

"Yeah, but you still haven't said what you were doing at the bus station?" Kira frowned, which resulted in Cal returning to his monosyllabic answers until Sam pulled up on in the old car she'd been driving for as long as he could remember.

"Not quite sure how you beat me here, but I'm pleased

everything's okay."

"We're all good." He nodded, his arm still firmly around Kira's slim shoulder. It would be a long time before he'd be letting her out of his sight again. "Thanks to Cal."

"Yes, well, that's going to be another conversation entirely." Sam's lips narrowed as she turned to her nephew. Apparently, Kira wasn't the only one wondering what he'd been doing at the St. Clair bus station in the first place.

His cell phone rang. It was Joanne. He'd been keeping her updated the entire time, but obviously the waiting had been too much. Can't say he blamed her. He turned to Kira.

"This is your mom. I need to let her know you're okay. But you don't need to talk if you don't want."

"A-actually." She looked up, her emerald eyes filled with tears. "I guess I could say hi."

His chest hammered. A few days ago, his biggest fear was she'd want to spend too much time with Joanne, but now it didn't matter.

"She'd like that a lot." He quickly filled Joanne in and waited for her to compose herself before passing it to Kira.

Sam squeezed his hand. "We're going to head off."

"Okay," he said as Cal sauntered over to the car, shoulders hunched. "Don't be too hard on him. Whatever he was planning, he didn't go through with it. And for that I'm grateful."

Sam nodded before frowning. "Try not to blame Paige too much. She had no idea this would happen."

"I don't," he said truthfully.

There was only one person to blame. *Me.* He'd taken his focus away from Kira and had almost paid the price. His attention had been swayed by someone from out of town.

It couldn't happen again.

• • •

Paige hitched in a breath as he walked up the path. His stride was slow, and measured, his face ashen white. She didn't need to be a mind reader to know what he was thinking.

Who he was blaming.

He had every right to.

Out of all the places she imagined Kira might've been, heading off to Seattle to see Meg Mitchell wasn't one of them. It never would've happened if she'd succeeded in getting the author to come to St. Clair. Or if she hadn't gotten involved with Luke. Inadvertently forcing him to split his attention.

She stepped out of the store and sat down on the top step, bracing herself for what was to come.

"How is she?" She barely dared to ask. Sam had called to let her know Kira was safely back at the house, being fussed over by everyone, and Trina had sent her a couple of text messages, as had Jacob. The only person she hadn't heard from was Luke.

"She's okay. A bit tired and confused. Upset she didn't get to the book signing." He lowered himself onto the step below her.

"About that." Paige wrapped her arms tightly around her chest. "I just want you to know how sorry I am. I had no idea she'd even think of going to it."

Guilt caught in her throat.

If anything had happened to her…

"Don't." He held his hand up to stop her. "This isn't your fault, it's mine. I let myself get distracted. And not just with last night. Every time we're together, I lose all reason. Paige, I'm sorry. I can't afford to do that again. My daughter has to come first. I…hell—" He broke off, his face drained. "What I want doesn't matter."

She willed herself not to cry. Besides, it was her fault, too.

I should've stuck to the plan.

Say no when I want to say yes.

"I understand. I really do," she said. She'd grown up with a father who never even gave her a second thought. Who pretended she didn't exist. The irony of falling for a guy who couldn't be with her for that very reason wasn't lost on her.

Then there was the more painful realization.

His ex-wife was back. He's seen her. Spoken to her, and never said a word.

Because I was only ever a distraction.

"I just hope my family does. We weren't as discreet as we thought we'd been. I know they were hoping it'd work." He leaned forward, molten silver eyes catching hers. Tiny prisms of gray flashed as his mouth twisted into an apologetic line. He grazed her hand with his. It was featherlight, but seared into her skin more deeply than fire.

"They'll come around," she said.

"You don't know my family," he said, and something in her twisted. Because she did know his family. And she adored them. With their easy banter and their fierce loyalty. It made her long for things she hadn't even known existed. "I'd better get back. Joanne arrived last night. She's staying at the bed and breakfast. Today the three of us are going to sit down and discuss things properly. It's what I should've done right from the beginning."

"Tell Kira I'm pleased she's okay."

"I will." He stood up.

The dull light was stark as he went. So much of their relationship had taken place at night, backdropped by a magical black veil. But now in the harsh light of day, Paige could see it for what it really was.

Something between two people who should've known better.

Her head pounded, and her body was weighed down with stones.

As he drove away, she was joined on the step by Dr. Penny

Groves, resplendent in an orange power suit not unlike the ones Paige had worn on her cross-country trip.

Oh, sweetie. I'm sorry. I guess this is the other shoe dropping.

Paige closed her eyes and didn't even try and stop the tears from falling.

Chapter Nineteen

"You're never too old to wear rhinestones, drink whisky, or mess up." **Just Say No**

"I think it's fair to say people have heard." Her words echoed like a gunshot through a desolate, deserted canyon. She still had a similar amount of sales, but it wasn't the same. The smiles weren't as big, the chatter not as genuine. And it seemed like her B.S. membership had been permanently revoked.

"They'll come back around," Laney said from her perch on the counter, her bright face tight. Despite Jacob's apology for leading her on, it was obvious it had hurt.

Something I know a thing or two about.

"Maybe," she said, even though it was a lie.

Luke said he didn't blame her, but it was hard to believe.

She'd been the one to swoop in and give his daughter big ideas. That it was possible to meet her favorite author, even if that meant catching a bus on her own without telling anyone. And the rest of the town agreed. It was like stepping into a time machine, going back to her first week in St. Clair when Diana's legacy had still hung heavy around her neck.

But even Diana hadn't screwed up this big.

"I mean it, Paige. You're going to be okay. Though, I'm sorry about Luke."

"Don't be. I'm just going to file it in the *I Shoulda Woulda Coulda Said No* folder," she said, referring to Dr. Penny Groves's solution to when you messed up. Last night she'd sat the Belles down with a bottle of wine and told them what had happened. Though, they'd both confessed to having a pretty good idea of what had been going on.

I really need to work on my poker face.

"I'll add Jacob Carmichael in there." Laney sighed and slid off the counter, still managing to look ladylike in the process. "From now on I'm a man-free zone."

"If it weren't ten in the morning, I'd drink to that." She gave Laney a hug and walked her to the door. At least her friend's business was still thriving. The window of her store was an explosion of burnt oranges, sierra reds, and vibrant saffron, against a waterfall of waxy ivy leaves. And she had an influx of Thanksgiving orders to be filled in the next two weeks.

Unlike me.

Paige was the opposite of thriving. In fact, she was as far from thriving as was possible. She'd bumped into Luke twice, and both times it had been painfully awkward. Especially the second, when he'd been walking out of Patsy's with his family. It had given her a new understanding of hell.

Which is why I need to stop thinking about it.

The rest of the day dragged its heels, mocking her by slowing the minutes down, making each one last an eternity. A couple of stray tourists wandered in but seemed to pick up on the unspoken consensus that her store was no longer fun.

She didn't even bother to move when the doorbell next went.

"Hey, Paige."

"Kira?" Her head shot up. It had been eight days since the drama. Eight days since Trina had been the one to call and say Kira needed a bit of time to adjust to seeing Joanne. She'd tried to reassure Paige, but the subtext was clear. *It's your fault.* "W-what are you doing here? Does your dad know?"

"He's cool. I told him I wanted to see you. I hope you're not mad at me?"

"Mad at you?" Tears threatened to leak out of the corner of her eyes. "Oh, honey, I'm the one who messed up. I know how much you wanted to meet Meg Mitchell, but if I ever thought you'd do something so dangerous—"

"I know." She let out a small sigh. "Dad's told me loads of times how bad it was. I didn't mean to make everyone worry. Though it was pretty awesome that I sat on the bus with Cal for an entire hour."

"Definitely a bonus, though hopefully you don't need to be on a bus to replicate it."

"Actually, he sits with me at lunch. You should see Hailey and Maxie's faces!" Kira giggled as she began to automatically neaten up the greeting cards.

"I bet they're both impressed." She reached under the counter for the parcel that had arrived yesterday. "I've got something for you."

"Really?" Kira said as she carefully peeled back the brown paper to reveal book one in the *Desert Witches of Numara* series. She flipped open the pages, and her eyes brimmed with joy. "It's signed. To me. *'Dear Kira, Thank you for being my number one fan. Love, Meg Mitchell.'* And there's two love hearts." Her fingers traced the writing, as though checking it was real. Her entire face shone with excitement.

"I'm pleased you like it." Warmth filled her chest. She could never make it up to Luke, but at least she could give his daughter what she'd wanted.

"Like it? I love it!" Kira hugged the book. "How did you get it? D-did you meet her?"

She shook her head. "Sadly, no. But I made a few calls and eventually spoke to her. She was definitely one of the nicest authors I've talked with."

"You spoke to her?"

"I did. Oh, and she said to tell you she's had a sneak peek at the movie and Trent Burton is *perfect* as Aaron."

"She. Did. Not." Her eyes were wide as saucers.

"Yeah, she did." Again, Paige couldn't help but smile at Kira's endless enthusiasm. It bounced off the walls and filled all the spaces with color and joy. *Is that what I've been missing?*

"I've hung out with my mom a few times," she suddenly said, and Paige's heart began to ache. Even being on the outside, it was impossible not to know Joanne had been staying in town, getting to know her daughter again. "She's been pretty nice. Though she cries a lot."

"I imagine the crying will stop after a while," she said. An unexpected wave of sympathy for the other woman washed through her. She'd been doing her fair share of crying in the last week, too.

"That's what Gigi says. I was still kind of mad at her, but then I remembered what you said about your dad. You never had a choice. So, yeah."

"Oh." She clamped down on her tongue to stop the unwanted tears from once again falling. "That's great. You deserve it."

"Thanks." The young girl gave her a wobbly smile as her phone beeped. She let out a pained sigh. "I've gotta go. That's Jacob checking up on me. They're all worried I'm going to run away again—which, for the record, I wasn't even running away, I was running *to* something."

"I'm sure they'll ease up." She followed Kira out the door, though she wasn't sure. It would be quite some time before all the people in the young girl's life recovered from the shock of not knowing where she was.

"I hope so. And hey, don't forget you're taking me to the movie when it comes out. And the popcorn."

"I won't." Paige crossed her fingers as it hit her just how impossible life in St. Clair would be from now on.

The idea of not being with Luke again—especially naked Luke—had been unbearable, but she'd assumed in time she'd get used to it. Like a limp (or the kind of open-heart surgery a person never *ever* recovered from). And that having the Belles, Audrey, and Victor would be enough.

But now it dawned on her.

It wasn't just him, it was his entire family. They were the fabric of the town. Which meant she'd see them all the time but not really be part of their lives. Because she didn't belong there. She never had. All the things she'd tried just to make herself fit in. To try and convince people she was like them. It hadn't been enough.

She was still an outsider. One who'd put Kira in jeopardy. One who'd fallen for a guy who couldn't give her what she wanted. Again.

She picked up her phone and scrolled down to Ellen's number. Then she sent her a text.

About that job. When can I start?

• • •

"Dad, she's here. I just need to get my books, then I'm ready."

"You're going to lunch, how many books do you need?" Luke said as his daughter half carried, half dragged a large bag behind her.

"I wanted to show Mom what I've been reading." She still faltered when she said 'mom', like she was trying out a new word and wasn't quite sure if it was right. That she was even open to it filled him with pride. Kira was fearless. No two ways about it. He picked up the bag and pretended to sag under the weight, which earned him an eye roll. "Exaggerate much?"

"Hey, I'm not the one with—" He peered in and frowned. "Three copies of the same book?"

"One's the signed edition, one's a paperback, and one's a hardback," she explained in a slow, patient voice. "Oh, and I just remembered I wanted to show her my Harry Potter collection. I'll be right back."

He carried the bag out to where Joanne was leaning against the car. She still refused to come into the house she'd once lived in. In a way, he was pleased. Not quite sure he was ready for that yet.

Correction. I'm not ready for any of this.

The first few visits had been with Trina and Stu tagging along, to make sure Kira was okay. But this was the second visit without them. He tried not to show his concern as he reached them.

Owen's arm was protectively wrapped around Joanne's shoulders. Color had returned to her face, and it looked like she'd put on some much-needed weight.

"She's just getting a few more books," he said by way of greeting as he opened the back door and deposited the first bag in. "You might've noticed she loves reading?"

"She did mention it once or twice." A wry smile danced around her mouth. "She's been talking about the bookstore a lot. And Paige. Is that someone—"

"No," he cut her off. He wasn't prepared to talk to himself about Paige, he was hardly going to do it with his ex-wife.

Besides, what's done was done.

And it was for the best.

For Kira.

Though, he'd been right about his family. His siblings had grilled him endlessly about it, while Olive had just shrugged and handed him yet another skein of wool to roll. He didn't know which had been worse. Scrap that.

Worse was Paige's face.

Resignation.

She'd known as well as he had it was the right thing to do. If only the right thing wasn't so damn hellish.

"Sorry, I didn't mean to pry."

"It's okay." He shrugged it off. Besides, he was getting used to being surrounded by people who pried.

A phone rang, and Owen answered it.

"I've got to take this," he apologized, stepping away from them both.

"He's being doing locum work, but now he's applying for a permanent job. We both are," Joanne explained, her voice cautious. "When we got back, we weren't sure if...well...if it would go well." A choking sound came from her throat. "Thank you for trusting me, Luke."

"I'm not sure I do." He leaned against the car.

"You do." She turned to him, her mouth in a serious line. "Or else I wouldn't be here. You're a lot nicer guy than you give yourself credit for."

"I can't be that nice." The words were out before he could stop them. The agonizing knowledge that'd been tormenting him for the last two weeks. "If I'm so great, then why couldn't you share your darkness with me? Let me help you? Hell, even tell me what was going on?"

The silence throbbed and flickered like an un-tuned channel.

"I couldn't share it with myself—I wouldn't even admit anything was wrong, so please don't keep blaming yourself. I was the one who didn't let you in, and I'll never stop being sorry about that."

He swallowed as Kira came racing out of the house, with yet another bag even larger than the last.

"I'm ready," she yelled before coming to a halt in front of them. "Hey, Mom."

"Hey yourself." Joanne's smile was pure brilliance. Transforming her face and putting back the softness, reminding him of the woman he'd once loved. And once hated. He was in neither place now, but as her words played in his mind, there was a chance there might be room for friendship. With Kira as their common link.

• • •

"No."

"What do you mean, no?" Paige said as Melanie shook her head. Dusty curls fell around her shoulder like something out of a hair advertisement. She was attractive at the best times, but when she smiled it was a whole other level. "Are you teasing me about the book?"

"I loved that book. I actually need to order a few more copies from you. I'm giving it to people for Christmas." Melanie upped the wattage on her smile as she stood at her front door. It was a sweet house, six blocks away from the store and with a large garden and picket fence.

"Then I don't understand. You told me that this town would crack me and when it did, you'd be standing here with a check. Well, here I am. You win. Consider me cracked. I'm heading back to New York."

To a job I hate, and a town that suddenly seems far too large.
None of which was the point.

Her decision was made.

Audrey and Victor had been surprisingly supportive, promising to come and visit as often as possible. Ellen had already started barking long-distance orders at her, as if she'd never left. All she needed was to sell the bookstore and organize the removal guys to collect her stuff. Then she'd have to buy a few more power suits to make up for the ones she ditched, and her transformation back to her old self would be complete.

Like it had never happened.

Except apparently selling the bookstore wasn't going to be as easy as she thought.

"I'm heading to Europe," Melanie said as she waved her arm for Paige to follow her inside. "Thanks to you."

"What did I do?" she asked before noticing the house was empty of furniture. "And don't you live with your mom?"

"God, you really are out of the loop." Melanie gave her a sympathetic smile. "My mom's gone to stay with my sister in L.A. for six months while I go traveling. With Jacob. We're putting all the furniture in storage and renting this place out while I'm gone. We leave just after Christmas, so I'll stay with him until then."

"Wait? What?" Paige sank down to the floor. Hopefully it would make her understand what was going on. "You got the book to help you say no to him. Then you said you loved the book. *And* you ran out on him at the Big Fish. What am I missing?"

"I did love the book, and I did say no to Jacob." Melanie sat cross-legged next to her, as Jacob suddenly wandered into the room wearing a pair of low-slung jeans and no shirt. Though, there was something different about him.

The restless energy that usually rolled off him was gone. He was calmer. Happier.

"But I refused to accept her no." He leaned forward and thoroughly kissed Melanie before giving Paige a shy smile. "Okay, there were also chocolates, flowers, and my famous pec display. I tell you that's the way to anyone's heart."

"The flowers and chocolates, yes. Pec display, no." Melanie shook her head, though it didn't stop her running her fingers over his broad chest. "He told me he wasn't going anywhere. That he'd rip the whole damn book up if it would help, it was so sexy. When Kira went missing, it was a real jolt. He said it was time for him to stop goofing around, and I should be his girlfriend. Real girlfriend."

"You guys are serious?"

"We are." Melanie's voice lost its teasing tone as she held up a delicate gold chain. "This belonged to his mom. He said it was the only way to prove he's changed. Well, that and suggesting we go traveling together."

"I know how much she's always wanted to see the world." Jacob's fingers interlaced with Melanie's, and she nestled into his shoulder.

"I'm sure we'll be back, but I don't know when," she added. "As much as I'd love to buy the store, I can't."

"Oh. Well, that's okay. And I'm happy for you. I really am." She instinctively gave Melanie's hand a little squeeze before Jacob dragged her into a three-way hug.

Everyone was getting what they wanted. Which was good. Seriously good.

If only it didn't remind her how badly her own happily ever after had gone.

"What are you going to do about the store?" Melanie frowned. "Because apart from me, you were the only person who showed any interest in it."

"I guess I just have to hope someone else out there's as desperate as I was." She sucked in a deep breath and tried not to think about just how rock bottom she'd hit.

"Paige," Melanie suddenly said. "I know I was a bitch when you first arrived, but I am sorry it hasn't worked. I really thought you were going to make it."

So did I. She plastered on a smile and walked out into the night. *So did I.*

• • •

That's a lot of shoes you have there. Is it to make you run away faster?

Paige didn't bother to answer as she dragged a suitcase from underneath the bed. Dr. Penny Groves had been bothering her all day with her one-liners and handy tips on how to get her life together.

They'd be handier if they actually worked.

She picked up the heels she'd been wearing the first day she'd met Luke, before quickly wrapping them in a shoe bag and tucking them away. To stop the memories from taking her places she didn't want to go. It had been like that all day as she packed and sorted. Audrey had swung by to help but had just left to meet Victor for a drink. She'd invited Paige to join them, but she'd refused.

If she was going to leave St. Clair, she needed to do it sooner rather than later.

Besides, just because Melanie didn't want to buy the store didn't mean her plans had to change. She'd already spoken with the original listing agent, who was swinging by tomorrow with a sign to put in the window.

You know I didn't expect you to give up so easily.

"That's because you clearly haven't examined my track record." She looked up, planning to throw a silver sandal at the good doctor. Instead, she was greeted to the sight of Olive standing in the bedroom doorway, a bemused expression dancing on her lips.

Her face heated. "I thought you were someone else. How did you even get in here?"

"Your mom was leaving as I pulled up. She said it was okay to come in. Who did you think I was?"

"Dr. Penny Groves." She sighed. It had been a long day. Too long to try and cover up her own brand of crazy.

"As in *the* Dr. Penny Groves?" The older woman's eyes were lively.

"That's the one. I might've been having a few imaginary conversations with her," Paige admitted, resisting the urge to laugh. *No wonder it hadn't worked out here.*

"Is that who advised you to sell up and leave?"

"You don't understand. I messed up everything. Poor Luke. His worst nightmares came true because of me," she said, not bothering to ask how Olive knew she was selling. This was St. Clair. Everybody knew.

"Nonsense. We all had a terrible scare, but Kira's safe, happy, and hopefully learned a lesson or two. His worst nightmare is none of those things. Now, I love my grandson and am damn proud of the man he's become. But he's not perfect. For the last ten years, he's been lying in a cocoon—praying that he doesn't grow wings."

"That's a very strange analogy." Paige wrinkled her nose as she cleared the suitcases off the sofa so they could sit.

"I admit it's not my best, but here's the thing, change comes to us all whether we like it or not. Luke can no more stay in his cocoon than Kira can keep being fourteen. To take all the blame is crazy. What happened wasn't your fault."

"I wish I could believe that. But they would've been better off if I'd never come to town."

"And what about you? Would you have been better off?"

"I—" She opened her mouth and then shut it again. Despite the last two weeks, it still couldn't take away from how happy she'd been in St. Clair. How right it felt to live there. "I keep trying to be part of this place, but it's not working. Community Patrol's no longer an option, and there's only so many times I can clean Robert."

"Sweetheart, do you think any of us were born with a

gold card declaring we belong here? The way we all fit in is by being who we are. Stop worrying about what you can't do and start doing what you do best. What makes you special?"

I'm excellent at falling for unavailable men.

Oh, and my ability to see imaginary authors is on point.

"The truth is I'm not special at anything."

"Really?" Olive raised an impressive eyebrow.

"It's true." She let out a tired breath as her phone pinged with a text. It'd be from Ellen. She'd already sent at least thirty about a cantankerous TV chef, and she suspected there would be plenty more to come. Well, for once it could wait. "Fine. The only thing I can do reasonably well is handle authors."

"So do that."

"I'm going to. That's the whole reason I'm moving back."

Okay, it was some of the reason.

"No." Olive shook her head. "I mean do that here."

"I tried, remember?" she protested. "With Meg Mitchell. And we all know how badly that failed."

"You tried once? How many people get things right the first time? You should've seen my first attempts at knitting. Disastrous. And the first year when I had to care for my three grandchildren after their mom left and my son died? It was messy. I'm talking tears, and snot, and door slamming messy. None of them wanted to be there, and I was far too old for the job. I failed so many times." Olive's green eyes shimmered with misty tears.

"I-I didn't know that." Paige's throat went dry.

"Show me a person who doesn't have a sad story in them." Olive patted her knee, her hand wrinkled and papery from a life lived and lessons learned. "If you want to stay here—if you truly want to feel like you belong—then stop asking what people want and start asking what you can give them. Don't be like Luke in his cocoon. Wake up. Start being you."

Oh. That's fantastic. Do you think I could use that for

my next book? Dr. Penny Groves appeared, notepad in hand. Then she wrinkled her nose in an apology. *Sorry. I can see you're having a moment.*

She blinked, and the doctor disappeared, but Olive was still sitting there, serene and wise, with just a hint of a smile around her mouth.

Her heart hammered.

Start being me.

It was both giddy and terrifying.

She'd spent so long pleasing other people. Her mom. Her boss. Her ex-fiancé. And yet if she didn't start pleasing herself, what was the alternative?

Going back to the old life I hated. The one I was desperate to leave.

A spark of hope nudged her, but it was dampened by the question that'd plagued her every minute of every day.

"What if he never forgives me?"

"There's nothing to forgive. Luke's problem is he's never been able to forgive himself. And you staying or going isn't going to change that. He needs to figure it out on his own."

He's not the only one.

For the first time in her life she needed to figure out how to stop pleasing the people around her and start pleasing herself.

"Thank you." She hooked her arm through Olive's, and they slowly walked down the stairs.

"Don't thank me. You're the one who'll be doing the work. And the first on your list will be to cancel the realtor and show the town you mean business."

"Actually, there's something else I need to do," she said as Olive climbed into her car and drove off. She retrieved her phone and sent Ellen a text message.

There's been a change of plans...

Chapter Twenty

"From small words, great things grow." **Just Say No**

"I still can't believe that in less than twenty-four hours, Dr. Penny Groves will be here," Laney said from her spot on the ladder, where she was hanging long garlands of ivy from the beams of the town hall.

Twenty-four hours and I still have so much to do.

Paige's stomach contracted. The last week had been a blur of activity, and Laney wasn't the only one having a problem accepting the big day was almost there.

When she'd first decided to stay in St. Clair, she'd been determined to convince Meg Mitchell to change her mind about doing a book signing in the small town. It hadn't worked, which was when she'd decided to be audacious. It probably helped she was a little drunk thanks to Sam's scrumptious rum gateaux.

She hadn't gone via Dr. Penny Groves's publicist. Hadn't even tried to pull any strings. Instead she'd written to the author herself and told her just how much *Just Say No* had changed her life. She'd gone on to describe St. Clair, complete with all the locals, and ended the email by saying how much everyone in the small town would love for Dr. Penny Groves to do a book signing.

No one had been more surprised than Paige when the notoriously private author replied, saying she'd be in the Pacific Northwest the following week and would love to do a signing.

A signing that was tomorrow.

"What if no one comes?" She scanned her to-do list for the zillionth time.

"Then you'll be eating sliders for the next year," Sam said as Laney climbed back down the ladder, and all three of them looked around the hall.

A stage and podium were at one end, while rows of chairs had been neatly placed. At the other end was a signing table with boxes of books set up in a large display.

So many boxes.

What if it's like my first day in business and I don't sell any of them?

Her original plan was to host it in the bookstore before realizing it was just too small. It had been Laney who'd suggested the town hall. Her friend had helped transform it into a gorgeous winter jungle of waxy green leaves and pale white flowers draping down the walls and hanging along the beams. Sam had volunteered to do all the catering, along with a little help from Patsy. Paige had done the rest.

Hustling like she never had before.

Once the hall was finished, Paige locked it up and said goodbye to the Belles before heading out to Victor's house. The author would be staying in Victor's newly converted cottage and was due to arrive in the next hour.

The charcoal-gray exterior and white trim made it fresh and inviting, while large potted plants dotted the entrance. A winding path through a cottage garden led to a sweet bench seat.

Luke had done an amazing job.

She swallowed hard. No matter what she did, all roads led back to him.

It had been two weeks since they'd spoken, though she'd seen him in the distance from time to time. He'd looked just like he always had. Slightly grumpy, in a hurry, and without too much time for people who weren't his immediate family.

People like me.

In the past it would've cut deep, but after her conversation with Olive, she'd forced herself to accept that if she wanted a future there, Luke would have to become part of her past.

And, while she wasn't quite ready to turn cartwheels, the black despair had left her. Replaced by mild gray funk. It was a step in the right direction. *And who knows, in about two hundred years I'll be feeling like my old self.*

"There you are." Audrey poked her head out of the cottage and waved. "I've just been giving it a final inspection."

"It looks amazing." She followed her mom in. The cottage was beautiful, with polished wooden floorboards, clean lines, and white walls capturing most of the light.

"Doesn't it just. And by the way, I've just been speaking with Olive, and she said all the accommodation in the area's booked out. Not to mention the wine tours. I had to name-drop to get Dr. Penny Groves onto one. I think she'll enjoy it."

"I hope so." Paige crossed her fingers. The author had admitted one of the reasons she'd agreed to the proposal was because Paige had promised she'd leave feeling refreshed and revived.

"I'm proud of you, sweetheart." Audrey suddenly squeezed her hand. "What you've managed to do is nothing short of a miracle."

"I guess all my people-pleasing's finally come in handy," she said, unused to getting a compliment from her mom.

"You say that like it's a bad thing." Audrey frowned. "Why would you think that?"

Paige scratched her head. "Because I seem to have spent my life running around after people. Patrick. Ellen. James—"

"Me?" Audrey added in a sad voice. "I hate that I was a burden to you. But Paige, your ability to make friends with people—to help them. That's not a bad quality. It's something wonderful. I don't have it, your brother certainly doesn't, but you do. That's what makes you special."

Tears shimmered in Audrey's eyes, and Paige's throat tightened. "I had no idea you thought that."

"Well, now you know." Her mom's voice was gruff as she brushed away a tear.

"Thanks." Paige's own eyes moistened, but before she could say anything else, her phone rang.

It was Nancy, her tattooed customer, who'd stepped up to do the graphic design work for the signing. The results had been amazing.

"Everything okay?" she said.

"Yup. I've just picked up the banners for tomorrow. They look ace," the woman confirmed. "But you might want to know Smith and Marlon are queuing up in front of the town hall with blankets, a tent, and a thermos of whisky. Apparently, they heard it was a thing."

She repressed a chuckle.

Her two elderly regulars had been excited about the signing, and despite promising them front row seats, they obviously didn't want to miss out. "Thanks. I'll call Myra and get her to pick them up."

"Cool. I'll see you tomorrow," Nancy said before ending the call.

"Problem?" Audrey looked at her, but Paige just shook

her head as a car drove toward the cottage and came to a halt. A woman stepped out. She was in her mid-fifties with coppery hair, smooth skin, and eyes the color of walnuts.

Dr. Penny Groves.

And unlike in Paige's imagination, there were no kaftans or ball gowns. She was wearing wide-legged black trousers, a fitted jacket, and a pair of cute pink suede shoes.

"You're here!" Paige found her voice. "You're really here."

"I really am." Dr. Penny Groves let out a throaty laugh and held out her hand. "It's nice to meet you."

"You, too." She grinned, her panic and worry leaving her. For better or worse, this was really happening.

• • •

"Look, there's another one." Kira pointed as they drove through town. Luke kept his vision firmly fixed on the road, though it didn't take a genius to know what his daughter was talking about.

What the whole damn town was talking about.

Tomorrow's book signing with Dr. Penny Groves.

The posters were everywhere he turned. A constant reminder of Paige. Still, true to his word, he'd stayed away from her. It was easier that way. He'd actually stayed away from as many people as he could. Because despite not telling anyone what had happened between them, the whole town seemed to know.

Which meant too many people asking too many questions.

"Can we go?" His daughter persisted when he didn't respond. "You're always saying we should support local businesses. Plus, everyone else will be there. Trina, Gigi—"

She paused, but Luke knew what name was coming next.

Cal.

He took in a deep breath.

As if he needed more problems.

"I'll think about it," he said as he turned down their street and into the garage.

"Thank you." Kira bounced along next to him, while clutching at her own copy of *Just Say No*. "It will be my first real book signing."

He raked a hand through his hair. It had been two weeks since Kira had climbed on a bus to go to Seattle on her own, and even though it was all in the past now, the fear of it happening again still haunted him. The guilt of taking his eye off the ball, even for one second.

"Okay, fine, kiddo. We can definitely go. Happy?"

"You bet." She grinned, wrapping her arms around him for a hug, before darting off to her bedroom to no doubt text Cal with the update. Somehow, he had the feeling he'd just been played. Still, as long as she was happy and safe, that's all that mattered.

He spent the rest of the night typing up quotes and working on the marina plans. Despite the money they'd raised in the Big Fish, they were still way off target. At this rate the new jobs he'd wanted to create for the town wouldn't be ready for the next hundred years.

Too tired to keep his eyes open, he headed to bed and fell into a dreamless sleep before Kira woke him the next day.

"Come on, we don't want to be late. People are already in line outside the town hall."

"What?" He groaned and rubbed his eyes. "Isn't this thing at the bookstore?"

"You need to get out more, Dad." Kira eye-rolled him. "The store's way too small. This is going to be massive. *Which is why you need to get up.*"

"Okay, okay. Just let me grab a shower," he said and

waited until she'd let out a world-weary sigh before closing the door. An hour later, he drove down the main street of St. Clair and blinked. Cars were parked for miles in each direction, and a long line of people snaked up the street around the corner from the town hall.

What the hell.

"There's one." Kira squealed with delight as she pointed.

"You do realize we're seven blocks away." He frowned, but Kira was already unbuckling her seatbelt and hugging her book to her chest. He let out a soft mutter and climbed out after her.

He blinked as they followed the trail of people walking to the town hall. Over half of them were out-of-towners, all clutching books, their voices excited.

"Come on." Kira tugged at his sleeve. "It's starting soon. I don't want to miss it."

He increased his pace to keep up with his daughter. The line was moving into the hall, and they were about to join the back of it when Olive waved them over.

"Luke, I wasn't sure if you'd be coming." She slipped her arm through his and led them inside.

He caught his breath. The hall was filled with trailing vines of ivy and the sweet perfume of clematis, while up on the stage was a huge cardboard cutout of Dr. Penny Groves along with two pink armchairs he recognized from her store. Kira let out a yelp of excitement and raced over to where Cal was moodily leaning against the back wall.

Servers darted in and out of the crowds, holding up trays of champagne and soft drinks, while others carried plates of sliders. The air was filled with pungent spices and excited chatter.

"That makes two of us," he said. "My daughter had other ideas. I can't get over this turnout. Where did all these people come from?"

"Here and there." Olive shrugged with a smile as she led him over to where Trina and Stu were valiantly saving two extra seats. "Turns out Dr. Penny Groves never does signings, so when word got out, people started booking. Every spare room in the town's been sold out, not to mention charter trips, wine tours, and even bicycle rentals."

This is insane.

Jacob and Melanie were over on the far side of the hall, in a tangled embrace. To the right, Smith and Marlon were being herded by Myra, who was laughing at something they said. Hell. Even Nancy Whitman was there, with her tattooed boyfriend. People he'd known all his life. People who'd never come along to a single town meeting, but they were out in force for Paige's book signing.

"If you hadn't been living under a rock, you might've known this," Trina chimed in. He rubbed his jaw as the room went quiet, and Paige walked out onto the stage.

Her blonde hair fell down around her shoulders in a shimmering curtain, while her fitted jeans and pale pink sweater hugged her curves.

She's beautiful.

A few people hollered, and she gave them a shy wave before reaching for the microphone.

"Hi everyone. Thank you so much for coming to meet the one and only Dr. Penny Groves."

On cue, the author walked out on the stage, and the crowd went wild. It took several minutes for Paige to calm everyone down before the pair of them sat in the chairs. And for the next hour Paige asked the famous author a series of gentle but probing questions that kept the audience in hysterics.

When they brought it to a close, the applause was thunderous, and the pair took a bow.

"Thank you," Paige said, a little out of breath, her cheeks flushed. "We'll take a fifteen-minute break and then Dr.

Penny Groves will start signing books."

People got to their feet, the chatter rising into the air in a cacophony. Kira was over with a group of friends laughing, and Olive slipped away to chat with her book club. He walked around the room, nodding to people he knew and squeezing past the many he'd never seen before, as they all lined up at the signing table.

It was too much.

He pushed his way through the crowd and stepped outside. Fall was almost behind them, and the vibrant leaves had turned to dull brown mush beneath his feet. He let out his breath. St. Clair was his home. The place that had always given him a sense of purpose. Except now something was off.

Footsteps came up behind him, then someone swore under their breath. A hint of vanilla drifted in the air, and he stiffened. Paige.

"I-I didn't see you there," she stammered as he turned.

She was struggling with two large boxes, and the smile she'd been wearing on stage was gone. Replaced by a wary frown.

No points for guessing what the cause was.

Or who.

"Just taking a break." He reached for the top box. Judging by the weight, it was more copies of *Just Say No.* "Hey, congratulations on the event. It's amazing."

"Oh." Delicate color hit her cheeks. "Thanks. I didn't think you'd come."

"It was Kira's idea," he said, and the color increased in her face. *Crap.* "I'm happy I did. I had no idea it was going to be so big."

The tension in her jaw lessened, and she gave him an achingly familiar smile. "You and me both. I'm still a little stunned."

"Olive was saying Dr. Penny Groves never does publicity.

Whatever you told her must've been pretty good."

She shut her eyes and wrinkled her nose. "Actually, I told her the truth. About how I ended up here. Why I wanted to stay. Did Victor tell you she's staying in the cottage?"

Well, I'll be damned. The Airbnb wasn't such a bad idea after all.

"That's great," he said before letting out a bark of laughter.

"What's so funny?" she demanded.

"Nothing," he said before shifting his weight as the irony hit him in the chest. "I always thought I was the one who was meant to save the town. Bring back business that didn't rely on the whims of tourists. I thought that being born and bred here somehow made me better. Which is probably what blinded me to the truth."

She caught her breath. Her navy eyes a thousand shades of blue. "Luke, that's crazy. The work you're doing on the Marina is amazing. It's definitely going to help save the town."

He shook his head as the tension in his chest suddenly lessened. "It's just occurred to me that the town doesn't need saving. It just needs new people with different ideas. People like you, Paige."

Her mouth opened, and he longed to kiss her.

Her breath hot against his skin, body pressed to him. But he couldn't. Nothing had changed. Kira had to come first. *Why is this so damn hard?*

"Thank you, Luke." Her voice was a whisper, her eyes filled with understanding. She licked her lips. "I know we can't…well…that's all in the past. But you once said you'd be my friend. I hope that still stands."

He swallowed, his gaze never leaving hers. "It does," he lied, wishing like hell things could've been different.

Chapter Twenty-One

"No, no, no." **Just Say No**

"I dare you to say your Thanksgiving was worse than mine," Zoe complained as Paige scanned a box of books into the system. "Because unless you have three drunk uncles, a breakout of food poisoning, and a nephew who likes ripping the upholstery on a three-thousand dollar sofa, then I'm going to win."

"Crap. I'm sorry, Zo," Paige said, wishing she could give her friend a hug. Despite her tough front, Zoe was still an emotional wreck when it came to dealing with her family.

That was me a few months ago.

"Don't be sorry, just tell me you had a better time than I did."

"Actually, I did." Laney had spent Thanksgiving with her sister-in-law, but Victor had invited her, Sam, and Cal to his house and proceeded to spoil them rotten. Something in her heart had filled at the sight of the ex-biker and her mom celebrating their first holiday with all the excitement of kids.

Well…kids with a fondness for whisky chasers, silk sheets, and making out in public.

James had even deigned to call and tentatively agreed to a Christmas visit, staying in Victor's cottage.

"And how's the master plan shaping up?"

"Amazing. Would you believe publicists are now ringing me to set up signings? The next author is Susan Kempers. Her crime novels are intense. You should come."

"I'd love to, but I'm busy doing important city girl stuff."

"I haven't even told you the date. You're going to have to come up with better excuses."

"I've been giving you my best work," Zoe complained. "When I said I'd self-combust if I left NYC zip code, that, my friend, was comedy gold. Besides, wouldn't it be better for you to come here? At least you won't have to worry about bumping into your crime-fighting ex-lover. Are you still thinking about him?"

Only every minute of every day.

She swallowed. Luke's face came into her mind unbidden. It did that a lot.

When she'd seen him at the book signing, a small spark of hope had flared in her chest. That he'd change his mind. That things could be different. The irony hadn't been lost on her that she'd just spent an hour in conversation about the power of no, and yet she'd still secretly been hoping he'd say yes.

"No. I'm fine. I swear it."

"Excellent. You've now assured me you're fine about seven hundred and ten times. I think that's a record. You know, it's okay not to be fine."

"That's not an option." She shook her head. If she allowed herself to go down the rabbit hole a second time, she might not come back out. "Besides, I'm—"

"Let me guess? Still fine?" Zoe finished. In the

background was a commotion, and her friend muttered something. "I've got to go. Disaster on the helpline. Hang in there. I love you."

"Thanks, Zo. I love you, too." She finished the call.

She might not have had the traditional family, but she and Zoe had always formed their own little unit, and it was only now she realized how important it was. Her improved relationship with Audrey and James had meant the unit had expanded. Not to mention Sam and Laney.

It wasn't quite how she imagined her new life in St. Clair would be, but it certainly wasn't as bad as the darkness she'd been lingering in two weeks earlier. And with that she flipped open her laptop and brought up a YouTube clip on how to replace a leaking faucet and got to work. After all, while she couldn't make her own life perfect, she could at least stop a tap from dripping.

. . .

Luke jogged along the road, his muscles groaning in protest. It was three weeks until Christmas, and bustle was all around him. Houses dripped with decorations, curls of smoke poked out of chimneys, and the air was filled with cinnamon and ginger floating out from organized kitchens.

He ignored it all and ran. To release the knot of tension he'd been dragging around with him like an unwanted skin.

Kira was spending half a day with Joanne, and while it was still nerve-racking every time he said goodbye to his daughter, a slow trust was developing.

And the rest?

No. There is no rest.

Liar.

He increased his pace and swore as he raised his head. The Belles of St. Clair stared back at him, three buildings huddled side by side, their pastel colors breaking up the otherwise gray day. *Hell.* He'd done it again. His mind had wandered, and his traitorous feet had taken a right turn, leading him to Fireside Books. To Paige.

He tightened his jaw, and he turned around.

Not that she'd notice. The town was still talking about the book signing. He'd even caught Mrs. Gilbert reading a copy of *Just Say No* when he returned Trevor last Tuesday night. He was probably the only person *not* reading it.

Still, he was happy her store was as busy as she'd longed for it to be.

And that she was fitting in. Especially since he'd heard how close she'd come to leaving.

Was he a selfish ass for wishing she had?

Don't even answer that. Besides, he suspected even if she'd been out of sight, she wouldn't have been out of mind.

He increased his pace and was panting when he reached Patsy's diner, where Jacob was waiting.

"Careful there, or you'll have a body like mine," his brother said by way of a greeting as he pushed open the diner door, and they both walked in. Patsy was busy at the far end of the counter, so they found their own table and sat down.

"Yes, but I'll never have the spray tan," he retorted, taking in the Day-Glo skin tone.

"There's nothing wrong with personal grooming. Melanie says…"

Luke bit back a groan. Ever since his brother had convinced Melanie to take him back, he'd begun quoting her on a daily basis. Still, he was happy. And hell, but he'd miss him when he went to Europe after Christmas.

"Ah, the Carmichael boys." Patsy appeared at the table and poured coffee without being asked. Steam curled up around the rim of the cup as he reached for it. "If I weren't saying no to men right now, I swear I'd drink you both in."

"You're reading the book?" Jacob's eyes lit up. "Isn't it amazing. I had no idea I was hiding my pain behind a sea of yeses."

"Preach." Patsy gave a reverent nod. "To discover my true self was only a 'hell no' away has been liberating."

Luke stared at the pair of them. Would they notice if he banged his head against the table?

"You okay, big brother?" Jacob's lips twitched in amusement. He turned to Patsy. "You'll have to excuse him, he still hasn't read it yet."

"Nor is he going to," Luke added as he pulled some bills from his pocket and got to his feet. "And I've just remembered I've got a meeting."

"Sounds to me like someone's still not owning their no," Jacob tutted.

Luke didn't reply as he stalked outside.

A bunch of tourists were all holding copies of *Just Say No*, and his mood worsened. He glared around the parking lot before remembering he hadn't driven there. Fine. *I jogged here, I can jog home.*

The familiar rhythm of his breath and the pounding of his feet against the road helped drive away the pent-up frustration.

The irony was that while Paige had been desperate to belong, these days he was the one struggling to fit in. He sped up. He'd hoped after things had settled life would go back to normal. Olive had laughed at that idea and told him some nonsense about a cocoon, and how change was inevitable.

Well, I'm not buying it.

Besides, what was so bad about staying the same?

It had given Kira the security she needed after Joanne had left town. And even though he knew *why* she'd left, it didn't alter the fact he'd been the one to keep their daughter safe for ten years.

Something niggled at the back of his mind.

Would things have been different if Joanne had told him the truth about the darkness consuming her? He shrugged it off. He'd never know.

The niggle was there again.

His muscles ached and heart hammered as he sped downhill until the curve of the harbor came into view. Whatever the niggle was, it didn't matter. What's done was—

He came to a shuddering halt as an image slammed into his mind.

At the bottom of Olive's garden on the night of her birthday.

The moon low, and the air filled with vanilla perfume. Paige's perfume. It was when she'd haltingly told him about her strained relationship with a father who dismissed her. Of how her creep of an ex-fiancé cheated on her. Of how her life in New York had been gray and overpowering. Of how she'd moved to St. Clair to find a place to belong. To take away the loneliness that surrounded her.

Shit.

She'd shown him her dark place. Something even his wife hadn't been able to do. And what had he done?

Pushed her aside. Just like everyone else had.

Said he didn't have room in his life for two people.

Greedy, selfish bastard.

Shame sucker punched him. Smashing into his throat and leaving him gasping for breath.

How had he been so freaking stupid? So scared to change that he'd ignored her. Hell, he'd watched his one amazing kid be open to meeting the mother she could hardly remember. *And I've been too scared to even see the woman I love.*

Double shit.

He loved her. But he knew that. Ever since the book signing, when she'd stood on the stage, light radiating around her. He'd known it and tried his best to swallow it down.

He'd screwed up.

Without consultation, his feet turned in the direction of her store. Pebbles flew up from the path as he raced along, his heart pounding in a two-four beat.

Tell her the truth. Tell her the truth.

The jagged stab of a stitch impaled the side of his gut, but he kept going.

The three historic buildings danced before his eyes as his breath ripped out of his throat. He paused to gather his thoughts. *Tell her the truth. Tell her how I feel. Tell...wait. Why's the door open at six at night?*

"Paige?" He took the stairs in two short strides, his run forgotten. "You here? Is everything—"

The arid stench of burnt plastic hit him. Adrenaline flared as he grabbed for the throw hanging over the back of one of the chairs and wrapped it around his face. There was no sign of flames, but the air was still heavy with lingering residue, so strong it caught in his throat and pricked his eyes.

"Paige?" He raced through the store and into the empty office. Adrenaline turned to panic as he hurried to the basement. The old wooden stairs groaned under his weight. The cloying remains of smoke were heavy in the air. It was pitch black, and he didn't dare put on the lights in case that was the cause.

Shit.

He fumbled for his phone and flicked on the flashlight. The remains of a charred circuit box clung to the brick wall like ivy, while a pile of blackened, tangled ash lay beside it. *No. No. No.*

"L-luke," a faint voice drifted over, so light he almost missed it. *She's alive.*

"I'm here." He turned his phone in the same direction. She was crumpled on the ground in an unnatural angle.

Streaks of charcoal smeared her gorgeous face, and her blonde hair was spread out around her. Nearby was a used fire extinguisher, and just past her was a small stepladder.

He was by her side in a flash. Down on the ground, checking her pulse while dragging his phone up to his ear. He hardly recognized his own voice as he called it in. Then he threaded his fingers through hers.

"It's okay, you're going to be okay. You hear me."

"What are you doing here? I don't understand."

"It's a long story, but right now we need to get you fixed up. Everything's going to be fine," he said, hoping like hell it was the truth.

"My arm hurts," she mumbled.

"I know, but I'm right here." He sucked in a ragged breath, sitting in the darkness until the emergency service sirens split the night. She tightened her grip on his hand, then passed out, leaving him alone and hoping like hell he'd found her in time.

Chapter Twenty-Two

"Think of yes as your fair-weather friend. No is the one who'll sit beside you when the nights are dark and endless."
Just Say No

Everything hurt.

Paige tried to shift, but her body wouldn't work, and when she opened her eyes light stabbed at her retinas, sending blinding hot pain into her skull. She closed her lids and tried to figure out what was going on. If it was a dream, it was a bad one. If it was a movie, then she wanted her money back. If—

"It's okay," a familiar voice said. "You had an accident. You have a broken arm, three stitches on your cheek, and a bruise on your ass that'll stop you nude sunbathing for a month."

Zoe?

She tried her eyes again. This time the pain wasn't as intense.

"Hey." Her friend's voice brightened. "I thought I saw signs of life. No, don't move. The nurse will be back soon. They need to give you a concussion test."

Paige tried to speak, but her throat was dry. As always, her friend read her mind and was instantly by her side, pouring a glass of water.

"You know, that was quite a routine you had going on there. Apparently, you tried to put out a fire, then fell over a stepladder."

What the hell is it with me and ladders?

Zoe held the cup up to her mouth, each sip burning her throat. As she drank, her friend continued to fill in the blanks. The accident had happened last night, and she'd been in the hospital for over twenty-four hours.

"Apparently drugs *really* knock you out. Which means you might need to rethink your dreams of being a hardcore badass," Zoe continued as Paige shifted into a sitting position and examined herself. One arm was heavily bandaged, the tiny stitches in her cheek hurt like fire, and her throat was coated in glass. "But seriously, you scared the freaking shit out of me, Paige Taylor. I told you this place was no good for you."

"And I told you I'd get you down here," she managed to speak. "If I knew it'd only take a small fire and a silly fall, I might've—"

"Please do not finish that sentence," Zoe warned. "My nerves can't take it."

"I still don't understand what you're doing here? Actually, how did *I* even get here?"

Zoe grinned. "Oh, you'll like this part. Your crime-fighting ex-lover found you in your basement. He called the hospital, and they called me. I guess you still had me down as your next of kin. I spoke to Audrey and decided to fly over."

"Slow down." Paige tried to hold up her broken arm before realizing it hurt. She raised an eyebrow instead. "You've been talking to Audrey?"

"Well, yeah. She's been here the entire time. So has half the town. Including a very cute vet called Marc...which we'll just put a pin in for now and come back to later. The main thing is you're okay."

"I hope you're using that term loosely," she said, her throat still burning. Before Zoe could answer, a doctor and nurse appeared. There were questions, prodding, and a concussion test before she drifted back off to sleep.

As she dozed, flashes of memories came back.

She'd been down in the basement trying to fix the water faucet when there was a spark from the circuit box. Next minute there were flames everywhere. She'd managed to get it under control with the fire extinguisher, but with no lights, she'd tripped back over the stepladder she'd been using earlier in the day.

Pain had seeped into her body, and through the haze Luke's voice had filtered in. But until Zoe had told her he'd been the one to find her, she'd thought it was nothing more than her overactive imagination.

This time when she woke, it was to the delicate scent of flowers. She opened her eyes.

The room was filled with dozens of bunches of flowers, most with Laney's trademark style, as well as balloons. There was a jar of Mrs. Gilbert's jam, and the mouth-watering aroma of butter and cocoa coming from a box nearby could only mean one thing. Patsy's cookies. Next to them was Sam's famous strawberry shortcake.

And so many cards. She randomly grabbed one.

Limericks are fun
But haiku gets the ladies
Get well soon. Marlon

Watery tears sprung to her eyes as she picked up the next one. It was from Smith, asking her to please excuse his friend and wishing her the best. Nancy's card included a press-on tattoo of a mermaid, and Olive's book group had sent her a giant card with a naked man inside. Of course they had.

She blew her nose as she read through the rest, only stopping when Audrey walked into the room, her face pale and lined with worry.

"Oh, honey, you're awake. Thank goodness." She eased Paige into a sitting position and busied herself fluffing pillows, checking tubes, and pouring water. Once a nurse, always a nurse. "Good news is you don't have a concussion and can come home tomorrow."

"Yay," she said before remembering the fire. She let out a groan. "Do I have a place to go back to? Did the fire—"

"It didn't spread," her mom said quickly. "Before you fell, you managed to put it out. There was damage."

Repair bills flashed through her mind.

She doubted fire damage could be fixed with a YouTube clip.

I'll have to close the store.

Then something else occurred to her. "Oh God. My next book signing. Is in a week. Just in time for Christmas shopping. I need to cancel it."

"Cancel it?" Zoe walked back in the room. "You think I've traveled all this way for nothing? I was promised a book signing."

"Yes, but—" she tried to protest before her mom started to laugh.

"It's okay, Paige. Next week's signing is going ahead," her mom said.

"How? If my circuit box is gone then I won't have electricity, let alone water, because I couldn't figure out how to fix the faucet." *Plus, I'm pretty sure I look like an extra in a horror movie.*

"You don't have to worry." Zoe put her arm around Audrey's shoulder. "Thanks to something called B.S., which doesn't mean what I thought it meant. Anyway, Fireside

Books is full of contractors making sure it's all up and going."

"It's all been Luke's doing," Audrey added.

Luke?

Her throat tightened. "Is he here?"

Zoe wrinkled her nose. "No. Though if you're ready for visitors, there are some people waiting outside. Would you like to see them?"

She tried to hide her disappointment. There was no reason for him to be there. Nothing had changed. Except now she was actually the woman who fell over ladders, making her even more of a liability.

Thankfully, her disappointed face must've looked like her pained face, and Zoe didn't comment as she opened the door. One by one her friends stepped in. Laney, Sam, Victor, Kira, Olive, Trina and Stu, Smith, Marlon, Myra, Nancy, Patsy, Marc—though judging by the way he stared at Zoe, he had an ulterior motive.

No Luke.

By the time visiting hours ended, she was exhausted, and fell asleep almost immediately. There were no dreams, just a strange floating sensation. Like the mattress was made of marshmallows. She wriggled deeper and was just about to conjure up a marshmallow pillow when there was a scraping noise.

She reluctantly opened her eyes, expecting to see a nurse. It was Luke.

He was sitting on a hard chair, his head bowed forward while his hands rested on the back of his neck. To someone who could barely lift her arm, it was like a complex yoga pose. Then she glanced at the clock on the wall.

It was three in the morning.

Okay. Definitely dreaming.

"Paige?" He raised his head, his face illuminated against the pale-green light of the appliances dotted around the room. "Shit. I hope I didn't wake you?"

"What are you doing here?" she said, simultaneously trying to sit up while wishing for a hat to hide her hospital bed head.

And makeup. Where was Dr. Penny Groves and her lipstick collection when she needed it?

"I went to school with Paula, the night nurse. She let me in."

"You B.S.'d your way in here?"

"I wanted to check you were okay." An uncertain smile crossed his lips, and color returned to his face.

"You're not here to lecture me on my inability to be around ladders of any description?" she said, trying to keep her voice light. *Why does he have to look so beautiful? And at night. Nighttime is my weakness.*

"You gave everyone quite a scare." He nodded to the door, as if asking permission to stay. She tilted her head in agreement, and her skin prickled as heat from his body reached out to her.

"Zoe said you found me."

"I have a magnet to your kind of trouble." His voice broke into a low animal growl. "Hell, Paige. You could've been seriously hurt."

"That would explain the intense pain every time I move," she said, as a dark shadow raced across his face. "I'm fine. I'm going home tomorrow...and speaking of home, Zoe and Audrey told me what you've been doing. I don't even know what to say."

"You don't need to say anything. It wasn't just me. It seems like the whole town has been through your store in the last couple of days, wanting to help out. The only thing missing is you."

A lump formed in her throat, and she closed her eyes.

She'd been doing so well, staying focused on her business.

Convincing herself it was for the best, but being close to him...well...it just kind of sucked. Especially since they had a deal. A deal he'd had no trouble keeping. He'd managed to stay away from her—

Wait. She inched her way farther up the bed.

"How did you find me?"

"When you weren't in the store or your office—" he started to say, but she cut him off.

"No, what were you doing there in the first place?" she asked as his face rippled with conflicting emotions.

"I wanted to—" He stopped and shook his head. "Look, I'm not sure we should be talking about this now. Paula said even though you're getting out tomorrow, the drugs have knocked you around. I should let you sleep."

"No." She reached out with her good arm and caught his hand. "Tell me why you were at the store?"

"I went there to tell you I was a complete dick. I messed everything up, and it's been torturing me—like hot steel under my fingernails. I wanted to tell you I was scared to change. That the fact I hurt you kills me inside."

"Oh." Her whole body burned with energy, numbing the pain and replacing it with exhilaration. "That's a lot of stuff."

"There's more. I went to tell you I'm sorry." His liquid silver eyes were haunted as he tentatively touched his fingertip to hers. "I thought I only had room in my life for one person. That if I took a risk, it could backfire—"

"A-and what do you think now?" She was almost too scared to speak in case it broke the spell and she woke up and discovered it was a dream. *Then again, if it were a dream he wouldn't have any clothes on.*

His touch was still featherlight, yet her entire body began to shake. "Paige, I love you. And I understand if you don't want to see me again. B-but I had to tell you. You and my daughter are the two most important people in the world.

And if I made you feel like that's not true, then I'm sorry."

She swallowed as Dr. Penny Groves's face blurred in her mind. *Just Say No.*

He was telling her everything she wanted to hear. But that's what Patrick had once done. And how many times had she let his words convince her he was different? That he'd changed?

It had been a hard-won lesson. She dug her nails into the palm of her hand.

"I can't be with someone who's going to dump me at the first sign of trouble. I'm not sure I want to risk that kind of hurt again." Tears stung in her eyes, and he flinched.

"I deserve that. Hell, if anyone had treated Kira the way I treated you—" He broke off, and raw pain flashed across his face. "You let me into your life, but I never let you into mine. Truth is most of the time I'm scared shitless that I'm screwing up. What if it was my fault Joanne left? And what if I did that to you?"

Is that really what he thinks?

She knew the answer to that. He tried to carry everyone he loved. To make sure they were okay. Safe. Happy.

He doesn't love often, but he loves deeply.

Something in her broke.

Like a wall crumbling away.

"If I'd left St. Clair, it would've been on me, Luke. Not you," she said. His eyes were heavy with fatigue, from all the things he'd been carrying around with him. "And you're wrong."

"Wrong about what?" He stiffened, as if the words had surprised him.

"Wrong that you didn't let me in. I got to see you with your daughter. Your family. Your town. You can't hide that kind of truth."

He was still, as if unsure what to do next. Then he let out a frustrated growl. "I'm not good at this stuff, Paige. But if that's the case, I hope one day you can see the truth about us. I love you. It's not going to change. I messed it all up, but if you're ever able to forgive me…well…I'll be here."

She wanted to freeze this moment. To examine it from every angle. To remember it forever. But if she did that then he'd never kiss her. And that would be a tragedy.

"Say that part one more time," she croaked.

"You and my daughter are—"

"Nooo." She shook her head, heat rising through her entire body. "The love part."

The darkness left his silvery eyes, and his mouth twisted into a smile. "I love you."

"I love you, too," she whispered. She would've said it a second time, but he leaned forward, his mouth gently brushing hers. His breath was warm against her skin, and fireworks exploded in her chest. He kissed her a second time before pulling away.

"And now I'm going to sit in that chair and you're going to get some sleep, because Zoe and your mom will hand me my ass if they discover I've kept you up all night."

"Don't tell me you're scared of them." She slid her hand into his, trying to tug him back to her.

"Only a little bit. But you do have a big day tomorrow. Moving back home and getting ready for your next book signing."

"Is this really happening?"

His mouth was back on hers, his hand trailing gentle lines down her face and along her neck. "Unless you're hallucinating and don't remember anything in the morning. Please don't be hallucinating."

"I'm not." She pressed her mouth to his and let out a contented sigh. Tomorrow they'd be able to tell their friends and family, but for now it was just the two of them. Right where they belonged.

Epilogue

"We all deserve to be happy, so don't stop chasing the things you believe in." **Just Say No**

"Paige, look what I found in the basement. Can you believe it?"

"Not even a little bit," she said as Kira dragged up a life-sized cutout of her new favorite book character. A dragonshifter called R'Tunga. "I guess you should probably find a good home for it. What about your bedroom?"

"Are you sure?" Kira said doubtfully as she peered around the bustling store. "It's kinda mean not to let everyone see him."

"Yes, but if you let everyone see him, they might try to touch him. Or even worse. Kiss him."

The young girl's face blanched an adorable shade of white, and Paige planted a kiss on her head. Kira gave her a quick hug before taking a selfie with R'Tunga.

"You're right. Do you think dad will mind?"

"Absolutely. But you're only fourteen once. You have to make the most of it."

"What are you two scheming about?" Luke walked through the front door. Then he let out a mock groan as he saw the cutout. "Give me strength. Do you really think this is funny?"

"A little bit," she said as Kira wrapped her arms around his waist while simultaneously taking the car keys from his hand to load up her latest haul before he changed his mind.

Once she'd darted outside, he tugged Paige forward and kissed her hard on the mouth. It'd been four months since the accident, and kissing him never got old. Nor did seeing him naked. She melted into him, almost forgetting where they were until there was a coughing noise from behind them.

"Really, Paige. Is this acceptable behavior from a business owner?"

"James. I thought you weren't arriving for another couple of hours. The signing isn't until tomorrow." She blinked before hugging her brother. They weren't much of a hugging family, so it was a work in progress. He untangled himself, but there was a small smile on his face.

"Yes, but darling Fi and the kids were dying to get here and see you and Mom. They're at her house now, but I wanted to drop off the champagne for the big day. I was having lunch with a couple of corporate guys yesterday, and neither of them could believe you managed to lure Dr. Penny Groves down here not once but twice."

"Paige can be very persuasive when she wants to be." Luke's fingers entwined in hers while he chatted with her brother. They were joined several minutes later by a radiant Zoe and a smitten Marc.

While her friend still complained St. Clair was far too small for a city girl like herself, she'd become a regular visitor thanks to her growing relationship with the vet, who now rented Paige's upstairs apartment.

Her smile widened as Sam and Laney poured into the store, carrying cakes and flowers respectively for tomorrow's book signing. They were followed by Olive and her Fifty Shades of Grey Rinsers. She'd planned to set everything up tonight, but the small town had other ideas. Everyone began to call B.S. as they picked up boxes of books to carry them to the town hall, when Luke reached for her hand and pulled her into the privacy of her office.

"Everything okay?"

"No complaints." He shrugged as he took her hand in his and studied her finger. Then his hard gaze found hers. "Though there's one thing that could be better."

"Too many people in the store?" she said, recognizing the gleam in his eye. It wouldn't be the first time they'd made out in there.

"I was thinking your finger's too bare."

"What?" She frowned as he dropped onto one knee. Her mouth fell open, and her heart pounded. "No, you can't be."

"Yes, I can be." He nodded, his gaze still holding hers as surely as his strong hand was wrapped around her fingers, like they were precious. *Like I'm precious.* Tears prickled her eyes.

"You're going to make me cry."

"Never intentionally." He stood back up and gently wiped the tears away and kissed her mouth until she was giggling. Then he lowered himself back to the ground and looked up at her. "Paige Taylor, will you do me the honor of becoming my wife?"

"Luke." Her voice was a little above a whisper. "I can't believe this is happening. I don't even know what to say."

Um, hello. Imaginary Dr. Penny Groves coughed. *You have my new book right in front of you. I'm signing it tomorrow. That might give you a hint.*

She glanced at the cover. *Just Say Yes—The Power of Being Open to Change So You Can Get Exactly What You Want From This Beautiful Life.* Then she smiled and pressed her lips to his. His arms snaked around her, and her pulse went into overdrive. "Yes, Luke Carmichael. I say yes."

Acknowledgments

A super big thank you to my editor, Candace Havens who is nothing short of a miracle! I'm so grateful that you can always find the real story, no matter how well I try to hide it! And a big thank to Liz Pelletier for seeing the potential in this series, as well as to Crystal for always keeping me on track.

As ever, Christina Phillips and Sara Hantz are my two secret weapons and they continue to save my sanity on a regular basis. All while wearing tiaras. You two are the absolute best.

To Molly and Arthur, my two in-house technical advisors when it comes to weird things on the internet. The fact that the pair of you have also grown up to be story loving, movie obsessed kids makes me so happy!

And to my husband, Barry. You survived yet another book. I honestly couldn't have finished this one without you.

About the Author

Amanda Ashby was born in Australia but now lives in New Zealand where she writes romance, young adult, and middle grade books. She also works in a library, owns far too many vintage tablecloths and likes to delight her family by constantly rearranging the furniture. She has a degree in English and Journalism from the University of Queensland and is married with two children. Her debut book was nominated for a Romantic Times Reviewers Choice award, and her first young adult book was listed by the New York Public Library's Stuff for the Teen Age. Because she's mysterious she also writes middle grade books under the name Catherine Holt, and hopes that all this writing won't interfere with her Netflix schedule.

Discover more August titles...

THE JULY GUY
a Men of Lakeside novel by Natasha Moore

A summer fling might be the only thing that gets art professor Anita Delgado through the next few weeks. When she meets sexy salvage specialist Noah Colburn, he's tempted by her offer of a no-strings fling for the four weeks she's in town. But he's running for major of his hometown of Lakeside, New York, and the gossip mill is notorious for ruining even the most upstanding reputations.

KNOCKED-UP CINDERELLA
a novel by Julie Hammerle

It was only supposed to be a one-night stand, but now I've gone from one-working-ovary to co-parent in the time it took a stick to turn blue. Ian Donovan may be a richer-than-hell venture capitalist, but he's no Prince Charming ready to sweep me off my feet. Good thing I don't need him. I've been doing fine on my own for forty years, and I'm not about to start changing that now.

ADVENTURES IN ONLINE DATING
a novel by Julie Particka

For Alexa McIntyre, the answer to everything comes down to numbers. Three sons. One divorce. One great life...except her boys are getting older and they really need a man around. Enter the number twenty, as in after twenty minutes with someone she knows whether or not she wants them in her life. So, she hatches a plan to meet any man who remotely strikes her interest—for a twenty-minute date at her favorite coffee shop. It's the perfect way to find her perfect match in the most efficient way possible.

JUL - - 2019

Biv

GR

Apr 2023